Crosse My Heart

Kate Sweeney

CROSSE MY HEART
© 2015 BY KATE SWEENEY

All rights reserved. No part of this book may be reproduced in printed or electronic form without permission. Please do not participate in or encourage piracy of copyrighted materials in violation of the author's rights. Purchase only authorized editions.

ISBN 13: 978-1-935216-73-5

FIRST PRINTING: 2015

THIS TRADE PAPERBACK IS PUBLISHED BY
INTAGLIO PUBLICATIONS
WALKER, LA USA
WWW.INTAGLIOPUB.COM

This is a work of fiction. Names, characters, places, and incidents are the product of the author's imagination or are used fictitiously, and any resemblance to actual persons, living or dead, businesses, companies, events, or locales is entirely coincidental.

CREDITS
EXECUTIVE EDITOR: TARA YOUNG

COVER DESIGN BY TIGER GRAPHICS

Acknowledgments

Acknowledgments are always hard for me. Not because I don't know who to acknowledge, but because there are just so many people who help me with every story. Whether I'm aware of it at the time or not.

My sister Maureen always helps me, especially with the mysteries, murders, and vampires (which she wants me to write again). She's always there to kick things around.

And the readers who constantly boost my ego and get my creative juices flowing. You are all priceless.

To Tara, my editor. I made a comment in this story that she was persnickety, in a good way. And it is good because I trust her to do her thing so well, I can concentrate on the creative process, which has nothing whatsoever to do with good grammar or syntax. Thanks, Tara.

And finally, to my partner in crime, Robin Alexander—an excellent author and a great gal. While I loved living in Louisiana, South Carolina is proving to be just as beautiful without the humidity!

To so many others, thanks so much.

Chapter 1

"Syd is still sleeping, Vic."

"What do you mean she's asleep, Harry?"

Harry Doogan scratched his balding head. "I'm not sure how many ways ya can mean that—"

"Oh, get out of my way. Move it. And what did I tell you about calling me that vulgar nickname?" She raised her cane in his direction.

Harry bowed at the waist. "My apologies, Mrs. Crosse. Doth thou want me ta wake Miss Sydney from her slumber?" He grinned as he chomped on his unlit cigar and peered down at her. "And might I say, you are impeccably dressed this morning. What color is that? It matches your eyes."

Victoria Crosse absently ran her fingertips across the fabric. "Really? It's cobalt and..." She narrowed her eyes. "I don't like you. You're a thief, and if it were up to me—"

"Me thinks thou dost protest too much." Harry buried his hands deep in his trouser pockets and continued grinning. "Milady."

"Just because my daughter taught you how to read, don't get nervous."

Harry laughed then. "I do like you, Vic."

"Oh, you old fool." She marched past him down the long hallway.

"Mrs. Crosse...Ma'am, Syd was out late," Harry said and stopped abruptly as she turned on him.

"Womanizing, I suppose. All she's good for these days," she said over her shoulder as she continued down the hall. Her cane, which she really didn't need, made an annoying click on the hardwood floor. "My only child. And she's a lesbian. Why her father left the company to her, I will never know. She's never there." She came to the double doors at the end of the hall and pushed them open.

Over in a huge four-poster bed, a very well-tanned woman lay sound asleep on her stomach. Her arm and leg were thrown off the side of the bed, and the sheet dangerously exposed her flank. She grumbled as her mother came into the room. The clothes, carelessly strewn all over from the evening's escapade, were kicked out of the way as her mother sat in the large overstuffed chair by her daughter's bed.

"Good grief, don't you ever wear pajamas?" Victoria hissed. She reached over with her cane and pulled the covers over her thigh.

The woman put the pillow over her head. "Harry, I thought I said no strangers."

"But, boss, it's your mother," he said, looking at her.

Victoria rolled her eyes. "Hired another rocket scientist, Sydney?"

Harry looked honestly hurt.

Sydney took the pillow off her head and opened one eye. "She meant that affectionately, Harry." She then peered at her mother. "Good morning, Mommy. What brings you over here at this ungodly hour?" She put her head down again and closed her eyes.

"Ungodly? It's ten in the morning, you idiot. Get up, I need to talk to you." She slapped Sydney's flank with her cane.

Sydney groaned loudly. "Harry, call security and have this woman removed."

"Sydney, Jonathon Pickford is missing," she said seriously.

Sydney groaned. "Harry, look under the bed, then call security and have this woman—"

"Sweetie, I'm serious." Her tone was now quiet but firm.

Sydney opened her eyes and looked at her mother. She reached for her robe. "Coffee, lots of coffee, Harry."

Harry made a quick exit as Sydney stood and tied her silk robe and struggled into her slippers.

"Okay, Mother, you have my full attention," she said, running her fingers through her thick auburn hair.

God, how she looks like her father, Victoria thought affectionately. Sydney was forty-eight, with a touch of gray at her temples, just like her father. Tall and slender, with the same arrogant air that her father had. Only Sydney pulled it off better because she was a gentle soul, whereas her father was a pompous jackass.

When Harry came in with the silver coffee set, Sydney raised her eyebrows. "Are we expecting the queen?"

"She's here," Harry said out of the corner of his mouth.

"Well, at least you have class," Victoria said, taking the delicate cup from Harry.

"Thank you," Harry said.

"I was talking to Sydney."

Sydney laughed as she poured a cup of coffee. "She got you good, Harry."

"You get that from the Cameron side of the family, don't forget it," Victoria said with a smirk.

"Yes, madam." Sydney bowed obediently. "Now, you aggravating woman, what's this about Jon Pickford?"

"He was supposed to be in Chicago yesterday morning. We were to have lunch and go to that fund-raiser together. I called his house in Seacliff. They hadn't seen him in two days. His car was still in the garage, his briefcase in the foyer, but he was nowhere. It's like he disappeared..." Her voice trailed off as she drank her coffee.

Sydney got up, put on her black horn-rimmed glasses, and walked to the big window overlooking Lake Michigan; she let out a deep sigh. "It is a beautiful summer day. Boats are all over the lake. I can almost see Gary, Indiana. Although I can't imagine anyone actually wanting to see Gary—"

"Sydney, what do we do?" Victoria interrupted her.

"Do? What would you like me to do, Mother?" she asked, adjusting her glasses.

Victoria groaned. "First, find a nice woman. I still cannot believe I hear those words coming out of my mouth." She rubbed her temples. "I'll never get an heir."

"Not the conventional way," Harry mumbled as he looked to the ceiling.

"You can leave," Victoria said to him.

Sydney chuckled quietly and drank her coffee; these two had been sparring for months.

"But I'd be happy if you could stop running all over downtown Chicago chasing women. Then maybe you could see that perhaps something is wrong. It isn't like Jon not to check in. You know that. When he and your father worked together, Jon was the responsible one. He would never purposely worry anyone. Not like your father..."

"Father was a bit of a cad. Charming and great at the business, Mother, but a first-class womanizing cad." Sydney walked over to her, sat on the arm of the chair, and put her arm around her. She kissed her head and said, "Okay, Vic ole gal, how about I take a trip to Seacliff, Michigan, and have a look myself? I really don't have anything to do today, being Saturday."

Victoria stood and groaned. "It's Friday, you fool."

"It is?" Sydney asked in amazement. "Well, that's even better. I haven't missed the weekend. See? Things are looking up."

Her mother took a menacing step toward her as she pointed her cane.

Sydney took a step back and raised her hands. "Be careful, that thing may go off. I'm leaving in one hour." She then lowered her hands and gave her mother a loving hug. "Hey, I don't want you to be angry with me," she said affectionately and looked down at her.

Victoria smiled and pulled on the lapels of her robe and kissed Sydney's forehead. "You are my only child, and I love you dearly. However, if you turn out like your father, I will have you shot."

"Understood."

Victoria shook her head as she walked out of the bedroom. She called over her shoulder, "Call me from Seacliff."

"Well, Harry, it looks like I'm taking a road trip." Sydney finished her coffee. "Though it's probably a waste of time."

"I dunno, Syd. Your mom looked pretty upset."

Syd waved him off. "Agita. Check the door."

Harry ran to her bedroom door, peering down the hall in both directions. "All clear. She's gone."

"Great." Sydney dashed to the other room and pushed open the double doors.

"This place always amazes me," Harry said, following her into the library, gazing at the enormous room filled with bookshelves, a gas fireplace, comfortable chairs, and a large desk.

"Yes, and it hides my favorite part." Sydney walked to the section of bookshelves and pushed on the corner. The shelf gave way and opened. Sydney walked into a hidden room with four computers and every electronic gadget imaginable.

"Money well spent." She sat at one computer, flipped it on, and sat back, adjusting her glasses as she waited. She then typed in several commands and watched the screen. "Speaking of money well spent, there's a phone on the desk over there for you."

"For me?" Harry picked up the cellphone. "But I got one."

"This is the latest version. I programmed the GPS on it so we always know where the other one is."

"Like spying?"

"Well, not exactly. Well, yeah, I guess, exactly. But remember last month when you were stuck in that building, and I couldn't find you? If we had these phones and yours was on, I could have known where you were. I suppose I could have just downloaded the app for it, but what's the fun of that? I love new technology."

"Wow. Okay. It's all set to go?"

"Yep. Just keep it charged and on."

"Okay. Hey, ya got anything?" Harry asked, peering over her shoulder.

"So far nothing from the authorities in Michigan. Jon's been missing for forty-eight hours." She adjusted her glasses once again as she printed out the information. "Well, I'm going to shower. Then we'll get a plan."

Sydney showered and wrapped herself in a comfortable terrycloth robe. When she entered the bedroom, she noticed her bed had been made, and Harry was in the process of taking the coffee tray. "Harry, really, you don't have to make my bed."

"But you never do," he insisted. "Don't take offense, but you're a bit of a slob."

"Hey," she said, placing her hands on her hips. "You're in my custody now. We made a deal with the judge. I hire you to be my driver, my assistant, if you will. And in return, you don't steal or pick locks anymore, remember?"

Harry grinned as he chomped on his cigar. "Yeah, I remember. You really came through for me. Thanks."

"Well, you're welcome. I was glad to do it."

"But you're still a—"

Sydney raised her hand.

"You're still not very neat," he amended.

"I can deal with that. But be careful. I can still call the judge. You know, he's a friend of the family. Get lost, will you, and let me get dressed. Oh, can you call Eddie? I think I'll take the Cessna instead of driving."

Harry stuck his nose in the air. "I think I'll take the Cessna. Should I have the caviar ready?"

"The judge, Harry!" Though Sydney tried to be stern, she let out an amused chuckle; she really liked Harry. She remembered four years ago when Lt. Jack Riley, Chicago's finest, called her.

He and Sydney studied criminology together at Northwestern. Jack became a cop; Sydney used her knowledge and inherent ability to aid her friends when needed. On several occasions, Jack had asked Sydney for assistance and always asked why she never became a cop herself. Sydney would become serious, well as serious as Sydney Crosse could be, and tell him she hated guns.

Jack had told Sydney about Harry, an aging petty thief caught once too often. Jack Riley had a soft spot in his Irish heart for the old crook. Sydney knew the judge. If something didn't happen, Harry would be tossed away for a long time. Together, he and Sydney did what no one else would do. They took a chance, and because of Sydney's money and social status and because the judge once dated Sydney's mother, Sydney got Harry. This was Harry's life sentence. Harry had been with her since and would never leave—Harry was a loyal thief.

"Syd? What the hell are you thinking?"

"What? Oh, I was thinking of how we met."

Harry laughed then, still chomping on his cigar. "That was a close one." He pulled out his phone. "I'll call Eddie."

While she watched him talk to Eddie, she took the time to regard her "charge." He was average height, a thin man with thinning white hair, and an occasional cigar, which he didn't light. When Harry Doogan smiled, his eyes lit up his entire face. He had a constant look of mischief about him, which Sydney adored.

"Okay. Eddie will have it all gassed and ready to go."

"Good. Go pack a bag."

"Huh?"

"How would you like to come with me to beautiful Seacliff? We have some good summer weather, and you need a vacation. We'll find Jon. He's probably lost in his woods. Then we'll have the rest of the weekend. We'll chase women," Sydney suggested with a wide grin. "That should torque my mother."

Harry was honestly taken aback. "You want me to go with you? On a vacation?" He looked like a little kid, then he let out a gruff cough. "Well, you do need me, boss."

Sydney smiled. "Yes, I do. Now go pack a small bag. Hurry up," she said impatiently.

She packed her laptop, picked up the printout, and locked up the library. If needed, she could plug into her extensive library, which she'd compiled over the years. A criminal library where she could cross-reference anything, anytime. It was indeed quite extensive and expensive. These were her private files that only she, Harry, and Jack knew about. She could log into them anywhere in the world, and she'd helped Jack countless times.

Sydney was whistling as she neatly packed her clothes. It took her a while to figure out what to bring. There was no excuse not to dress well. Besides, it threw everybody off. She'd rather have her mother think she was a womanizing clothes freak than have her worry every time she got herself embroiled in a mystery, which was the reason for her late night.

One of her friends, a socialite and a past lover, had a problem. She was getting phone calls, letters, that sort of thing and asked for Sydney's help. Over the last two weeks, Sydney figured out who it was and almost got herself shot in the back. The bullet just missed her. Jack finally showed up, and together, they subdued this character. However, that was too close. It was a good thing her mother didn't look at her blazer that morning; she would have seen the bullet hole that went clean through.

She finished packing and looked up at the doorway. There stood Harry in a bright blue and red outlandish shirt and red slacks.

"Whattaya think?" Harry asked and turned around.

Every sense was offended. Sydney was dumbfounded. "The ladies will go wild. I don't think they'll be able to stand it."

"Thanks. You look like a million bucks."

"You think so?" Sydney gazed in the mirror, giving her reflection a jaunty smile. "I like these pleated slacks. They make my hips look slim."

"Like they need slimming. Ya need to put a little on dem bones, Syd. And quit staring at yourself in the mirror."

"Oh, keep still." Syd grabbed her lucky brown leather jacket, which she got from her mother's friend whose aunt was a WASP in World War II. She had flown the supply planes along with other brave and patriotic women. Sydney treasured this jacket above any other possession. She slipped on her sunglasses and glanced in the mirror once again. "I feel like Amelia Earhart."

"And ya look like ZaSu Pitts."

Sydney whirled around. "I don't know who that is, but with a name like that, it can't be good."

Harry let out a belly laugh. "She was an old comedic actress. Her face had a lot of character, my mother used to say."

"Hmm." Sydney ran her fingers through her hair one last time. "Let's get this over with. I'll meet you downstairs. Will you grab my bag?"

"You got it."

"Jon Pickford, you'd better be trying to get some peace and quiet from your mercenary family and that's all."

But he missed the charity engagement with no word to her mother.

That bothered her. Perhaps it wouldn't be such a waste. She truly hoped she'd find Jon sitting at home with a tumbler of scotch in hand.

Was it too much to hope for? Probably.

Chapter 2

Sydney bounded down the stairs only to be met by Harry, who had a sick, apologetic look on his face. She followed his glance to find her mother sitting in the living room; a small piece of luggage sat at her feet.

"Mother?" Syd asked slowly. "What are you doing here?"

"I'm going with you. We'll be there in three hours if you hurry up."

"Uh, no, you're not."

"Uh, yes, I am," Victoria said.

"I was thinking of flying..."

"That rat trap? You can't be serious."

"It's in great shape. Eddie's kept it in prime condition. It's all gassed up and ready to go." Harry stepped back when he received the glare. "Mrs. Crosse."

"Mother..."

"I'm going. Even if it has to be in that antique flying contraption. I've called Keith and Tina to let them know we're coming." Victoria pulled out her cellphone. "And now I suppose we have to tell them we're flying. It's a good thing Jonathon shared your love of flying. He still has the hangar and the runway. It would be more convenient to land there than at the airport."

While Victoria was on the phone, Harry leaned into Sydney. "Who are Keith and Tina?"

"Jon's children. And children being the operative word. You know grownups that never grew up."

"Gotcha." Harry watched Sydney, who seemed to be lost in her thoughts. "Hmm. So this Jon guy has a runway?"

"Well, he had a hangar and runway put in behind his fifty-acre home. The town of Seacliff gladly agreed since Jon donated the library and the courthouse."

"Ah, how you rich live."

"Yeah. Some don't know how to handle it."

"Like his lazy kids? Grownup snots, huh? My old man would know how to handle that."

"Yes, well, I'm not sure corporal punishment is the answer."

"All right. We're all set." Victoria placed the phone in her purse. "Keith said the runway is ready, and he's called the airport."

"Eddie has already taken care of everything," Sydney said. "I suppose you're not going to change your mind?"

"I am not." Victoria looked at the small bag in Harry's hand. "What do you think you're doing?"

"I'm going with you," Harry said defensively, almost clutching his bag. "Syd invited me."

Sydney stepped in to seize the moment. "So now do you still want to go?"

Victoria tore her gaze from Harry. "You're not getting rid of me that easily. Let's go."

Sydney hung her head in defeat; she and Harry dutifully followed Victoria.

"Harry, my bag," she said over her shoulder.

"Yeah, it's your bag. You—"

"Just pick it up, please," Sydney implored him. "And let's get this over with."

"So much for chasing women this weekend." Harry groaned when he picked up Victoria's suitcase. "What the hell does she have in here?"

Sydney winced as she watched her poor mother try to get into the small confines of her vintage Cessna.

"Syd told ya to stay home." Harry tried to assist Victoria. "Vic, this was a mistake. It ain't first class."

Victoria yelled over her shoulder. "I've warned you about your familiarity."

Harry chomped on his cigar as he stood behind her, pushing her in. "And I'm about to get more familiar if you don't get in," he said with a deep groan. He then grinned evilly as he placed both hands on Victoria's derrière and gave a gentle nudge.

Victoria let out a screech, nearly flying into the seat.

"Mother, please." Sydney stuck a finger in her ear. "Are you all right?"

"I am not. Harry Doogan, you did that on purpose."

Harry sported an innocent tilt of his head. "What did I do?"

Sydney lowered her sunglasses. "Harry, will you please get in so I can get this thing off the ground?"

Finally, they were in the air. Sydney settled back; she loved to fly. There was such freedom in the air. She glanced at Harry, who fiddled with an old lock—this was their game together.

"Okay, do it again," Sydney said as she piloted the Cessna over Lake Michigan.

Harry sighed. "Okay, watch."

He blew on his fingers, then rubbed them on his shirt. He then put his hand on the tumbler of the small lock. "Ya listen—click, click. Then a lower click." He put his ear to the lock and turned the tumbler slowly back and forth. He gave Sydney a smug look and pulled on the latch, and the lock opened.

Sydney was impressed. "Amazing. Do it again."

From the backseat, Victoria let out an irritated sigh. "Sydney, would it be too much to ask you to concentrate on flying this deathtrap?"

"Mother, please. I'm trying to concentrate," Sydney called out.

Harry sighed and repeated. After several lessons, Sydney felt she was ready. "Okay, my turn. Hold the wheel."

Harry turned white. "Are you nuts? I can't fly this thing."

"Sure you can."

"No, he can't!" Victoria yelled.

"Yes, he can. Hold your wheel," Sydney said confidently.

Harry rubbed his hands on his pants and gingerly took his wheel.

"Now easy, easy. Just watch that little horizon line, keep it level. Now…"

She tried the tumbler back and forth, listening, pulled on the latch, nothing. Sydney tried several times with no luck.

Harry, however, was having the time of his life. "I'm actually a pilot."

"You're actually an idiot. Both of you," Victoria added.

Sydney was frowning, pulling on the latch. "Yes, yes, you're doin' fine," she said absently and certainly not watching Harry. She tried the tumbler again, and finally, it worked; she pulled the latch, and the lock opened.

"Hey, I did it!" Sydney beamed and saw a maniacal look on Harry's face; she heard the bloodcurdling screech from the backseat.

All at once, Harry pulled the wheel back to him slightly, and the plane rose.

"Harry," Sydney said quietly.

Harry laughed and pushed the wheel away from him, and the nose of the Cessna dipped.

"Harry," Sydney said with a bit of urgency.

Harry turned the wheel, and the plane glided to the left, then back. He giggled like an insane person.

"Sydney!" Victoria cried out. "For heaven's sake."

"Okay. Harry, you're freaking out my mother." Sydney nervously leaned over. "Crashing this plane is not an option."

Harry stopped giggling and turned red. "Right, boss."

The remainder of the short flight was mercifully spent in light conversation. Victoria seemed to relax because Harry was not allowed at the controls again.

After checking in with the local airport, Sydney flew to Jonathon Pickford's huge lakefront home.

"Merciful God," Victoria whispered as the plane landed.
"See? Safer than driving," Sydney said, cutting the engine.
"Can you please just get me out of this sardine can?"
Harry let out a genuine laugh. "You're a good sport, Vic, er, Mrs. Crosse."
"Oh, keep still and give me a hand. And watch that hand, Harry Doogan."
"Yes, ma'am," he said with a deep bow.
"Where is everyone?" Sydney asked.

As if on cue, Tina came out of the house, waving enthusiastically as she met them halfway. She was just as Sydney remembered: as tall as Sydney, with long blond hair that, if Sydney remembered, Tina spent a good deal of money to keep it the same color. And she was in perfect shape, spending her father's money to maintain her narcissistic lifestyle.

"Yeeouzah, who's that?"
"Tina," Victoria said with disdain. "And keep your eyes in your head."
"Sydney!" Tina called out with a wave.
Sydney dropped her bag as Tina ran into her arms. "Oh, Sydney, I'm so glad you're here."
"Are you?" Sydney asked with a wry chuckle.
Tina pulled back. "Dad is still missing," she said with a sniff.
"What happened? Where's Keith?" Sydney asked quietly.
"In the house." Tina noticed Victoria then. "Oh, hello, Victoria."
Victoria smiled sweetly. "I'm doing very well, thank you for asking. You still haven't heard from Jonathon?"
"No, we haven't. Let's get inside." Tina led the way toward the back of the house.
"How's Keith doing?" Sydney asked, slipping her arm under Victoria's.
"He's as upset as I am, naturally," Tina said, sniffing once again.
"I'm sure," Victoria mumbled.

Harry was glad he was relegated to handle the luggage, better that than get into a caustic conversation with Vic.

As they walked into the living room, Sydney noticed Keith standing by the fireplace, brooding.

"Keith," Victoria said.

He turned and offered a thin smile. "Victoria, how are you?" He walked up to Victoria, kissing her cheek. "Sydney."

"Keith."

"And who are you?" Keith asked, offering his hand.

"Harry Doogan. A friend of the family," Sydney said, staring at Keith. Useless, Sydney thought. She never really cared for him. Spoiled rotten whelp. He was taller than Tina and had sandy blond hair and blue eyes. Only thing he was good at was spending his father's money, from what Sydney remembered. He went to Harvard and learned absolutely nothing. He was nearly forty and still a little boy.

"Nice to meet ya," Harry said, shaking his hand.

"Victoria."

Syd froze when she heard the soft, affectionate voice. She honestly thought she'd never hear that voice again. A flood of memories crashed through her mind, just hearing her voice.

"Grace," Victoria said softly. "Hello, dear. You look wonderful."

Syd finally turned around. And there she was. Grace Morgan. The only woman she ever loved.

Grace arched one eyebrow when she looked into Syd's eyes. "Well, well. Sydney Crosse, I thought you were dead."

So much for love…

Chapter 3

"Not dead, Grace. Just missing." Sydney kept her hands in the pockets of her fashionably pleated slacks. The last thing she wanted was for Grace Morgan to see her hands shaking.

Syd was painfully aware of Tina's superior smirk and her mother's withering glance. She didn't know which was more annoying at the moment. But it was Harry's confused posture that had her chuckling.

Grace avoided eye contact with Sydney and regarded Harry. "Hello."

"Hi. Harry Doogan. Friend of the family. That's how I've been introduced so far," he said kindly, taking her hand.

"Well, if you're a friend of Victoria's, you're all right in my book," Grace said sweetly, smiling at Syd. "I adore that shirt. Grace Morgan."

Harry continued to shake her hand. "I knew that red hair meant you were Irish," he said with a wink.

"It's more of a strawberry blond now," Tina chimed in. "Isn't it, Grace?" She playfully wagged her finger at Grace. "I warned you to wash away the gray."

"Can we discuss your father?" Victoria sat in a chair by the fireplace. "What, if anything, have you found out?"

Tina sat on the couch; when she started to cry, Keith sat next to her and explained. "Dad's been missing since Tuesday night. He had dinner with Grace. No one's seen him since."

Syd noticed the old familiar signs of impending anger; Grace's lips pursed as if biting off a sarcastic retort.

Sydney regarded Grace and asked softly, "How do you know Jon, Grace?" She poured her mother a cup of coffee and handed it to her; she saw the warning glance and winked. She then picked up a sandwich and took a bite.

Harry followed her lead and snagged a sandwich, as well. He offered one to Victoria, who declined.

"I'm his attorney."

"You remember that Grace is a lawyer, don't you, Syd?" Tina asked.

Syd ignored her as Grace continued. Syd knew after all this time she and Grace still had one thing in common—they both disliked Tina and Keith.

"Jon and I were working on a contract regarding all the land he owns in the Upper Peninsula. So I was really the last one to see him, I suppose. As Keith said, we had dinner on Tuesday." She stared at her hands. Sydney said nothing as she watched her.

"I heard Brianne say they thought of taking some boats out on the lake, close to shore, you never know," Keith said. His voice trailed off sadly.

Syd noticed that Grace stiffened when Keith mentioned Brianne. "Brianne still the sheriff here in Seacliff?" Syd asked.

"Yes. She just got re-elected," Keith said.

Syd nodded. "Grace, when you left Jon, how was he?"

"He was fine. Looking forward to signing the contracts. He seemed happy," Grace said.

During this discussion, Syd watched Tina, who bristled angrily as she listened to Grace. There was no love lost between them, it seemed. She didn't remember any animosity between them before. But then it'd been years since Syd had anything to do with any of them.

"Where are you staying?" Grace asked.

"Oh, you'll stay here, of course," Tina said, pasting on a smile. "We have plenty of room. We insist, don't we, Keith?"

Keith looked like he'd rather slam his head in a car door, Syd thought.

"Of course. We'd love it."

"Well, I have to get back to the office for a little while." Grace walked over to Victoria and kissed her cheek. "It's a horrible reason, but it's very good to see you again, Victoria."

"I agree, dear. We'll see you later."

"It's nice to meet you, Harry."

"Same here."

Grace then turned to Syd. "I suppose it's inevitable to see you, as well, Syd."

Syd was about to say something when Grace abruptly walked out of the room.

"Well, that was uncomfortable," Keith said with a smug grin as he looked at Syd.

"Let me show you to your rooms." Tina pushed her way in between Keith and Syd.

They followed Tina up the winding staircase. "Victoria, I'll give you this room. There's plenty of room and a private bath. Mr. Dooley—"

"Doogan."

"Oh, sorry. Mr. Doogan, you and Syd can go right across the hall. The bathroom is at the end. How's that? Cozy?"

"Very," Syd said with a sweet smile.

"I'll leave you to get settled in. I think Brianne is coming over later, hopefully with good news."

"Tina, I might want to go into town. Can I borrow a car?" Syd asked.

"I can drive you," she offered.

"No, thanks, I'd rather go alone."

"Sure. Take the red Mercedes in the driveway. The keys are in it."

"Isn't that a little trusting?" Harry asked her.

"We're not worried. Nothing ever happens in this drab place." Tina laughed as she walked down the stairs.

"I'm exhausted," Victoria said. "If you hear anything, Sydney, please let me know."

Syd kissed her forehead. "I will, Mother. I think I'll go into Seacliff and—"

"I suggest you stay away from Grace," Victoria said sternly. "She didn't seem too happy to see you." Victoria reached up and patted her cheek. "You can hardly blame her, can you?"

"Nope, I can't. It was a shock to see her. I don't know why. I figured she still lived here. I—"

"You...?" Victoria gently prodded.

Syd let out a dejected sigh. "I don't know."

"Well, that's a start. Harry, do your job and take care of my daughter," she said as she opened her door.

"Yes, Mrs. Crosse."

She glared at him. "Are you making fun of me?"

"No," he said defensively. "I meant it."

"Good. Come to my room when you get back."

"I will," Harry said with a wicked grin.

Victoria slammed the door.

"You really know how to get under her skin." Syd patted him on the back.

"It's so easy." He followed Syd into her room.

"Um, Harry, you have your own room."

"I know." He sat in the overstuffed chair by the window overlooking the property. "I'd like to hear about Grace."

"I don't want to talk about it."

"That's obvious 'cause you never mentioned her. Now give."

Syd sat on the bed and groaned. "It's really none of your business."

"Don't matter. I got all day." He sat back and put his feet up on the ottoman. "From the beginning."

"I was born—"

"Very funny."

Syd huffed petulantly and grabbed a pillow. "She grew up here. My family used to come here for summer vacation after Jon bought this place."

"You've known her that long?"

"Yep. She worked at an ice cream shop by the lake. I remember her always looking tired. Even as a kid, she was so serious. She always wanted to be a lawyer." Syd chuckled quietly. "I used to kid her about it all the time. Anyway, one summer she wasn't there, and I realized she was eighteen and went off to college. I didn't see her for almost two years. And you know when you get older, family vacations are less. I was never...and she was always so focused."

"Knew what she wanted, and you didn't?"

"Yeah. I worked for my father after college for a few years. Anyway, I saw her many times when we'd come here for whatever function Jon had. Graduations, family stuff like that. It wasn't until about nine years ago when she came to Chicago. I found out from my mother she was in town, and we all met for dinner. And well..." Syd shrugged. "We got to talking, then we saw each other a few times, then we saw each other more and more."

"And ya fell in love with each other?" Harry asked softly.

"I suppose. Yes."

"What happened?"

"I fucked it up and got scared. Grace was so real, so grounded, and I was all over the place. So I broke it off. And she said to call her when I grew up, if I ever would. I think those were her exact words. She always wanted me to be honest. Always challenging me." She laughed then. "She'd always say 'cross my heart.' Only she used cross like my last name, ya know Crosse."

"I get it." Harry laughed along. "So did you cross your heart and tell her the truth?"

"No. I was a coward and blamed her for being so stuffy and serious. Never wanting to have fun, always work. But she was kind and generous. A good woman. Not like me. Rich, carefree. Didn't want responsibility."

"You're not like that, Syd."

She shot him a glare. "How the hell do you know? You don't know me, really."

"Yeah, I do." He sat forward. "You were scared and stupid. Now maybe ya got a chance. Ya never know."

"I have no chance."

"So you do want another chance."

Syd frowned deeply. "No, I didn't say that. I'm fine. It's been too long, and besides, she was seeing Brianne…"

"The sheriff? Hmm. That would make it difficult."

"Oh, why are we talking about this? Damn you. It's been too long, and she's…" Syd threw the pillow against the headboard and stood. "I'm going into town. I'll be back. Watch my mother, will you?"

"Sure."

"And quit smiling like a jackass. This isn't funny!" She angrily grabbed her jacket, then slammed the door.

The red Mercedes convertible did indeed have the key in the ignition. The top was down; it was a warm, sunny day. Syd backed down the driveway and took off. It was a short drive into Seacliff.

When Lake Michigan came into view, Syd relaxed, taking a deep breath and slowly letting it out. All this talk about the past irritated her; she wanted it to stay right where it was—in the past, where it belonged. As she drove into town, she passed a small building. The shingle outside read, *Grace Morgan, Attorney at Law.*

She stopped at a red light and noticed Grace walking down the street, reading a newspaper and eating an apple. Her long thick hair blew freely in the wind. Damn it. As Sydney continued to watch, Grace bumped into the garbage can in front of her office, not watching where she was going. She then tossed the apple core into the can and disappeared into the building. Sydney chuckled slightly and looked away. "Damn it."

Syd drove by her office and parked in a public lot by the lake. She sat there for a moment, watching the seagulls diving at some paper bag on the beach. She closed her eyes and took a deep breath of clean air, so unlike downtown Chicago. She remembered her childhood summers here in Seacliff. As she told Harry, she used to come here on vacation with her parents.

Sydney was very fond of Jon and his wife, Emily. Since he was in business with her father, they were constantly seeing them, which was all right with Sydney and her mother, who adored both of them, as well.

When Emily died nearly ten years ago, Syd's mother cried for a week. Now she had to go through all this with Jon missing. She looked down the street and decided to go to her fate and walk to Grace Morgan's office.

"Pardon me," Sydney said quietly as she walked in the small office. She looked at the name plaque. "Debbie?"

"Yes." Debbie looked up and smiled. "May I help you?"

"I'd like to see Ms. Morgan, if possible. She's not expecting me, but if you tell her Sydney Crosse would like a moment." She smiled and took off her sunglasses.

Debbie gazed at her with her mouth open.

Syd leaned forward. "Debbie?"

Debbie blinked and laughed nervously. "Shertainly." She shook her head. "Sure, certainly, one minute." She backed up and walked down the hall.

Syd twirled her sunglasses. "I still got it. Now if that will work on Grace."

Again, she was hoping for too much.

Chapter 4

Grace read her briefs, eating another apple. She looked up when Debbie's red face appeared.

"Grace." She came in breathlessly. "There's a woman to see you."

By Debbie's appearance, Grace knew exactly who it was. She let out an angry growl. "Don't tell me—Sydney Crosse."

Debbie laughed. "Yes. Grace, she's adorable. Those blue eyes and—" She turned around and bumped into Sydney, who was standing right behind her.

Sydney held her elbow to steady her. "Whoops, careful."

Debbie chuckled nervously and skirted out of the way.

"May I?" she asked and looked at Grace.

"You're already in. But thanks for asking." She offered Sydney the chair in front of her desk.

Syd looked at it and dusted it off before sitting down. Grace bit off a sarcastic remark as she watched her.

Syd crossed her long legs, twirling the sunglasses, as she looked around the office.

"Meet with your approval?" Grace asked, sitting back in her chair.

Sydney stopped and looked at her. "Would it matter?"

"Long ago, it might have."

Syd looked as if she might say something. Grace shuffled papers on her desk.

"It's very comfortable. Your clients must feel like they're right out in the woods."

Grace couldn't decipher if she was being honest or sarcastic. "Thank you. I'm taking that as a compliment. Syd, I'm very busy. What can I do for you?" she asked professionally. Although it was hard not to look into those godforsaken blue eyes.

Sydney's smile faded; the sparkle left as she got serious. It changed her look entirely. She now looked older, Grace thought.

"What do you want?"

"I...I don't know."

"Some things never change." Grace angrily shuffled the papers once again.

"You're going to give yourself one helluva paper cut if—"

"Oh, shut up!"

Syd's eyes bugged out of her head as she quickly sat back.

"You come here, flirting with my assistant, thinking all you have to do is flash the grin and all will be forgiven. Well, it's not."

"Grace—"

"Do you know how long it's been?"

"Six years, two months, and four days," she said softly.

Grace was breathing like a bull. They both stared at each other for a long moment.

"I know you're here because of Jon."

"Yes. I told my mother I'd look in to it, and she insisted on coming with."

Grace laughed then. "That does sound like Victoria."

"What were you working on with Jon?"

Grace got up and paced by the window. "We had dinner on Tuesday. We sat for five hours finalizing this venture. We were to meet in my office Wednesday afternoon. He was to sign that contract for the land deal in the U.P. worth millions, preserving the forest and wildlife we both love so dearly."

"I know you always wanted to be in conservation," Syd said.

"I did. And now, being an environmental lawyer, I got my wish. Using the law to make sure the forests are kept intact. Jonathon agreed on this. When he decided to turn his hundred acres into a state park and wildlife refuge, I was thrilled. I had worked with him for four long years. Making sure all their bases were covered, no stone was left unturned. It was an ironclad contract. I spent so many long nights with my head in the law books." She turned around to Syd. "I just don't know why he would do this."

"There's got to be a logical reason. He just wouldn't run off. Jon's not like that. There has to be a reason. Someone knows something. We have to find out."

Grace listened to Syd; she folded her arms across her chest almost in a protective gesture. "You sound different."

Broken from her thoughts, Syd looked up. "Different?"

"Yes. You seem, I don't know."

Syd let out a sad laugh. "Grown up?"

Grace grinned in spite of herself. "I suppose so."

"Maybe I have. Look, I have a friend back in Chicago. A cop who—"

"You have a friend who's a Chicago cop?"

"A lieutenant. We went to college together."

"I see. He studied criminology, and you chased skirts." When she saw the hurt look on Syd's face, she relented. "I'm sorry. That was out of line."

"No," she said with a sigh. "It's more the truth than I like to admit. Look, Grace, I was so wrong."

"About what?" Grace asked, absently picking up a pen on her desk.

"About, well, everything I guess. I was—"

Grace let out a low growl when Debbie knocked and walked in.

"Am I interrupting?"

"Your timing stinks," Grace said, avoiding Syd's laugh. "What is it?"

"Brianne's here," she said in a worried voice. "With some gentleman."

"Who?" Grace asked.

"I don't know. Brianne didn't introduce him. I think he's a cop."

Grace chewed at her bottom lip. "Give me a minute, Debbie." She looked at Sydney when Debbie left. "It has to be about Jon."

"Of course. Can I stay?"

"Yes, I...that's fine."

They both looked up when Brianne walked in with Debbie right behind her.

"Sorry, Grace. I told Sheriff Gentry to wait..."

"That's all right, Debbie. Thanks."

Debbie glared at Brianne, who just grinned. Her grin faded when she recognized Syd.

"Well, well. Sydney Crosse. What are you doing here?"

"Hello, Brianne. It's nice to see you too." Syd grinned in return. "I'm here about Jon. My mother's worried."

"And you're such a good daughter," Brianne said, holding her hat in one hand; the other lazily rested on her sidearm.

Behind her, the gentleman let out a harsh cough.

"Oh, sorry. This is Detective Webster from the state police."

The detective looked at Syd. "And you are?"

Syd smiled. "A friend of the family. Sydney Crosse from Chicago."

"Detective, how can I help you? I'm hoping it's about Jon."

Detective Webster coughed. "How well do you know Jonathon Pickford?"

Grace nodded. "Well enough, I suppose. I'm his lawyer."

"When was the last time you saw him, miss?" he asked without emotion.

She frowned as she watched him. "Tuesday night. We had a business dinner," she started and could see the corners of the man's mouth turn up. Irritated by the implication, her temper was starting to boil. She looked at Brianne. "Would you like to tell me what's going on?"

"Grace..." Brianne started and reached for her hand.

Detective Webster cut her off. "Ms. Morgan, Jonathon Pickford has been missing for forty-eight hours. He was last seen with you."

"That's common knowledge, Detective," Grace said. "We're all worried about him."

"Can you come down to the station with us?" he asked, not really needing an answer.

Brianne shot him an ugly look. "That won't be necessary right now. Grace," she started, putting her hands on Grace's shoulders. "It's okay. We'll find him."

Detective Webster stood there like a robot. Brianne turned to him. "She's not going anywhere, Detective." He regarded Grace then. "Drop by the station tomorrow morning, okay?"

She nodded as if in a trance. Brianne kissed Grace's forehead, and they were gone. Grace walked around and sat behind her desk. "Why do they want me to come to the police station?"

"It's routine. They're trying to track down his movements, that's all. Don't worry."

Grace chewed at her bottom lip. "Where the hell is he?"

"Grace, maybe you and I can—"

"No, please...this is too much for me to think about right now. You can't...I—"

"No. I get it. You go ahead. I'm heading back to the house. I'll see you later."

Grace nodded and watched the door close behind Syd. She looked out the window to see her walk across the street. She tried to ignore how her heart raced when she first saw her and how all the memories of them came rushing back.

Memories she tried to forget. "Damn her."

Chapter 5

Once back at Jon's house, Syd found Harry and her mother sitting outside on the patio. Harry had a beer, which wasn't surprising. What surprised Syd was the cold bottle in her mother's hand.

"Since when do you drink beer?" Syd asked.

"It's ungodly hot," Victoria said.

"And I couldn't find the liquor to make madam a martini," Harry said.

Sydney chuckled. "Enjoying yourselves? This is an odd picture, let me tell you."

Harry looked up, smiling. "What did ya find out? There's beer in the little fridge over there."

Sydney grabbed a beer and sat down. "Well, Jon's definitely still missing, and Grace and Brianne are probably still an item." She took a long pull from the icy bottle.

"Hmm." Victoria did the same with her bottle.

"What does that mean?" Syd looked from her mother to Harry. "What have you two been up to?"

"Nothing. Just talking and drinking," Harry said, rocking in the chair.

"Mother?"

"You're a fool, Sydney."

"Thank you."

"You're welcome. Grace and Wyatt Earp are not an item."

"I don't care."

Harry snorted into his beer, which Syd ignored.

"But just for the sake of argument, how do you know?"

"I have my ways. You may not have spoken with Grace all this time, but that doesn't mean I haven't."

This revelation shocked Syd; she spilled her beer down the front of her linen blouse. "What? You talk to Grace behind my back?"

"Actually, you were in the room on several occasions. You were just clueless. And I might add self-absorbed."

"I'm not self-absorbed." Syd heard the petulant tone in her voice.

"Perhaps not now. You have evolved," Victoria said, holding her empty bottle up to Harry, "somewhat."

"Hmm. Where is everyone?" Syd asked.

"They both had a charity function in South Haven. They won't be back until later tonight. So we're on our own. What happened with Grace?"

"She had a state police detective in her office. He wants to question her about Jon."

"You sound concerned. It's logical, isn't it?" Victoria took the bottle of beer from Harry. "Thank you."

"You're welcome."

Syd watched both with a skeptical eye. "What is going on with you two? And yes, it's logical. I suppose I'm just worried. I think she wants to be alone. Or at least away from me."

"I can see that," Victoria said. "Well, let's get ready and go into Seacliff and have dinner. If I remember, Ernie's is a good place."

Harry's eyes lit up. "Don't have to ask me twice."

Ernie's was an adorable lakefront restaurant. Its nautical motif only enhanced its charm.

"Let's have a drink," Sydney said, guiding them toward the bar.

"Let's," Harry agreed and rubbed his hands together.

"Let's get a table," Victoria said, putting a hand to her silver hair.

"C'mon, Mother. Don't be a dud."

"Victoria, you look lovely this evening," Harry said, giving Victoria the once-over.

"Thank you. I wish I could say the same for you. Where on earth did you get that shirt?"

Harry looked at his red plaid shirt with the sleeves rolled up. "What? It's a summer fabric. Syd said so."

"Say that ten times." Syd hailed the bartender. "Can we get a table, please?"

"It'll be a couple minutes," the bartender said.

Syd leaned on the bar. "We'll order drinks right now, if that would be all right."

The woman grinned. "It's mandatory. What can I get you?"

"Harry, name your poison."

Harry laughed and slapped the bar. "Bourbon neat."

Sydney lightly hit the bar. "Excellent!" The bartender stood in front of her. "You heard the man, you delightful woman, bourbon neat. And two very, very dry Bombay martinis, straight up, three olives, if you please."

The bartender smiled and gave Sydney a wink and walked away.

Harry chuckled. "How do you do it?"

"They smell money, I'm afraid," Sydney said.

"No…"

"It's true," Victoria said in agreement. "What did you order for me?"

"Your usual."

"You could have asked."

"Why? I know what you like."

"Because, you fool, a woman likes to be asked. Good Lord, if you must be a lesbian, would you please…What am I saying?"

"I'm not sure. But I know what you mean. I get too controlling."

"Like your father. And look how that ended."

"Can you hoist yourself on the barstool?" Syd asked her.

"I can help," Harry said in her ear.

Again, this interaction shocked Syd. Her mother blushed to her roots.

"Shut up, you old fool. I can manage."

"Your table is ready," the bartender said. "I'll have your drinks brought to your table."

"Saved..." Victoria said. "You get the table."

Harry watched as she headed to the restroom. He then followed Syd to the table overlooking Lake Michigan. "This is nice. Like a vacation."

Syd raised her glass and toasted with Harry. "Here's to finding Jon," she said seriously.

Harry nodded. "And to your mother, a nice old broa—, er lady."

"Where did the old gal go to?"

"Restrooms."

"Ah. Well, to my mother. If you play your cards right, you never know," she suggested.

Harry looked shocked. "Boss, I could never get that lucky."

Sydney looked at him over her martini glass. "Don't bet on it."

Harry's smile had Syd turning in her seat. Victoria weaved her way to their table.

Harry jumped up and held out her chair.

"Thank you, Harry. Did you notice Grace?" Victoria took a sip of her martini. "Very good."

"Where?"

"She's just arrived...With Wyatt."

Sydney noticed Grace coming in with Brianne. She looked around while waiting to be seated. She caught Sydney's eye and coolly smiled. Sydney raised her glass slightly and gave her a smug grin. Brianne saw her and nodded.

Sydney further noticed Grace wore her hair up and a beautiful pair of—what Sydney was sure was—sapphire earrings. She knew they matched her eyes.

Syd tried not to watch them as they made their way to a table, thankfully, on the other side of the restaurant.

"What do you suppose is the attraction there?" Harry sipped his drink.

"Who cares?" Syd nearly put her eye out from the toothpick when she took a healthy drink of her martini. She snatched the toothpick and ate the olive.

"Who can tell?" Victoria said to Harry. "The course of true love…"

"Is constantly derailed," Harry said, holding up his drink to her.

"Too true," Victoria said, touching her glass to his.

Syd glared at both of them. "I should have left you on the patio."

"Whattaya think they're talking about? It don't look like love talk," Harry said, watching them.

"As if you'd know," Victoria mumbled into her martini glass.

"Okay, change of topic." Syd tore her gaze from Grace.

"Good idea," Harry said. "Tell me about Jonathon."

"Let's order first." Syd hailed their server; at the same moment, she noticed Grace watching her.

Syd knew Brianne was talking to her, but Grace seemed not to care. Finally, Syd had to look away when the server came to their table. She barely remembered what she had ordered for dinner.

"Okay, so fill me in," Harry said. "It sounds like you've known him and his family."

"Yes," Victoria said, toying with her water glass. "I met Jon when I met Sydney's father. They were college roommates and best friends."

Syd smiled affectionately. "They both had eyes for the prettiest girl at Northwestern, Victoria Cameron."

Victoria huffed indignantly.

Harry leaned on the table. "I can see that. I bet you were as good-lookin' as you are right now."

"And you're a rascal, Harry Doogan."

"Rascal?" Syd whispered. Syd hid her astonishment in her martini glass, which only had an olive in it. She quickly looked around for her server.

"I married David Crosse, and that as they say is that. Jonathon and David started TeleCrosse Communications forty years ago. Jon sold out to David ten years ago to devote the rest of his life to conserving his beloved acreage up here in Michigan."

"How many acres?" Harry asked.

Syd waited until the server set their plates in front of them. She cut into her steak as she continued. "One hundred acres of wild untouched forests. I personally think he was trying to cope with his wife's death."

"Yes. That was so sad. What a wonderful woman," Victoria said wistfully. "Emily Kennedy Pickford, they were married for nearly forty years. She died of cancer ten years ago. Left poor Jon with two children."

"Two mooches," Syd corrected her as she ate her steak. "This is delicious."

"He was a good husband and father," Victoria said softly. "Good Lord, I'm talking as if he's dead. Where is he?" She looked at Syd, who reached over and took her hand.

"I don't know, Mother, but I'll find out."

Harry reached over and took her other hand. "And I'll help Syd. Don't you worry."

"Thank you both," Victoria said. "Now let me go so I can finish my dinner."

The rest of the evening found Syd extremely anxious and preoccupied; she didn't even remember eating her steak—and she loved steak.

It didn't help matters when Grace and Brianne left before them. For a moment, Grace looked at their table. She waved to Victoria and smiled hesitantly in Syd's direction.

This was not going to be the weekend Sydney hoped for of finding Jon quickly, then having a raucous time in Seacliff.

It seemed nothing was going right at all.

Chapter 6

It was just about sunrise when Syd woke; she stretched and lazily threw back the covers. With the sun just coming through her window, she felt revitalized for some reason. She loved this time of day and decided to take a walk along the beach after a good shower.

Sydney took a deep breath of fresh air as she walked slowly along the shore. Lake Michigan was always a bit cold, but the water that lazily lapped on the shore was actually warm against her bare feet. Clad in shorts and a lightweight shirt, she carried her deck shoes and walked in the ankle-deep water.

As she strolled along the shore, she noticed an adorable house set off by itself. It looked old and majestic standing alone. Then something in the water caught her eye. A swimmer, a woman who looked like she was having difficulty, was about a hundred feet ahead of Syd, close to that house.

Syd ran along the shore. The woman was about thirty feet out, then she went under. Syd dropped her shoes, threw off her sunglasses, and ran into the water. She frantically looked around in waist-deep water; there was no sight of the swimmer. Christ, she thought. Then the woman came up, floating on her back. Syd quickly swam to her and grabbed her while the woman screamed and lashed out, smacking Syd across the face.

Struggling to help her, Syd yelled, "You're all right. I have you." She dragged the woman back to shallow water where she effortlessly held the drowning woman.

"Grace? I—" Syd shook her head to get the water out of her eyes.

Grace still struggled in her arms. "What in the hell are you doing? Put me down."

Syd only held her tighter and started for the shore. "Oh, no. I caught you, and I'm going to keep you. You beat any lake trout." The corners of her mouth twitched as she continued toward the shore.

Grace stopped struggling and said calmly, "Put me down, you arrogant…" Before she could finish, Syd threw her in the water; she came up coughing.

Syd laughed and offered her hand. "Sorry…"

Grace wrenched her arm away, glaring at her. "Sorry, my ass." She put her leg behind Syd and shoved as hard as she could.

Syd flew backward, landing in a splash in the shallow water. She sat there, laughing hysterically. "Where did you learn that? Is that the thanks I get for saving you? You looked like you were struggling."

"Saving me? You pompous ass. I was washing my hair," she said angrily with her hands on her hips.

Sydney noticed she was wearing a wonderful green bathing suit that complemented her reddish hair perfectly.

"Really? My mistake, I thought you were drowning. I must remember to wear my glasses," she said sadly. "Give me a hand." She extended her hand and laughed again as Grace marched out of the shallow water.

"Grace, wait," she called after her.

"God, you're full of yourself," Grace said over her shoulder.

"Oh, c'mon. I'm sorry. I…" Syd grinned and ran to catch up to her. "You live here?"

"Yes. Sit on the porch, you're all wet."

"You're not the first person to tell me that."

"And I'm sure I won't be the last."

"That's gratitude for you. I save you, and I—"

"No." Grace gritted her teeth. "You did not save me. I was washing my hair." Grace sighed deeply. "Would you like a cup of coffee?"

"Yes, please." Syd looked out at the lake. She liked it up here. It was quiet and peaceful.

"Are you falling asleep?"

"Almost. It's quiet up here." She took the cup from Grace. "Thanks."

"You're welcome," Grace said, avoiding looking directly at Syd. She walked over to the other rocking chair and sat.

"So Tina and Keith don't look like their father is missing. Are they still going through Jon's money?"

Grace nodded sadly. "Like shit through a goose."

Syd chuckled as she drank her coffee. "Mother's worried sick."

"I know. She looked so tired last night."

"Speaking of last night. Are you and Wyatt…?"

"Wyatt?" Grace said angrily.

"Oh, I—" Syd laughed nervously. "I'm sorry. I didn't mean."

"Oh, yes, you did." Grace rocked faster. "You have some nerve, Sydney. What right do you have, coming back after all this time?"

"I have no right."

"That's right."

"I know, I know. I'm sorry."

Grace breathed heavily through her nose. "God, you're infuriating."

"I'm sorry," Syd said softly. "I was wrong."

"Yes, you were."

"Maybe I should go."

Grace stood and took her coffee cup. "I was going to go to Jon's this morning. I can drive you back if you want to wait."

Syd's mouth dropped. "Uh…"

Grace rolled her eyes and walked away. "Don't fall off the porch. I'll be right out."

Chapter 7

Grace noticed the police car when she pulled into the driveway. Her stomach flipped anxiously.

"Well, let's get inside," Syd offered.

When Grace and Syd walked into the house, they saw Brianne standing in the library talking to Tina and Keith. Victoria sat in stony silence with Harry standing next to her; he looked sad. When he saw Syd, he shook his head. Grace felt like crying; she swallowed her emotions and walked farther into the room.

Syd ran up to Victoria and knelt in front of her. "Are you all right?"

Victoria nodded. "It's bad news, Sydney."

Tina cried into Keith's shoulder.

Grace walked up to Brianne. "What's happened, Brianne?"

"He's dead. Dad is dead. That's what's happened." Tina continued to sob, clinging to Keith.

"Is this true?" Sydney asked, frowning.

Brianne nodded. "They found his body south of here, on the shore, hidden by some rocks. Two kids thought they saw it on Thursday. When the kids heard about Jon's disappearance, they told their mother. She called. They found him early this morning. His body's at the coroner's now. The state police are combing the area looking for anything."

Brianne looked from Grace to Sydney. "Where've you been?"

"Fishing," she said absently.

Grace knew Syd probably wanted to tell Brianne exactly what she thought of her, but she saw the pleading look from Grace and relented.

"So what's next?" Grace walked over and sat next to Victoria.

"The state police are taking over. It may have been an accident. We can't know until the autopsy is done."

"I can't believe it," Grace said, shaking her head.

Brianne stood next to her, putting her hand on her shoulder. "I know, sweetie. I'm so sorry."

"How long will the autopsy take?" Keith asked, running his fingers through his hair.

"I'll check in with the troopers. I'll let you know," Brianne said. "I'd better get back to the office. I'll call you later." She gave Grace's shoulder a reassuring tug and was gone.

Tina wiped her nose with her tissue. "How can this have happened?"

"I don't know," Victoria said numbly. "But they'll find out." She looked at Syd, who nodded. "I think I'll go up to my room."

Syd and Harry helped her to her feet.

"I need to go to my office," Grace said.

Syd noticed how tired she looked and how her hands shook as she rubbed her forehead.

Grace kissed and hugged Victoria. "I'll keep in touch."

"Thank you, dear."

Grace turned to Tina and Keith; neither made a move to go to her.

"I'm very sorry," Grace said softly to both of them.

Tina merely nodded, wiping her nose with the tissue.

Syd glowered at both of them. Harry looked like he might vomit.

Grace awkwardly turned away from them. She looked at Syd. "I'll talk to you later."

"Okay. If you need me…"

Grace smiled and put her hand on Syd's forearm. "Thanks. I'll call you."

Grace numbly drove to her office. Although it was Saturday, she felt like keeping busy. She read her briefs and worked on her computer. It was one o'clock, and the day was gorgeous. She sighed unhappily and looked out her office window.

Then she saw Sydney at the traffic light. She had Tina's car and looked deep in thought as she waited for the light. She put her head back and ran her fingers through her hair. Then she looked over at Grace's office. Grace instinctively took a step back, hoping she didn't see her, and in the next instant, she hoped she did.

By one thirty, she decided to go home. She gathered her briefcase, opened the door, and ran right into Sydney.

"Oh, good. You're still here," she said.

"I was just on my way home," Grace started, and Sydney interrupted her.

"I just wanted to let you know how sorry I am about this," she said gently.

Grace couldn't help it; she suddenly burst into tears. She dropped her briefcase and covered her face with her hands.

"Oh, Gracie, I'm so sorry," she whispered.

Syd picked up her briefcase and took her keys. Syd put her arm around her shoulders, and Grace allowed her to usher her out of her office.

Once outside, Grace stopped and gently pulled away. "I'm sorry, I don't know why..." She hated herself when she started to cry again.

"Grace, please. I can't stand to see you cry. Let's go."

Syd's car was parked in front of her office. She took Grace's briefcase and tossed it in the backseat.

Grace got in without a word and put her head back. "Where are we going?"

"No one works on a beautiful sunny Saturday in June. We're going to the beach," Sydney said, smiling and stealing a glance at her.

"Really, I don't think..."

"No use, I've made up your mind. To the beach," she said firmly. "Mother is lying down. Harry is keeping an eye on things for me."

"Why?"

"Just because."

Grace put her head back and sighed, too sad and too tired to argue. They drove for a few minutes, then Sydney turned around.

"To be honest, I have no idea where I'm going. So let's go back to your place," she said, smiling.

Grace turned in her seat and glared at her. "Look, Sydney. That line might work on all the other women who are crazy for you, but not me. Stop this car right now."

Sydney was shocked. "Gracie…"

"Don't call me that. Stop this car."

"I'm sorry, please calm down. I was not suggesting…"

"I'm not kidding."

"Okay, I get it. I'll take you home. You can't walk from here," Sydney said firmly.

The remainder of the drive to Grace's house was quiet.

Syd pulled up on the side of the house and stopped. Grace got out and slammed the car door. She picked up her briefcase and noticed a picnic basket on the seat.

Sydney looked at it, then at Grace. "I saw you in your office. So I stopped and bought a picnic lunch and a bottle of wine. I knew how upset you probably were over Jon. Believe me, I was thinking of nothing else but having lunch with you. I honestly couldn't remember a better beach than this."

Grace said nothing as Syd put the car in gear.

"I am truly sorry. Perhaps next time."

She watched as Syd pulled away. "Damn her!"

Grace threw on her bathing suit and decided to go for a swim. She grabbed her towel and headed to the beach. As she walked into the shallow water, she knew it would be chilly, but she didn't care. Diving in, she caught her breath just a bit as she came up swimming.

As she let out a contented sigh, she looked at the beach and sighed heavily. There was Sydney Crosse spreading a blanket and adjusting her chair.

She watched Syd as she slipped out of her cover-up, exposing a sexy one-piece bathing suit. Grace damned her racing heart as memories flooded back. Memories of them when they were younger and in love. Or so Grace thought.

Sydney Crosse was still in very good shape as she walked into the lake, then dove in. And as she remembered, Syd was an excellent swimmer.

"Well, you're not as good as I am, you narcissistic boob."

Syd was just getting out when she noticed Grace swim up to her. "Hi."

Grace walked out of the shallow water. "Hi. Look, I'm sorry. This whole thing..."

"I deserve everything you deal out. Let's forget it. I'm starving, and I know you haven't eaten all day."

Grace followed her to the blanket on the beach and sat at one edge. "I'm really not very hungry."

"Liar. I remember your appetite." Syd opened the bottle of wine and poured two glasses, handing one to Grace. "I've got fried chicken, potato salad, and fruit. That's all I could get from the market down the street."

"Thanks." Grace took a sip of wine and relaxed. "I do love it here."

"I know you do. Jon did too," Syd added quietly. She ate a chicken leg, tossing the bones in the bag. "It had to be an accident."

"I hope so. I don't know what to do if it wasn't."

"Find out why and who."

Grace watched her; Syd looked deep in thought. "What are you thinking?"

Syd looked up. "Oh, nothing, really. Well, I suppose I was thinking who'd want to kill Jon and why. But it was probably an accident." She dusted off her hands and picked up some grapes. "Tell me again about the contract."

"We worked together for years. Jon was a great conservationist, and he wanted to leave something behind. He was worth at least twelve million dollars and wanted to make his life worth something. Ever since Emily died, he was lost. Tina tried to get closer to him, but I believe she only tried to get in Jon's good graces. It's no secret Tina and Keith are supreme disappointments. I think those were his exact words."

"How much was Jon planning on leaving to the Conservation Department?"

She shrugged. "Honestly, I only know what we discussed. If there was more, I'm sure it's in his will. I was just happy to help him do this." She looked around the beach and the lake. "Pretty soon, the lakefront will be gone. This beach will recede, and someday, being the wonderful species that we are, we'll destroy all of it with buildings and shopping malls. We'll cut down every tree and rape the land in a ravenous frenzy for money, lousy money." Grace lifted a handful of sand and let it sift gently through her fingers.

"I've forgotten how passionate you are regarding this. I admire you."

Grace didn't respond; she sipped her wine.

"I'm sorry, Grace," Syd said softly.

Grace looked at her then. "Why? I get that you didn't love me anymore. But how could you not talk to me all these years? Weren't we more than that? Be honest with me."

Syd chuckled sadly. "Cross my heart?"

Grace smiled. "At least you remember that. Yes, cross your heart, Ms. Crosse."

"I was never very good at being an adult. And you took to it so eagerly." Syd gulped the wine in her glass. "I got scared."

Grace tilted her head. "Scared of what?"

"Scared that you'd see I was all show and no stay. I knew how to dress well, how to act in society with the right people, but I had no idea how to love you."

"That's how you looked at yourself. That's not what I saw."

"It couldn't last. You knew what you wanted—"

"I only wanted you," Grace said quietly, sifting sand through her fingers.

They sat in silence for a little while. Grace hid her grin when she watched Syd absently drawing in the sand.

"I know it's been a long time. And you probably won't believe me. Can I tell you something without you getting angry or slapping me?" Syd asked.

"I'm not sure. I guess you'll just have to give it a try."

"I never loved anyone after you." Syd glanced at Grace, then looked back at the sand.

"You're right. I find that hard to believe. You know I talk to Victoria from time to time. There was a woman named Rita, I believe, then Andrea and—"

"I didn't say I was celibate. I said I never loved anyone. And while we're at it, you…"

"Me what?" Grace asked lightly; she picked up a peach and took a bite, wiping the juice off her chin.

"Brianne Gentry," Syd said.

"What about her? And quit sticking your jaw out."

"You're not in love with her?"

"No," Grace said simply. "What does it matter to you?"

"It doesn't."

"Then why did you ask?" Grace held up the bottle of wine. "More wine?"

"No," Syd said quickly. "Thank you."

"Sydney," Grace said, setting the bottle down. "You can't get angry with me when we haven't spoken in years."

"Who's angry?"

"You are," Grace said quietly.

"I am not." Syd picked up some sand and tossed it back down.

Grace cocked her head. "Tell your face."

Syd hung her head and chuckled. "I give up."

Grace laughed along. "Don't give up. I've always gotten a kick out of irritating you, but we should go."

They started to clean up their picnic. Syd reached over and gently grabbed Grace's wrist. "Can you irritate me later, maybe?"

Grace laughed then. "Maybe."

Chapter 8

Harry waited for Sydney in her room. He paced back and forth, looking at Sydney's computer. He plugged it in, but after that, he hadn't a clue what to do. He looked at the laptop angrily and paced once again. He ran to the door when it opened.

"Thank God!" he said.

Sydney laughed. "What the devil are you doing?"

"Where have you been?"

"I was with Grace. Where's Mother?"

"She's in her room. Poor woman's been crying all afternoon."

"I should go to her."

Harry grabbed her by the arm. "Not yet. Jack Riley called, said to tell you to read your eel. What the hell is that? Some sorta code?"

Sydney narrowed his eyes and watched Harry. "Read my eel? Have you been drinking?"

"No!"

Then it dawned on her; she laughed and sat on the edge of the bed. "You old nut. Read my email." Sydney went to the computer and turned it on, then logged in.

Harry watched as Syd concentrated on the computer screen. "Anything?"

"Jack sent something on Tina and Grace, but Keith would have to wait until tomorrow. No big surprises. Basic information on Grace and Tina. Wonder why I have to wait for something on Keith."

"That's it?" Harry asked. "Boy, when he called, Vic was all over me wanting to know who it was. I said it was nothing, but I know she didn't believe me. I hate lying to your mother."

"She's fine. Has the sheriff come by at all? I need a shower."

"Yeah, the sheriff came by. Boy, was she pissed off when I told her you went to see Grace."

"Really? Good. What happened?"

"Well, she comes by about an hour ago and talks ta Keith. I try to listen, but they're talkin' low. I don't hear anything, then the sheriff leaves. Keith goes to his car and takes off, and Tina leaves to find you." He threw his hands up. "That's all. I figure they're all upset about the father. Everybody's edgy around here. I wanna go home."

"No. Did Brianne say anything about the autopsy?"

Harry leaned against the dresser. "Well, she says the coroner is mostly done."

Syd pulled out a change of clothes. She whirled around to Harry. "Already?"

"I guess. The sheriff says they should know by tomorrow exactly how he died."

"I can't believe an autopsy can be done that quickly. Hey, I have an idea. Tomorrow morning, we take a drive to that beach and take a look where they found Jon. I need to get a picture of this place in my mind. I'm having a hard time believing Jon drowned. What was he doing that far from home? Jon was an excellent swimmer. I know Lake Michigan has horrible undertows, but Jon has lived in this area all his life. Why now does he have a problem swimming?" Sydney shook her head. "It just doesn't jibe, Harry. Something's not right."

Harry looked very worried as Sydney put on her robe. "I have a feeling you're gonna get mixed up in somethin' here."

"I know, and you're gonna help."

Harry shook his head and chewed on his cigar. "And how are we going to deal with your mother?"

"We'll think of something. Let me go check on her, then we go out for dinner and regroup."

After showering, avoiding her mother's question about Jack's call, and calming Harry, Syd was really ready for a drink. It also surprised her that Tina and Keith were nowhere to be found. Her mother mentioned they went to make funeral arrangements. The feeling that something was just off with this entire situation still nagged at her.

But once again, they decided to have dinner at Ernie's. The hostess saw them coming and miraculously had the same table. Victoria was impressed; Syd figured it was the ginormous tip she left.

"I sincerely hope Grace is all right," Victoria said. "I don't like to think of her alone right now. You know she has no one in her life."

Syd leaned forward. "Mother, how do you know these things?"

"I told you."

Syd narrowed her eyes. "Just how often do you talk to Grace?"

Victoria grinned and stirred the toothpick in her martini glass.

Harry rested his chin in the palm of his hand. "I adore you."

Syd watched them closely. "The universe is all out of whack. I can't handle you two anymore."

Suddenly, Victoria waved frantically. Syd turned to see Grace standing by the hostess. Grace smiled and waved, then made her way to their table.

"Did you plan this?" Syd asked her mother.

"Naturally. Left to you, you'd make another monumental mistake."

Harry stood when Grace approached the table. "Well, don't you look lovely? Don't she look lovely, Syd?"

Syd nodded. "Very." She glared at her mother. "I hate you."

Victoria laughed and sipped her drink. "You love me. Grace, sit down, dear."

"Thank you, Victoria. Good evening, Syd."

"Hello."

"How are you? Save anyone lately?"

Syd clenched her teeth while listening to their conversation. She had to admit, however, she'd take the ribbing from Grace instead of the painful angry look she received when they first saw each other at Jon's. She watched Grace, who was talking to Victoria while Harry found something on the table very interesting.

"What are you doing?"

"I like this little curly thing of butter they have here. I've never seen anything like that. How do you suppose they do this?"

"The butter grows like that."

Harry waited for a moment. "Very funny."

Syd laughed, but she looked at Grace, who dabbed her eyes with her napkin.

"What's wrong?" Syd asked.

"Nothing. I just can't believe this is happening," Grace said; she took a deep breath. "It's just surreal."

"I know what you mean," Victoria said. "Though I had a bad feeling when he didn't show up in Chicago. I have to say, I didn't expect this." She reached over and took Grace's hand. "We'll help you through this."

"Thank you. I suppose all we can do is wait to see what happens next."

"Hey, Syd, who's that with Keith?" Harry motioned to the front of the restaurant.

Sydney looked by the door to see Keith with an attractive woman, dark hair, nicely dressed. He had his arm around her waist, and he kissed her on the cheek as they waited for their table.

"Grace, do you know who that woman is?"

She looked over her shoulder. "That's Marcy Longwood. She's the family lawyer."

"I thought you were Jon's lawyer," Syd said.

"I only do the legal work for this contract. I'm an environmental lawyer."

Syd buttered a roll while she watched Keith.

Keith had a possessive air about him; he kept touching this poor woman. Marcy seemed to initially enjoy the attention, then she casually picked up his hand off her arm and placed it on the table and patted it affectionately. Keith frowned like a child and drank his cocktail quickly.

Syd laughed. "What a whelp."

Dinner was as light as it possibly could be, given the circumstances. And the evening ended much too soon for Syd when Grace announced she was leaving.

Afterward, Syd sat at the table stirring her coffee, knowing her mother and Harry were watching her.

"What?" she asked, concentrating on her coffee cup.

"Are you going to be an idiot all your life?" Victoria asked evenly.

"Is that a rhetorical question?"

"Seriously, Sydney. When are you going to grow up and tell Grace you were a colossal ass and apologize?"

Syd looked at Harry. "You're supposed to be on my side. What do you have to say?"

"Not much," Harry said. "Your mother's doing a good job. I think I'll just watch."

"Coward," Syd mumbled.

"You have to make this right. Grace still cares for you."

"Oh, how do you know that?"

"One has to be blind not to see the way she looks at you. Tell her, Harry."

"She's right, Syd. Grace lit up like a firefly when she saw you tonight."

"You're both whacky." She set her coffee cup down when her hand visibly shook.

"You're very blessed. You learned well from your father and Jon. I wish I could say the same for Tina and Keith. They were spoiled, really spoiled. They lacked for nothing. You, on the other hand, understood the value of money. It was something you worked hard for and wasn't handed to you. Even though you inherited a fortune, you've never abused it."

"Except the wardrobe," Harry said absently.

Syd laughed then. "Well, one must dress well."

Victoria ignored their playful banter and continued, "For not having a brain for business, I must admit, you've handled yourself well with the company."

"That's because I hired a good VP, who in turn hired exceptional managers. I knew nothing of that. But I knew Father and Jon poured their lives into that company. It's not my cup of tea, but that doesn't mean I can't take care of it. I trust them to take care of it."

"Your father trusted no one." Victoria sighed sadly. "He surrounded himself with lackeys who'd spy on his employees. But you trust your executives. You give them responsibilities and pay them a deserving salary for their good work. The fact that TeleCrosse Communications stock has skyrocketed is due mainly to their work."

"Due completely to their work," Syd gently corrected her. "And I'm very grateful. And I show that gratitude in their salaries, which I can well afford."

"If you're gonna throw money around, that's the best place," Harry said. "Besides, it frees you up to—" He looked stunned when Syd glared at him. He offered an apologetic grin.

"Frees you up to do what?" Victoria asked innocently. "To spend your time with that policeman?"

Now Syd was stunned. She swallowed convulsively. "What, um, what are you talking about?"

"Oh, please. You two are so transparent. Running around Chicago like something out of a dime mystery novel. I'm well aware of what you've been doing with Jim Kelly."

"Jack Riley," Harry offered.

"Whatever." Victoria waved dismissively. "Just what do you think you can do?"

"I, well, I don't know."

"I know you took those criminology and those dreadful anatomy classes at Northwestern. I still think it was a tremendous waste of time and money." She regarded Harry. "And what do you have to say?"

"Me? Nothin'. I think Syd is a great gal. She has a big heart, which I think she inherited from her mother. She helps her friends when they need it. She takes care of a multimillion-dollar company at the same time. She's never caused you any trouble. Never been in the papers. And she doesn't burp in public." He leaned in and smiled at Victoria. "So you might wanna cut her some slack, Vic."

Syd's hand flew to her mouth. Her mother just blinked.

Syd frantically looked around for their server. "Check, please!"

Chapter 9

Sydney woke Harry early the next morning. She showered quickly and dressed, then knocked at Harry's door.

Harry opened the door. "What?"

Sydney chuckled. "You grump. Good morning."

"It was a late night with your mother."

"C'mon, get dressed. We have a crime scene to visit," Sydney said. "What are you wearing?"

Harry looked offended. He wore the most outlandish pajamas. Sydney looked shocked. They were red and white striped with a red collar and cuffs.

"My sister got 'em for me for a birthday present. Don't laugh." He let out loud yawn. "Lemme shower. I'll be right down."

"Fine. I'll leave my mother a note. Hurry up."

It was a sunny, clear day as they drove south to the rocks where Jon's body was found. They found them with little difficulty. It was indeed secluded. The huge rocks stood about eight to ten feet high and stretched about fifty yards before ending abruptly. The waves now lazily lapped up to them. When it was windy, the whitecaps were sure to angrily crash against the rocks. Sydney and Harry made their way to the beach and looked around.

"What're we lookin' for?" Harry scratched the back of his head.

"Anything, anything at all. If he was murdered—and I think he was, don't ask me why just yet—the murderer had to leave something behind. If he was killed here," Sydney said, looking around the area. "Maybe he was killed somewhere else and left here. Perhaps he drowned, and his body washed ashore. I just don't know."

They combed the area for well over an hour. Suddenly, Harry stopped. "Syd, maybe this is nothin'."

Sydney came quickly to his side. "No such thing," she said seriously.

They squatted down and looked at an end of what looked like a thin cigar. It was in between two big rocks. Sydney squeezed her hand in between. She slipped and let out a painful grunt when she cut the palm of her hand on the rock.

"You okay?"

"Yes, yes." Irritated with herself, she carefully pulled the butt out and held it up, looking at it. Its end was neatly squared off.

"Don't look like a normal cigarette or a cigar ta me," Harry said, looking at it. "Your hand's bleeding."

Sydney gave the cigar a curious look. "What's the name for those little cigars? Damn. Both ends are squared off. You don't need to clip them. It's an old type name." Sydney closed her eyes. "It's on the tip of my tongue."

"Lemme see."

"My Uncle Max used to smoke them all the time. This looked like the same one."

"Oh, I know." Harry snapped his fingers a few times. "Cheroot," he said triumphantly.

"That's it. A cheroot. Got a handkerchief?"

"Yeah." He pulled it out of his back pocket and handed it to her.

"Since when?" Syd asked, holding it up.

"Since your mother. She nagged at me. I couldn't take it no more."

She took the handkerchief and gently put the cheroot in it and closed it up.

Harry looked doubtful. "You really think that's somethin'?"

Sydney shrugged. "Look around. We've been combing this place for an hour. Did you see any butts lying around? Did you see anything? This place is very isolated. Look how long it took us to get down here. The police were here all day yesterday. And look at the cheroot. You smoke cigars. Does it look old or soggy?"

Harry looked at it, then bent down to sniff it. "Boss, I can still smell tobacco, not much, but I can smell it."

Sydney smiled and looked out at the lake. "Something's wrong here. I can smell that, too."

"Let's get breakfast. I'm starved. You gotta get something for that hand."

They found the closest diner and ordered a quick breakfast.

"I'm sure the autopsy is done, and I know we won't be able to see it," Sydney said, examining the bandage on her palm. "We've got to see what's on that report. Perhaps Brianne will let a little out, but she's the sheriff. She won't say much. Definitely not to me, anyway."

"How are you going to see the autopsy report?" Harry said with a mouthful of pancakes.

"I just don't know, but I'll figure it out. I wish the state police weren't involved. I might be able to get around Brianne, but not the state police."

"Syd, what if they determine it's an accident?" Harry asked, finishing his pancakes.

Sydney looked out the window of the diner. An ugly feeling crept over her.

"Getting one of your feelings?" Harry asked.

"Yeah. I can't explain it. When I know something, I just know it. And unfortunately," Syd tossed her napkin down, "it wasn't an accident. I wish with all my heart it was."

"I wonder how everyone is doing this morning."

"We should probably get back. I'm sure my mother is up. I hate to leave her with Tina."

When Syd pulled into the driveway, she noticed Grace's Jeep. They found Grace and Tina on the patio.

"I thought I heard voices," Sydney said, smiling at Grace. "Good morning."

"Good morning," Grace said, avoiding eye contact.

"Where's my mother?"

"In the kitchen. She's making breakfast."

"My mother cooks?" Syd looked toward the kitchen.

"Where have you been and what happened to your hand?" Tina asked.

Sydney looked down at it. "I went jogging and tripped and fell against some rocks."

Tina seemed to accept the explanation, but of course, Grace gave her a dubious look, which she avoided.

"Good, you have coffee." Syd poured a cup for herself and Harry.

"Mornin', Irish," Harry said, smiling.

Grace smiled back. "Good morning, Harry, Sydney. Where did you go jogging?"

"Oh, just by the beach."

"In deck shoes?"

Tina noticed them, as well. "Fashionable, Sydney, but not practical."

"Well, I was never one for practicality. You know me. It's all about the fashion. So have you heard anything from Brianne?"

"Not yet. Grace and I were just talking about Dad. We both agree that the coroner had better have some answers."

Sydney gave her a curious look. She sounded like she was reading from a cue card. Good grief, she thought, her father just died. Tina could show a little more sadness or remorse than the brief tears she shed when Jon's death was announced.

"Syd?"

She looked up when all eyes were on her.

"Your phone. Someone is texting you," Grace said.

"Oh." Syd pulled out her cell. It was from Jack—he had information on Keith that he would email to her the next day. "Hmm."

"Anything wrong?" Tina asked.

"Oh, no, no." Syd put the phone in her pocket. "My bookie."

Grace offered a smug grin. "My ass."

Syd looked up when her mother walked out onto the porch. "Good morning, Chef."

Victoria raised an eyebrow. "Don't be insolent. Good morning. Harry."

Harry stood and pulled out a chair. "Good morning, Vic. You look rested."

Victoria sat with a groan. "I slept very well. The beds are very comfortable, Tina. Where's Keith?"

"He'll be down."

"Got home very late last night," Victoria said, looking at Syd. "Actually, it was early this morning."

"My ears are ringing." Keith walked out onto the patio. "Good morning, all."

At least he looked tired and worn, Syd thought. Though she wasn't sure if it was from grief or a late night with Marcy Longwood. She listened to the small talk until the doorbell rang. Everyone sat for a moment, hearing the bell ring again.

"Well, I'll get it," Keith said.

Though no one said anything, Syd figured they all suspected what it had to be. When she saw Brianne follow Keith, her suspicions were confirmed. She instinctively reached for Grace's hand.

"Morning, everyone," Brianne said, looking very dour. "I hope everyone is okay."

"No small talk, Sheriff," Tina said quickly.

Brianne ran her fingers through her short blond hair. "Okay. This is just the preliminary report. They're still waiting on tests to come back that may take a couple weeks." She ran her hand across her face. "It looks like Jon was murdered."

Syd was not surprised. Grace stared blankly at the table. Sydney noticed that Keith and Tina reacted a bit slower. Shock, she thought. Then Tina put her hands over her face and sobbed, turning to Keith, who held her.

Grace was white. "How?" Her hands were trembling.

"Primarily suffocation. There was sand in his mouth, throat, lungs, and nostrils. There was also lake water in his lungs and tissues..." Brianne started.

"That in itself doesn't point to murder, Brianne," Sydney interrupted.

"Look. I don't know what your interest is in all this, Crosse, but don't get in my way. And don't go snooping around. Not that I wouldn't want the state police or the FBI to arrest your sorry ass."

"That's not an answer. That doesn't point to murder."

"No, it doesn't, but someone stabbed him in the back of the neck with a very sharp instrument. They still haven't determined what it was. However, that's what finally killed him, the coroner thinks, anyway. Like I said, it's prelim, he's waiting on tests."

"God, I don't believe it," Grace said, leaning against the counter. "Jon murdered."

"What happens now? You find this guy, right?" Keith said, frowning and holding Tina.

Brianne shifted uncomfortably and glanced at Grace.

Sydney got a very, very bad feeling. She looked at Grace, who had her arms folded in front of her, staring at the floor. Syd's mind raced with all sorts of scenarios.

"There's something you're not telling us, Brianne," she said quietly.

Brianne shot a venomous look. "Look, Crosse, you can leave any time. This is a family matter."

Syd agreed. "You're absolutely right. Why don't we leave you three? Mother, Grace? Let's leave them alone. Harry, come along."

Brianne's face turned red. "Someday, Crosse, you and I will go 'round and 'round." She then turned her attention to Grace. "Grace, they found something on Jon's body. I need you to come down to the station."

Grace looked at her completely bewildered. "Why me?"

"I can't talk about it here. I'll wait outside. It's just a few questions."

"Don't answer any questions. I'll call Marcy," Keith said.

He went into the living room. Tina just stood there staring at Grace. Sydney watched everyone, then got very nervous.

"Okay," Brianne said, "come down to the station this afternoon."

Syd heard Brianne's almost pleading tone with Grace, who still stared in disbelief.

Brianne walked up to her. "It's just questions, I promise."

"All right," Grace said.

Brianne walked out with Tina following her to the door.

Sydney put her hands on Grace's shoulders. She just kept staring blankly. Sydney gently shook her. "Grace," she said firmly.

She blinked and looked up at her with tears in her eyes. "What's happening?" she asked in a small voice that broke Syd's heart.

"Listen to me now," Sydney said urgently. "Do not talk to anyone. Don't answer any questions until I get my attorney here. I'll call him. I'm sure he can be here this afternoon. On second thought, you're not leaving my sight until then. C'mon, we're getting the hell out of here."

Victoria agreed. "Now you're making sense." She took Grace by the arm. "Come along, Grace. Do as Sydney says."

Grace smiled weakly and followed her. Sydney went up to her room and grabbed her laptop; she met them on their way out.

Brianne stood by her patrol car talking to Keith and Tina. Sydney ignored all of them as she opened the car doors for Grace and her mother. She slipped in behind the steering wheel and started the car.

"Grace, where are you going?" Brianne asked Grace.

Sydney had enough of this woman. "Grace is going with us. She'll be at the station at three o'clock, Brianne. Now get out of the way, please. I don't want to run over your footsie."

Keith came over and pulled Brianne back. He looked at Grace and patted her hand. "Good idea, Grace. Get out of here for a while. I'll call Marcy and let her know. She'll help any way she can." He reached in and kissed her cheek.

Grace smiled at him and covered his hand. "Thanks, Keith, I'll be fine. I just need to get some fresh air."

"Where are we going?" Victoria asked.

Sydney glanced back at Grace. "Mind if we go to your house? I need to make a call or two."

"Of course," Grace said, trying to smile.

Syd noticed it didn't work very well.

Victoria and Grace sat on her front porch looking out at the lake. "I feel very young rocking in this chair."

Harry came out with iced tea. "Hope ya don't mind, Irish, I invaded your kitchen." He smiled and handed her and Victoria each a glass.

Grace looked up and chuckled. "Not at all. What's Syd doing?" She looked into her living room; Syd was on the phone pacing back and forth.

They all heard her say loudly, "Then call him in Lake Geneva and give him this number. I want a call in ten minutes, Richard."

"There's no need to bellow," Victoria bellowed.

Syd came out on the porch. "Were you yelling at me?"

"Yes. Who were you being so rude to?"

Sydney watched the lake. "God, I love this lake. I called my lawyer."

"Walter?" Victoria asked.

"Uh, no. I have a lawyer, Adam Bryson, for these types of things. He's in Lake Geneva. He'll call in ten minutes."

"Why are you calling your lawyer? I don't need a lawyer. I'm a lawyer. Really, Syd, I appreciate your concern, but Brianne is only doing her job. It's just questioning. You can't just fly in and take control of everybody." Grace stopped and put her hand to her forehead.

Sydney squatted next to her. "Grace, look at me."

Grace took her hand away and looked into those blue sparkling eyes.

"I'm not trying to control everyone. If I was, I'd have had a better chance with you."

Grace glared for a moment, but when she saw Syd's lips twitching, she laughed. "God, you're a jackass."

"She's got your number," Victoria said.

Syd chose to ignore her. "However, my instincts told me to get you out of there for now. If I've offended you, I apologize. But I'm calling my lawyer, and that's that."

"Well, maybe that's not that. Look, I know the law, and if I needed a lawyer, Marcy Longwood is a good criminal lawyer. So I don't need you..."

Syd walked over and leaned against the porch railing. "You're absolutely right. You don't need me. However, Marcy Longwood is the Pickfords' lawyer, and you're not a Pickford. And I have a feeling she's also sleeping with Keith. I just want to make sure you have someone who cares only about you. Besides me, of course."

From the living room, they heard the phone ring. Syd started for the door; Grace jumped up to stop her.

"Really, Sydney. This is my house and my phone. God, you're annoying."

Syd stepped aside and opened the screen door for her.

"Really!" she repeated angrily and answered the phone.

She came back and sat in a huff. "It's for you."

Victoria and Harry exchanged happy grins.

"Don't start, you two," Grace warned them as she rocked in her chair.

Sydney walked out on the porch. "He's already in the air. I'll go meet him. Remember, don't talk to anyone, and don't go anywhere."

Grace said nothing as Syd gracefully walked off the porch and drove away. "Arrogant jackass."

Victoria laughed. "Yes, she is. She gets that from her father."

"And not her mother," Harry said.

"How is it, Harry, that you work for Sydney Crosse?" Grace asked absently, rocking in her chair.

He chuckled and rubbed the back of his neck. "Lucky, I guess."

"Oh, I don't know. It seems to me that Sydney's the lucky one."

"Don't be too hard on her, Grace," Victoria said softly. "You and I have had our discussions, but I know you care deeply for her. And she you."

"I really don't want to talk about that time. Sydney made it clear back then. And sealed it when she never tried to contact me. We were more than that."

"But you never tried to contact her, dear," Victoria said. "If you were more than that, you could have called her instead of coming to me."

"It was her decision."

"And your pride."

Grace continued to rock back and forth.

"You're gonna take off in that thing if you're not careful," Harry said. "I think I'll go make some lemonade."

"He's a smart man," Grace said after he left.

"He's an old fool. But he's loyal to Sydney."

"So how do you know Syd still cares?"

"It's not so much of what she says, but what she doesn't. We've talked about all the running around she does. But she's never brought any of them home. Not one rocket scientist or nuclear physicist. Well, there was one who attended a massage college. There was no one, Grace. No one like you. You know she jokes about the 'cross my heart' thing you two used to say to each other."

"Some joke," Grace said sadly.

"How little you know of my daughter." Victoria put her head back and smiled. "I never understood her being a lesbian. I always thought it had to do with her father's philandering, something deep-seated that only she understood. She is like her father in one regard. They lack emotional evolvement. David never cared, really. Sydney cares too much, but she doesn't trust her feelings. And that I believe has to do with her father. But she does care. She cares deeply."

Victoria took a drink of iced tea and looked out at the lake. "This is really a lovely home you have. You got a good life, don't you?"

Grace looked out at the lake; she loved it here. Even in the winter. It was bitter cold, and she didn't care. "Yes, I do, Victoria, but sometimes..." She stopped abruptly.

Victoria smiled and looked at her. "I know. Sydney has a great many 'but sometimes,' too." She put her head back and rocked. "Life is full of them."

Grace smiled and rocked in her chair. "You're quite the philosopher."

"Oh, I don't know about that. But I know a thing or two."

Chapter 10

Syd found Adam sitting in the small airport looking over some paperwork. She laughed when she saw how he was dressed. Casual shorts and a short-sleeved shirt, deck shoes, no socks. He must have been in the middle of a barbecue when she called. Adam was an older man in his sixties. With gray hair and blue eyes, he was the consummate attorney who knew his craft well. For this, Sydney paid him handsomely.

He stood when Sydney approached.

"Good heavens, Adam, you have legs," Sydney said in mock astonishment.

Adam looked down. "By golly, you're right."

"I'm afraid I was rude to Richard. I should call him back and apologize."

Adam chuckled. "Don't worry. Richard already told me. He says you get it from the women with whom you associate."

"Well, I'm glad you're here. Let me fill you in quickly," Sydney said and ushered him to the car.

Sydney explained the situation on the way to Grace's. Adam listened and nodded as she spoke.

"So you see, I just have a feeling Grace is going to need you."

"I'll do what I can. You're on a first-name basis already?"

"I've known Grace. We…uh…"

"A fling?"

"No," Sydney said quickly.

"I see…"

"No, you don't. We had a relationship years ago. I'm only doing this because she's in trouble."

"I see."

"Stop saying that."

"Sorry."

Syd took the remainder of the drive explaining the situation to Adam. He was up to speed as they pulled up to Grace's.

Syd introduced Adam to her mother, then to Grace.

"It's good to meet you," Adam said.

"I think I'll have Harry take me back to the house. That way, you can talk in private," Victoria said.

"Thanks, Mother. I'll come by later."

Victoria kissed her cheek. "Behave."

Syd backed up. "O-okay."

After they left, Grace suggested they go inside.

"Well, Ms. Morgan..." Adam sat at the kitchen table.

Grace gently interrupted him. "Please, call me Grace."

"Then you must call me Adam."

Syd sat at the table, as well, and vowed silently to keep quiet and not interrupt Adam.

"All right, Grace. Tell me more about your relationship with Jon Pickford. We don't know what evidence they have, so we have to assume the worst. Now how did you know Jon?" he asked gently.

"I suppose I've known Jon all my life. Growing up here, it was hard not to know him and his family and friends." She glanced at Sydney for a second. "After I became a lawyer, we knew each other better. He came to me one day about five years ago with a fantastic idea."

She explained Jon's idea regarding his acreage and their years of planning and long hours making sure nothing was left to chance, no loopholes.

"So, last Tuesday at dinner, we went over the final contract. He was to come in on Wednesday morning and sign it, then I was to record it and set it all in motion. Unfortunately, he never showed," she finished and took a deep breath.

Sydney noticed Grace's hands trembling and fought the urge to reach over and hold her hand.

"Now I have to ask a personal question. Did you and Jon have any kind of relationship other than business or friendship?"

"No, we did not," she answered honestly.

Adam smiled. "Sorry. But somewhere down the line, you'll be asked that question, believe me. When and if you're asked, answer it just that honestly."

"Jon's son, Keith, wants me to use their family lawyer, Marcy Longwood," Grace said. "And Sydney doesn't think it's a good idea."

He shrugged. "Well, I don't know Ms. Longwood. However, if she is Jon Pickford's lawyer and her client now is dead and you may be implicated, there might be a conflict there that Sydney might find, well, not in your best interest. I don't often agree with Sydney. But in this instance, I believe she may be right."

Sydney grunted sarcastically. "Thank you, Adam."

"You're welcome." Adam looked at his watch. "Well, it's almost three. I think we'd best be going."

Sydney stood, and Adam put a hand on her shoulder. "Not you, my dear. You stay here and out of trouble. I don't need you and the authorities adding to anything here."

Sydney started to argue but relented when Adam gave her a stern look. "You've always trusted me, Sydney."

Sydney jammed her hands in the pockets of her shorts and said nothing.

Grace chuckled. "Adam, you have to let the world in on how you do that. Leaving Sydney Crosse speechless has to be an art."

"I'm just supposed to sit here and wait?"

"Yes."

Grace, against her better judgment, walked up to Syd and placed a hand on her cheek. "Thank you for all this."

"I want to go with you."

Grace smiled. "We'll be right back. Adam is right. You'll wind up getting into an altercation with Brianne."

"Flatfoot," Syd grumbled.

"You made my point." Grace reached up and kissed Syd on the cheek. "Thank you."

When she pulled back, she nearly laughed at the stunned look on Syd's face.

"Now who's left whom speechless?" Adam said, leading Grace out the door.

"Ready?" Adam asked as he opened the glass door.

"I suppose."

"You'll be fine."

Grace could tell Brianne was shocked when she saw Grace come in with Adam.

"I'm Adam Bryson, Ms. Morgan's attorney." He held his hand out; Brianne took it, still looking at Grace.

"I only wanted to ask you a few questions, Grace."

Adam smiled. "Sheriff, my client fully understands and will do everything in her power to answer any and all questions."

"This is Detective Webster from the state police," Brianne said.

Adam shook his hand, then they all walked to Brianne's office.

Brianne shifted uncomfortably and pulled out a plastic bag. "Okay, Grace," she started gently. "This was found in Jon's pocket. It's a page from a journal we think might be Jon's. It says in here that he was going to stop all the proceedings concerning that contract, and he hesitated to tell you, knowing how upset you were."

Grace was completely confused; Adam watched Brianne and Detective Webster. He decided he didn't like this man at all. He was watching Grace with a particularly ugly leer. He's made his mind up already, Adam thought. Thank God Sydney called him. He would never doubt her instincts again.

"What are you talking about, Brianne?" Grace asked bewildered, and Adam put a hand on her arm, watching Brianne.

"It says here, in Jon's own handwriting, that you were in love with him and he wasn't in love with you. That's why he was afraid to tell you." She looked at Grace almost apologetically.

Adam said nothing as he watched her curiously.

Grace was shocked. She sat back in her chair, speechless. Adam leaned over. "May I?"

Brianne slid the plastic bag over. "It's evidence."

Adam smiled. "Yes, Sheriff, I know." He picked up the bag and looked at the page. "How do you know this is Mr. Pickford's handwriting?"

Brianne sighed. "Keith, his son, acknowledged it, and he gave us a sample of his handwriting. It was all sent to the lab."

Adam gave her a sad look. "So you don't know if this is truly his handwriting. Correct?"

Brianne glared at him. "All indications..."

Adam put his hand up. "Where is this evidence kept?"

Brianne looked confused. "We keep all evidence and reports pertaining to any case in the evidence room across the street at the courthouse. Why? Please don't suggest that it might be tampered with."

"Why would you say such a thing? Do you have any further questions for Ms. Morgan?"

"Yes, I do," Brianne said and swallowed convulsively. "Grace, you were with Jon on Tuesday, correct?"

Grace was numb. "Yes," she said quietly.

"What time did you leave him?"

"We left the restaurant at ten, and he drove me home," she said. "And he didn't come in. He left, and that's the last time I saw him." She looked up at Brianne sadly. She was only doing her job, she thought.

"Are you finished, Sheriff?" Adam asked professionally.

Brianne glanced at Detective Webster, who nodded. "Yes, that's all for now. Grace, I don't have to remind you to stay close."

Grace nodded and stood.

"So you're saying you didn't love Mr. Pickford, is that it? And you wouldn't be upset that he didn't love you and ruin all your plans?" Webster asked.

Adam glared at him. "Detective, are you going to charge my client at this time?"

Brianne jumped in. "Nobody's charging anybody." She glared at Webster.

"Not yet."

"Thank you." Adam gently steered Grace out the door.

The drive back was quiet until Adam said, "Detective Webster is a flatfoot."

Grace looked at him and laughed until she cried.

Sydney saw the car pull up and quickly went over as Adam stopped. He gave Sydney a stern look. Sydney looked at Grace, who had been crying. Damn it, she thought. She opened the door for her. Grace looked up and gave her a weak smile.

"They think..." She couldn't finish. She buried her face in her hands and sobbed.

Sydney quickly put her arms around her. "Hey now. Don't worry, we'll figure this out."

"Let's go in," Adam said and walked to the house.

Sydney kept her arm around Grace and walked inside. She gently set her in a chair and got her a glass of water.

"Thanks."

Sydney turned and looked at Adam. "Okay, give."

"Sydney, you were absolutely right to call me."

Adam explained the whole process. Sydney paced as she listened.

"I could use a drink," Adam said when he finished.

Syd reached down and stopped Grace when she started to stand. "I'll get it. Tell me where."

"In the cabinet above the stove."

Syd opened the cabinet. "Scotch, gin. Good Lord, Grace, you have everything."

Grace laughed along with Adam.

"I'll have scotch, rocks," Adam said absently.
"Name your poison, Grace. Gin and tonic, if I remember."
"That's fine. Thank you."
Syd prepared the drinks, then sat at the table with them.
"Adam, you said the evidence was kept in the courthouse? Doesn't that seem illogical? Why across the street?"
"They've always done it that way," Grace said, taking a long drink.
Sydney sipped her drink and contemplated the situation. Finally, Adam put his hand to his forehead.
"Sydney, please, you're making me dizzy."
"Sorry."
"What's on your mind?"
Syd glanced at Grace. "I think something smells rotten here."
"I agree," Adam said, running the tip of his finger around the rim of the glass.
"She's being railroaded," Sydney said to him.
"Again, I agree."
"But why? Why me? I don't understand." Grace sighed and put her head back.
"Grace, there must be something you know or have, and whoever it is wants you out of the way. God, I want to see that report and that evidence. I need Harry," Syd said thoughtfully.
Adam nearly spit up his drink. "No, not a word. I don't want even an inkling of what you're thinking, and neither does Grace. This is not like the other times."
"What other times?" Grace asked.
"If you plan on doing anything to help, you better make damn sure you know what you're doing. If you do something and get either Grace involved or me," Adam warned, and Sydney nodded.
"Not to worry, Adam. I understand completely. I will act with extreme caution and discretion."
"I sincerely doubt that," Adam said sadly.
Grace regarded Sydney and Adam. "What other times?"

Chapter 11

"I'm sorry Victoria had to go back to Chicago," Grace said.
"I know. She completely forgot about the charity function. She'll fly back for Jon's funeral. Harry took her to the airport." Syd sat back, letting out a tired sigh and looking around the restaurant. "Ernie's is sure getting a workout this week."
Adam glanced at his watch. "Okay, where am I staying? It's getting late. And I'm sure Grace is exhausted."
"I'm sorry, Adam. You must be tired, as well," Syd said. "I got you into a bed-and-breakfast down the road. Millie's, I think it's called. I'll give you a lift."
Grace apologized when she stifled a yawn. "Red wine always makes me sleepy."
"It's not just the wine. You had a very full day. C'mon, I'll drop Adam off, then take you home."
Adam shook Grace's hand while Sydney paid the bill. "Get a good night's sleep, Grace. I'll see you all tomorrow."
"Thank you, Adam, for everything," Grace said, smiling.
"Don't thank me. It was Sydney's idea."

The short ride home was quiet after they dropped off Adam at the B&B. It was a beautiful night full of stars. Sydney opened her door and looked up. "What a beautiful night. How about a walk, or are you too tired?"
"No, a walk sounds fine."
Syd leaned against the car and took off her shoes, then rolled up the linen pants above her ankles. She tossed the shoes in the

car. "I love the feel of a sandy beach. You'd better take off those shoes."

Grace reached down to slip off her shoes and instinctively put her hand on Syd's arm to steady herself. Her fingertips tingled from the touch.

They walked in the darkness along the beach. Sydney played with the ring on her finger. "Nice night."

"Yes, it is." Grace was watching the road. "Someone was watching me this morning."

Syd stopped dead in her tracks. "What? Where?"

Grace pointed to the road. "Right up there. See where the tall weeds are? He stood there watching me swim, then he left. I couldn't see him or his car because of the sun."

She shrugged and looked at Syd, noticing the dark look in her eyes as she looked up at the street.

"What time was this?" she asked as they continued walking.

"About seven this morning," Grace said with a loud yawn. "Sorry."

"Swimming at seven in the morning again? Washing your hair?"

"No, I was not. Maybe I was looking for the lifeguard."

Syd laughed then. "I'm telling you, I thought you were drowning."

Grace laughed along with her. "I've forgotten how much we used to laugh together."

"We had some good times, didn't we?"

"We had a lot of good times."

"Until I screwed it up." Syd absently kicked at the sand.

"I can't argue with that."

"I don't suppose you'd like to skip over that part."

"Let's head back," Grace said.

Syd grudgingly followed her back to the house. They both heard a noise from behind her house.

"Grace," Syd whispered. "Stay here."

She started for the back of the house and felt something behind her. She whirled around to see Grace, wild-eyed. "You scared the shit out of me. Go back, you little nitwit."

"No," Grace hissed and held the back of Syd's blouse.

"You're wrinkling the linen, let go." Sydney slapped behind at Grace's hand. "Let go. Just give me a minute."

"Be careful."

"No, I think I'll be dangerous."

Grace held on to her arm. "I'm not kidding."

"Quit pawing me." Syd pushed her hands away.

Something was definitely at the back of the house. Sydney couldn't see a thing. Then as she got to the back, something screeched and jumped at her. She put her hands up as a cat hissed and jumped at her head.

Grace let out a scream, along with Sydney, who put her arms up to fend off the feline. She threw the cat off, then promptly fell back into the lawn furniture. The cat was quickly gone.

Sydney struggled to untangle herself from the attacking lawn furniture. "Christ, are these alive?"

"Are you all right?" Grace asked through her laughter. She reached down to pull her up.

"Good grief, it's dangerous around here." She grunted and looked around.

"Well, it's gone. The lawn furniture must have scared the hell out of it. Did you see how big that cat was? My God, it was as big as a mountain lion." She brushed off her slacks. "My good slacks. Do you have any idea how much these cost?"

Grace, for the first time in five days, threw her head back and laughed hysterically.

Sydney gaped at her. "Well, I'm glad I amuse you," she said and grabbed her arm. "C'mon, let's go before a herd of water buffalo decide to roam by."

"Thanks for saving me again," Grace said. "So why do all the women find you so irresistible? Honestly, I don't see it."

"That's because you're a smart woman, which is why I find myself ridiculously still in love with you. With other women, it's my money, pure and simple. I—"

"What did you say?" Grace looked like an owl.

"I-I don't know. What did I say? They like me for my money."

"No. You said you're ridiculously still in love with me."

"I did not."

"You did too."

"Is that bad?" Syd instinctively stepped back, just in case it was.

"I don't think so. I-I don't know."

"Wonderful!"

"Wonderful?" Grace now took a step back.

"It's progress. And that's all I can ask for right now." She took her by the shoulder. "I want to kiss you so badly right now, but I won't. I'm being honest. Cross my heart. Good night."

"G-good night," Grace called after her. "Now you're being honest? You could have kissed me!"

Sydney laughed as she drove away.

She stopped by the place where Grace said she saw the man watching her. She parked and looked around, but in the darkness, she couldn't see much. Then as she was about to leave, she saw it. Her heart drummed in her chest as she bent down and picked up the end of a small skinny cigar.

"This can't be." Maybe she was wrong. Many men smoked cigars. Maybe she was getting paranoid. She took out her cell, called Harry, and told him what she found.

"Look, I don't know if this has anything to do with anything, but I don't like this, Harry. I'm going to stay around here for a while."

"I'll be right there."

"Well then, bring some coffee."

Harry arrived with the much-welcomed coffee. Sydney sat on the hood of the car drinking. Harry noticed Grace's shoes in the backseat. He picked them up and looked at them.

Sydney chuckled. "Don't be vulgar. We went for a walk along the beach."

"And?"

"And nothing. It was a nice walk. And I told her I was still in love with her."

Harry spit up his coffee. "And how was that tidbit of information taken?"

"Well. I think. She seemed responsive."

"Did you kiss her?"

"No."

"Why not?" Harry shook his head. "Youth is wasted on the young."

"Oh, please. I can't just kiss her after all this time. Though I wanted to."

"You'll find the right time."

"So ya think this guy will show up?"

"I don't know. I'm probably all wrong. However, if I leave and something happens, I'd never forgive myself."

They sat there for a while longer. Syd had an idea.

"Harry, tomorrow, I want you to go to the courthouse and case the joint."

Harry gaped at her with his cigar hanging out of his mouth.

"Syd, you ain't serious?" Harry was shocked.

Sydney nodded. "I am. I want you to find out which room is the evidence room, how much security there is, and all that."

"Why?" Harry swallowed with great difficulty.

"Because, you old thief, you and I are going to get into that room and take a look at the evidence and that report. Now you go home and get some sleep. I'm staying here for a while. Tomorrow, you go into town and discreetly, and I must emphasize discreetly, find out all we need to know, then go and buy whatever you need." She pulled out her credit card and handed it to him.

"However, this must be clean and easy. I leave this to your discretion. If it's risky in any way, we think of something else. I will not take the risk of losing my best friends."

"Me?"

"Of course you."

"Okay then. I'll do it." He smiled and patted Syd on the shoulder. "Don't stay out here too late. Call me if anything happens."

Sydney drove back to Grace's house and parked a block away. She walked to the house, making sure all was secure. She looked at her watch; the illuminated dial read two thirty. She was exhausted as she sat in the rocking chair on the porch. She sighed comfortably.

"I'll stay for an hour or so, then go."

She put her head back, and with visions of Grace's smiling face, she fell sound asleep.

Chapter 12

Grace woke at five a.m. It was too hot to sleep. She got up and showered and put on a pot of coffee. Then she went into the living room and opened her shades. She almost died when she saw Sydney lying in the rocker. What in the hell was she doing? And for one horrible moment, she thought she was dead.

She didn't know whether to be relieved or irritated when Syd let out a deep snore. She gently opened the front door and stood there looking at Syd. She had said the previous night that she was ridiculously still in love with her. Cross my heart, she had said.

Syd's usual well-groomed manner was completely gone. Her expensive linen slacks were rumpled. And a lock of brown hair fell helplessly on her forehead. Grace did not resist the urge. She reached over and gently brushed it back off her forehead.

Syd stirred and didn't wake, but she mumbled something Grace couldn't make out. So many memories flooded back while she watched Syd sleep. This was one of her favorite pastimes— watching Syd sleep peacefully. So many wasted years. Victoria was right, it was just as much her fault as Sydney's for not communicating at all. They were certainly good friends before they fell in love, having known each other since they were young.

But for now. What in the world was she doing on her porch? She took a step back, and the floorboard creaked. Sydney sat up immediately and looked around.

Grace put her hand on her shoulder and chuckled. "Hey, hey."

Syd looked around. "Good grief. What time is it?" She blinked and rubbed her eyes. "Where the devil are my glasses?"

"In your lap. What are you doing here?" Grace asked, drinking her coffee.

"I'll tell you for a cup of coffee," she said with a grin.

"Fine." She shook her head and came back with a cup for her.

"Cream and sugar?" Syd asked.

"Yes. I remember."

"Hmm, thanks," she said, taking it from her.

"Okay, you've got your coffee, now answer my question."

Sydney moved and groaned. "God, this is not a good chair to sleep in."

"Sydney…"

"Okay. When I left, I drove to the spot where you saw the guy. And I found something that is probably nothing, but I just wanted to make sure you were okay. So I was just going to sit for a bit, but I guess I fell asleep." She smiled sheepishly. "Sorry."

"You stayed out here all night?"

"Well, no. Just for the last few hours." She put her head back and almost fell asleep again.

"Look, why don't you go on the couch? You look exhausted."

"No, I think I'll take a swim. Want to join me?"

"You don't have a suit."

"Well…"

Grace stood. "I have some shorts and a tank top for you. That should do. Come with me."

Syd followed her inside.

"I'll be right back."

Grace returned with the makeshift suit; she wore her green suit from the other day. She tossed Syd the clothing. "Meet you outside."

"Hmm." Syd held up the shorts. "I was thinking along the lines of skinny-dipping."

"Yes, I figured as much," Grace said over her shoulder.

Syd winced as the screen door slammed.

Grace waded in the shallow water waiting for Syd. She laughed when Syd walked out to the beach. The shorts were far too long, and the tank top hung nearly to her knees.

"You look adorable," Grace called out.

"These can't be yours." Syd gave Grace a raised eyebrow.

Grace smiled. "Never mind whose they are."

"Well, I look ridiculous." Syd gathered the bottom of the tank top and pulled it up, tucking it inside her sports bra to expose her midriff.

Grace tried not to notice how trim and muscular Syd had become. She didn't recall her being this fit. Comes from chasing all the women around Chicago, she thought.

Syd pulled the drawstring on the shorts as much as she could. "You know these are going to fall off!"

"Oh, quit complaining and get in."

Syd ran and dove in; she came up screaming. "It's freezing."

"Good Lord, you've turned into a weenie." Grace watched her swim toward her.

"I am not. There may be children around."

"We're alone, Syd. C'mon, let's swim. You used to be a good swimmer."

"I still am." Syd lazily swam toward her.

"Prove it." Grace started to swim to shore.

Syd followed her and grabbed at her ankle when she swam closer. Grace screeched and playfully kicked, hitting Syd square in the mouth. When she heard Syd cry out, she stopped swimming.

"Are you all right? I'm so sorry."

"Good grief. I think you loosened a tooth." Syd flexed her jaw. "You did that on purpose."

"I did not, Crosse. I'm just a better swimmer. Admit it."

Syd stood in the shallow water. "Say that again."

"Say what again? I'm a better swimmer."
She shook her head. "No. Say my name again."
"Don't be ridiculous." Grace smiled. "Crosse."
Syd put her hand over her heart, grinned like an idiot, and fell back into the water.

Grace laughed and reached for her. Syd came up laughing and playfully grabbed her around the waist. Grace put her hand on Syd's shoulder, but this time, she didn't push Syd away.

Syd was breathing heavily as she smiled at Grace "Hey, Grace," she whispered and gently pulled her close.

She pulled Syd's hair, then pushed her back in the water. "You need to cool off, Crosse." She laughed and started swimming for shore. "I'm a better swimmer." Grace got out first and ran for the house, still laughing.

Sydney pulled up the baggy shorts and took off after her. "Wait till I get my hands on you."

Grace stumbled, allowing Syd to catch up to her; she dove for her ankle, and they both fell laughing. Sydney pinned her on the sand and looked down at her. They were both breathing heavily. Grace looked up at her.

"Well, maybe this time you'll kiss me."

"Yes, I think I will." She bent down and gently kissed her lips. It was warm and wet and very tender, just as Syd remembered.

Grace sighed as Syd lowered herself next to her on the sand. "God, Syd. I've dreamed of this."

An electric feeling shot through Sydney when Grace whispered against her cheek. She pulled back, searching every inch of Grace's face.

"That bad?" Grace reached up to caress her cheek.

"Very bad." She kissed her again, this time with more passion.

Grace wrapped her arms around Syd's neck, running her fingers through her hair. The feel of Syd was still amazing after all this time. "Sydney," she whispered.

"God, Grace." Sydney moaned and kissed her neck, then her kisses traveled to the top of her breast. Gently, she pulled the straps of her bathing suit down to expose her breasts.

"Sydney." Her body shivered when she felt Syd's kisses. "Syd, Syd. We can't do this here."

Syd lifted her head. She kissed Grace while she adjusted her suit. "Okay. I'm not sure I can walk, but you're right. Let's get off the beach before we get arrested."

Once on her porch, they heard the phone ringing, and Grace ran in to answer it. Sydney brushed the sand off her body. "This is the worst excuse for a bathing suit." She looked up when Grace returned. "If we're going to continue swimming, I must get a decent suit. This is abysmal. What's wrong?"

"What? Oh, nothing. That was Brianne. She wanted to make sure I was all right. I know she was upset that I had Adam with me." Grace sat on her rocker.

"Listen to me. Something's not right here. I can't put my finger on it. But somebody killed Jon, and it wasn't you."

Grace stood and put her arms around her neck, burying her head into her shoulder.

Syd gently stroked her hair. "Shh now, everything will be all right. I promise you."

"How can you be so sure?"

Syd bent down and kissed the tip of her nose. "Because I promise. Cross my heart."

Grace let out a sob and clung to her. "It feels so good to hold you again."

Syd held her closer. "I feel the same way. I'm so sorry. I was such an idiot."

"Don't, Syd. Let's not try to blame." She looked up and smiled. "Let's just be very grateful we're getting another chance. We...we are, aren't we?"

Syd smiled and placed a soft kiss against her lips. "Yes, Grace. We are."

Grace pulled back, running her fingers down the fabric of the baggy shorts, stopping at the waistband. "These are abysmal."

Syd found it difficult to breathe; she leaned back against the porch railing. "Well, the...the color's not too bad." She moaned when Grace tugged at the drawstring.

"Grace," she said in a ragged voice. "What are you doing?"

"I know it's been a while, but if you don't know..." Grace leaned in and kissed her on the cheek, her lips traveling down to her neck.

"Oh, God," Syd whispered when she felt Grace's fingers boldly slip into her shorts.

They jumped when they heard a car door slam. Syd couldn't move; her legs were shaking, but Grace quickly stepped back when Brianne appeared.

"Brianne, what are you doing here?" Grace asked, running her fingers through her hair.

"I might ask her the same question," Brianne said angrily.

"I was invited," Sydney said, smiling.

Grace glared at both of them, feeling what was about to happen. "Both of you, stop it. Brianne, what do you want?"

Brianne continued to stare at Sydney. "I just wanted to make sure you were all right." She turned her attention to Grace. "Be careful with this one, Grace. Remember what we talked about."

"Brianne..."

Syd looked from Grace, who looked embarrassed, to the superior grin on Brianne's face, which she wanted to slap.

"Yes, I told her," Brianne said, jutting out her jaw.

"Just what have you told her?" Syd asked.

"We know all about your whoring around in Chicago. Grace agrees with me. You think you're so much better than us." She took a step toward Grace as if validating her statement.

Grace glared at Brianne and stepped away.

"I see." Syd grinned, then she folded her arms across her chest. "Had an adult conversation, did we, Brianne? And no one thought you'd amount to much. And here I thought you were just a knuckle-dragging flatfoot."

Grace stood in front of Brianne when she took a step toward Sydney.

"No need. I'll leave you two to do whatever you two do."

"Sydney…"

"I'll come back for my clothes." Sydney smiled at Brianne and walked off the porch.

She heard Sydney's car pull away. "Go away, Brianne." Grace didn't know if she was more mad with Brianne for making such a stupid statement or at Sydney for believing Brianne's stupidity.

"Did you sleep with her?" she asked rudely.

"Oh, shut up," Grace said, truly disgusted. "And go home."

She walked away, slamming the screen door behind her.

Chapter 13

Sydney stormed up the stairs and into her room, not stopping to acknowledge Tina, who was in the living room.

Harry walked in, yawning and scratching his head. "Syd, where you been? And how's come you get Vic's room with the private bath? Hey, you look terrible. Why are you in those shorts? And why are you wet?"

Sydney looked down at the hideous wardrobe and growled with self-contempt. "Harry, remind me. From now on, I am swearing off women. I mean it. I'll become a nun if I have to." She grabbed her robe and headed to the shower. "I tell you, I'm supremely, supremely I say, disappointed with Grace!"

Harry sighed and sat on her bed. "Aw, geez. What happened?"

Sydney took a deep breath and told him everything. She felt like she was going to confession. Harry nodded and listened. "Syd, Grace hasn't seen ya in years from what you said. Did ya ask her what they talked about? Did ya ask her anything?"

"How could I with Wyatt Earp standing there?" Syd stopped and came out of the bathroom. "She annoys me. That woman truly gets under my skin. I don't trust her. Never have."

"Probably 'cause she's got a snooker for Grace."

"A snooker?" Syd shook her head. "I need a shower."

Harry called out to her, "Ya know ya shoulda stayed and asked her." He heard the shower start. "She's gonna blow it again."

There was a knock at the door. Harry didn't even get a chance to get up. Grace flew into the room.

"Oh. Sorry, Harry, I was looking for Sydney. She left in a huff." Then she heard Syd's voice from the shower. She looked at Harry and put her fingers to her lips.

"Sure I could have asked," Syd yelled from the shower, "but why didn't she say something? Brianne, that moron. God knows what she told her. What the hell does Grace see in that flatfoot? I gave her more credit than that."

Harry ran his hand across his mouth to keep from laughing. Grace walked up to the bathroom door and stood with her arms folded across her chest, leaning against the doorjamb.

"Well, if she thinks she's going to play some game here. Shit, Harry, I even said cross my heart to her! She's probably trying to get back at me. That's it," Sydney yelled from behind the shower curtain.

Grace fumed as she casually walked over to the toilet and flushed it.

"Geezus Christ!" Syd yelled and threw back the curtain. She saw Grace and quickly grabbed the curtain to cover herself. "What in the hell are you doing here?"

"Playing some game with a witless, arrogant ass who isn't worth my time!" she yelled back at her. She turned on her heels. "See ya, Harry," she said, then stormed past Harry and out the door.

"See ya." Harry walked to the bathroom door while Sydney stood there with the shower curtain still covering her. Harry shook his head. "Nice going."

"What do you mean?" Sydney grinned. "Did you notice how her eyes sparkled when she called me witless?"

Grace stormed into her office. Debbie jumped ten feet when she slammed the door.

"Good morning!" she yelled at Debbie and headed for her office. She abruptly turned back to her assistant. "If that egomaniacal, arrogant..." She stopped and counted to ten.

Then calmly, she said to Debbie, "If Ms. Crosse calls or stops by, I've left the country."

"Adam Bryson is waiting in your office. He has an appointment," Debbie whispered.

"Oh, God." Grace rubbed her forehead and laughed. "What else?"

Adam stood when Grace walked into her office. "I'm sorry, Adam. I-I got a little sidetracked."

"That's quite all right. I'm early. I rented a car when I couldn't get in touch with Sydney. Everything all right?" he asked cautiously.

"Yes, thanks. Tough morning. How are you?"

He nodded. "Very well, thank you. Any calls?" he asked, sitting down. Grace sat behind her desk.

"No, nothing as yet. I just got in."

"You seem a bit preoccupied. Would you like to tell me?" he asked, almost fatherly.

Grace looked out the window. "How long have you known Sydney Crosse?"

"Oh, God, what has she done? Why?"

"Just wondering."

"It's none of my business. However, you're my client. You've got to focus here." He angrily shifted in his chair. "I'll strangle that woman."

Grace turned. "Sydney did nothing, really. I, well, you might as well know, we had a relationship. We haven't seen each other in years. It's just...oh, I don't know. She's still the most irritating and childish woman I've ever met. She probably should have stayed in Chicago with all her..." Grace let out an angry sigh and sat.

"I like you, Grace. I like Sydney, too. Sad thing about reputations. They follow you whether they're true or not. Believe me, Sydney Ellen Crosse is no saint. However, she is not the runaround maniac that people are led to believe. You must trust me. Sydney is not what she appears." He smiled, and she watched him.

"I know."

"You still care for her?"

"Against my better judgment. Yes."

Adam laughed along with her. "She is trying. And I mean in a helpful way, not an annoying way. And she wants to help you. So do I. So let's get back to the business at hand. Now…"

They both looked up when Debbie walked in. "Grace, Sydney Crosse is here. I told her you were in Guatemala, but she's not buying it. Maybe I picked the wrong country."

Grace sighed. "Oh, God. That woman."

Adam chuckled.

"Show her in," Grace said with resignation.

Adam smiled. "She is persistent. You have to give her that."

Debbie opened the door and laughed when Sydney wagged a finger in her direction. "You are a darling, but Guatemala?"

"Do you have to flirt with my assistant?"

Sydney flashed a charming smile. "No, but how else was I to get in to see you? I'm so sorry about this morning. I..." She came into the office and noticed Adam. "Oh. Uh. Good morning, Adam. How's the bed at Millie's?"

"Fine. We were just talking about you."

Sydney beamed. "You were?" She looked at Grace, who gave him a sour look. "In a good way, I hope."

"Yes, I was telling her how important it was for her to focus on her present situation and not be distracted." He gave Syd a fatherly glare.

Sydney looked like a scolded schoolgirl. "I agree. I will leave you two to your powwow. Oh, by the way, do you have the address and names of the kids who found Jon?"

Adam leafed through the papers. "Yes, and it was like pulling teeth to get it from the local authorities. I have no idea what's wrong with them. Here." He scribbled on a piece of paper, handing it to Syd. "What are you going to do?"

"Just take a drive and check things out."

"Where's your bodyguard?" Adam asked.

"Oh, he's…" Syd looked from Grace to Adam. "He's…"

Adam held up his hand. "I don't want to know."

"Good." She turned to Grace. "I apologize for the interruption, truly I do. Perhaps if it wouldn't be too much of a distraction, we could have dinner tonight. Adam can come along."

Grace looked into her eyes, then picked up the papers on her desk and shuffled them. "I'll see," she said evenly.

"Good. That's better than a poke in the eye." Sydney smiled. "Thank you." She looked at Adam and shook his hand. "Take care of her, Adam."

Grace stared at the door for a second, then sat down. "I never realized how bossy she was."

Adam concentrated on his file. "Yes. It's annoying. You'll get used to it because she truly means well. But it's annoying nonetheless."

Sydney drove back to the rocks where Jon's body was found. It was secluded, and she could see how his body could go unnoticed. However, she looked out at Lake Michigan, wondering what Jon was doing in this area. She looked around the surrounding area. Tall grass hid this beach. It was certainly not a place to go swimming. There wasn't much shoreline at all. Looking farther north, she saw a few vacationers in the water where the beach area seemed larger.

As she walked along the beach, she saw two boys running and pushing each other, laughing and calling each other names. Syd smiled as she watched them, wishing she'd had a brother or sister to play with growing up.

"Cut it out, you dork!" the little one said.

"Tommy, don't be a wiener," the older called back.

Sydney smiled. Ah, youth. She wondered how she'd sound calling her VP a wiener at the next board meeting. She'd have to try it out.

The older one threw the football, and it landed at Sydney's feet. She picked it up, and the older boy smiled. "Thanks, lady."

Sydney winked. "Sure."

The two boys played football on the shoreline while Syd watched.

"Michael Baker, what are you two doing?"

Syd turned to see a young woman walking up to them.

"We're playing, Mom."

"I hope they're not in your way," the woman said.

"Oh, no. I was just walking by. Kids are fun to watch. So much energy."

"Too much. Especially boys."

Syd noticed how tired the woman looked. "I'm Sydney Crosse."

"Lynn Baker. Those two ruffians are my sons."

"Mrs. Baker, do you live around here? I don't know if you heard about the gentleman that was found the other day…"

"Hold it. Who are you? We've answered all the questions we're going to answer. This whole thing was very upsetting," she said angrily.

It then dawned on her that Mrs. Baker's kids were the ones who found Jon. "I'm very sorry. I'm a friend of the man they found. I'm trying to find out who killed him. Are your boys the ones who saw him?"

"Look, they weren't sure what they saw. It was dark and late. Only…" She stopped.

Sydney looked at her anxiously. "We don't know each other, but my friend was murdered. That's what they're saying. If you can help, I'd be very grateful."

They walked over and sat at the picnic table on the beach. "Ms. Crosse, Mike said he saw a boat on the water. That's why they went to the rocks to begin with."

"What kind of boat?" Sydney asked patiently.

"He said it looked like one of those big boats, with the tall fishing poles on the back. I don't know what that means," she said, watching her sons play.

Sydney thought for a moment. "A charter boat, with down riggers. That's what he meant, I'll bet."

Mrs. Baker nodded. "He said it also had a big bell on it. I told the officer when she came back." Sydney looked at her then.

"What officer came back?" Sydney asked.

"They initially showed up, state police. We answered all the questions. A policewoman from...I can't remember gave me her card and told me to call if the boys remembered anything. When Mike remembered the boat, I called her then. She came back out and talked to him. She told us to forget everything and salvage our vacation, we wouldn't be bothered again."

"Did you keep the card, Mrs. Baker?"

"No, I got rid of it. But the name..." She tried to remember. "Jerkins...Jordon...no." She sighed, trying to think.

Sydney said slowly, "Brianne Gentry?"

She snapped her fingers. "That's it." She described Brianne to a T.

Sydney watched the boys playing. She looked up when Mrs. Baker touched her arm.

"What's happening, Ms. Crosse? This is my family we're talking about."

Syd patted her hand and smiled. "Nothing. Everything is fine."

"I couldn't stand anything else happening to this family." She looked at Syd. "My husband died eight months ago, cancer. This is the first vacation we've had. It's good for the boys. They miss him. He used to play football with them all the time."

"Where do you live?" she asked.

"Outside Ann Arbor, Michigan. Things are all different now. I'll have to go back to work." She looked at Syd. "I shouldn't be telling you all this. You're easy to talk to."

Syd thought for a moment, then looked at the boys. "Mrs. Baker, how much longer are you here?"

She watched her sons, smiling. "We leave tomorrow. I can't afford any more time."

She took out her business card and handed it to her.

Mrs. Baker read it. "TeleCrosse." She looked at Syd. "This is you?"

Sydney nodded. "When you get home, you call that number. Our company is always looking for good employees. That is, if you're not locked into Ann Arbor."

Mrs. Baker smiled but gave Syd a curious look. "You don't even know me or what I can do."

"You're the mother of two energetic boys. That makes you management material, trust me."

"I will. I will call," she said and gave a determined nod.

"Good. When you call, ask for Judy Wellman. I'll call her and let her know. She'll take care of everything. The move, finding you a place. How's that?"

"Sounds too good to be true. Why? Why are you doing this?"

"I've been very blessed in my life. I'm just starting to realize how much, even going through this tragedy with my friend. I just want to give back."

"Well, at least you can let me offer you something to drink."

"That sounds fine, thanks."

"I'll be right back. Will you watch the boys?"

"Sure." Sydney watched the boys playing along the beach. She had no idea what Brianne was doing, but she didn't like Mrs. Baker or her sons in this any longer. They had gone through enough. She made a mental note to tell Mrs. Baker to call if anyone contacted her before she left.

She was tired and sunburned but extremely happy when she left the Baker family, knowing they would come to Chicago and start a new life.

Then Sydney thought about Brianne Gentry. She would ask Adam if there was any mention of a boat in the police report he received. Maybe she was overreacting because she thought Brianne was a colossal idiot. No, there was something going on, she could feel it. So maybe the murderer got Jon on the boat and tossed him overboard. Jon was a good swimmer, though. They found sand in his lungs, mouth, and nostrils. How the hell do you get sand in your lungs, she thought as she pulled up to Grace's office. Not seeing her car or Adam's rental, she drove to Grace's house.

Grace was sitting on the front porch with Adam. She looked up when Syd walked onto the porch. "You're sunburned. What have you been doing?"

"Hi. Did you miss me?"

"What? No..."

Adam gave Syd a curious look. "What have you been up to? You have that gleam in your eye."

Syd laughed and explained her day. She noticed the deep frown that creased Adam's brow when she told them about the boat.

Adam looked at Grace. "Did the sheriff tell you about a boat?"

Graced shook her head. "Not a word."

"Something's going on here, Adam, I can feel it," Sydney said.

Adam agreed. "Well, be careful, Sydney. There's a murderer out there. Don't go getting yourself into another..."

Sydney shot him an urgent look, and he stopped.

"Another what?" Grace asked. "What are you doing, Sydney?"

"I'm not doing anything."

"Cross your heart."

Syd opened her mouth, then shut it.

"Adam said earlier you are not what you appear."

Syd glared at Adam. "You blabbermouth."

"What is it exactly that you do?" Grace asked her.

"About what?" Syd asked innocently.

"Don't be obtuse. Answer me."

"You worry too much. I have to take a shower. I'm all sweaty, and you know I hate to perspire. Oh, by the way, Adam, do me a favor. Call the office and tell Judy a Mrs. Lynn Baker will be calling. She's a new employee," Sydney said, walking off the porch.

Adam called after her, "What department?"

Syd turned and said impatiently, "I don't know. Find something. Good heavens, the company is big enough. Make sure she gets all benefits and a decent salary. Oh, and she'll be moving, so we'll take care of that and finding her affordable housing. She's got two football players to feed." She waved her hand and walked away. "And, Grace? I will pick you up at six. Look wonderful."

Grace sat there staring at the lake. "Look wonderful. What a pompous ass," she said to Adam.

He nodded. "Yes, she is. An expensive pompous ass." He took out his phone and dialed. "Judy, Adam, guess what? Yes, she's at it again. A Mrs. Lynn Baker. Her exact words were 'I don't know. Find something.'"

Adam took the phone away from his ear. Grace could actually hear yelling. Adam chuckled. "Judy, you want to tell Syd that?" He rolled his eyes at Grace, and she chuckled. "Goodbye, Judy." He put the phone in his pocket.

"Where were we? Ah, a very expensive pompous ass, I believe."

Grace put her head back and laughed.

Chapter 14

Harry went into Sydney's room. "Christ, she's taking another shower." He heard the shower turn off. "Syd? I'm here."
"Okay. Be right out."
Harry sat in the chair by the window overlooking the back property. "How the rich live."
Syd came out tying her robe around her. "Okay, give. What did you find out?"
"Well, it's a piece a cake," he said triumphantly.
Sydney looked at him. "You sure? Don't lie to me."
Harry shook his head. "Would never lie about this. We can be in and out in fifteen minutes. No worry." He winked, chomping at his cigar. "I got the skinny from the security guard, nice old guy. Place closes at five. Only one guard, another old-timer, George, and he's got a bum ear."
Syd eagerly sat. "Okay."
"Now Joe, that's the guy that spilled his guts, tells me there's no alarm on the building. The city council hasn't gotten around to it yet," Harry said, shaking his head. "The evidence room is on the second floor, back, second window. Basic lock on the door. No worry. The back door is a bit trickier, but I can handle that."
Sydney listened, completely amazed.
"Here's how I figure. We go in the back entrance. Up a flight, second door on the right. I pick the lock, we're in. Only problem, I don't know exactly where it's kept. That's what will take most of our time. Once we find it, you do your thing, we

put it back, we lock up. And we're outta there. Like taking candy from a baby, as they say," he said proudly and winked at Sydney.

"Harry, you astound me. You figured all that out in one afternoon?" she asked, truly amazed.

"Yep. And I picked up all we'll need. Cost you only a hundred bucks. Here's your card. Oh, and I had a corned beef sandwich and a beer."

She walked over to him and kissed his head. "You're worth a million corned beef sandwiches."

"So when do we do this?" Harry asked eagerly.

"Tonight, right about midnight. George should be asleep by then. It's imperative that we do not get caught. Understood?"

Harry nodded. "Understood. No worry. In and out." He smiled and rubbed his hands together. "Syd, I got the itch."

"That's wonderful, but no scratching in public," Sydney said and got ready for dinner.

Syd pulled up to Grace's at six on the dot. She was sitting on her front porch rocking away. She hadn't noticed Syd, who stood there watching her.

Grace wore her hair up and was wearing a cool, soft yellow sleeveless summer dress. She watched Grace as she stared out at her lake.

"You have a beautiful profile, Grace."

Grace smiled, still looking at the lake. "And you're still a flirt."

"How do you like my new outfit? I knew you were going to wear a dress and the exact right color for your hair, so I opted for summer slacks. You know, yin and yang."

Grace looked at her from head to toe. Syd looked beautiful. She wore her hair, as Grace remembered, on the short side, knowing the brown lock hung ever so slightly over her brow. Just enough for Syd to brush it away now and then. She wore a pair of navy slacks that had to be tailored and an ivory blouse that had to be pure silk or maybe linen. Grace had no clue. Syd was the clothes horse. Yes, she looked beautiful.

"It's all right."

"Just all right?" Syd's eyes bugged out of her head. "Do you know how long I vacillated on what to wear?"

"I have an idea."

Syd frowned deeply and put on her sunglasses. "Well, let's get this over with."

Grace laughed and walked up to her. She put her hand on Syd's cheek. "You are a beautiful narcissist."

"And that's supposed to make me feel better?" Syd grabbed her elbow. "C'mon, let's go."

Grace hid her grin as Syd drove down the highway; she was brooding.

"Where are we going?" Grace asked.

"There's a little place down the road that has great seafood. I thought you might like it."

"Adam?" she asked, looking out the window.

"Nope. No Adam. No Harry. No Keith or Tina. No one. Unless you want to go back and pick someone up."

Grace heard the sarcasm. "If you're referring to Brianne, then no. I do not want Brianne here. And stop pouting, for chrissakes."

"I'm not pouting."

"Oh, yes, you are. Look," Grace said, turning sideways, as much as her seat belt would allow. "I am going to say this once and only once. I am not involved with Brianne. I have never been involved with her. She wants it, I do not. We discussed you once. She was the one who mentioned the women you see in Chicago. We did not agree, as she said, and we did not talk about it again. Mainly because I told her I was not interested in her gossip!"

"Why are you getting so upset?" Syd asked calmly.

"Because you took off in a petulant huff—"

"Petulant?"

"And you didn't stick around long enough to let me explain. As usual!"

"As usual? What does that mean?" Syd glanced at Grace while trying to concentrate on the road. "Now see what you made me do? I just passed up the restaurant. If they give away my table…"

"Oh, who cares about a stupid table?" Grace said, nearly pulling out her hair.

Syd pulled onto the shoulder and turned around. "Well, it's an expensive restaurant, and getting a reservation is…What?"

"You're insane."

"I am not. I've taken tests before." Syd put the car in gear and headed back.

Grace groaned and rubbed her forehead. "All I'm saying is…Oh, what the hell. I don't know what I'm saying. I never did where you were concerned."

Syd winced at her sad tone. "Sorry," she said, not looking at her.

"Me too." Grace reached over and put her hand on Syd's knee. "Let's just have a nice dinner."

"Okay. Deal."

It was an adorable lakeside restaurant, small and quaint. A trace of elegance, but not stuffy. There was a small dance floor and about eight tables. Only two of them were filled.

"Monday is a slow night, from what I gathered." Syd led her to the hostess area. "I hope you like it."

The older woman looked up and immediately smiled. "Grace! Oh, my gosh. It's been such a long time…"

Syd's mouth dropped. She then glared at Grace, who avoided her completely as she held out her hand.

"Hi, Dana. It has been a while."

"It's been a year at least. It's so good to see you again. Wait till I tell Frank. I don't have a reservation for you, but…" She looked at Syd when she held up her hand. "Oh, you made the reservation?"

"Yes."

Dana looked at her book. "Crosse for two? You must be Crosse."

"Yes," Syd said sweetly. "It's my natural state."

Syd could tell Dana didn't get it, but she laughed along with Grace anyway.

"Well, you were specific. And I must tell you, it has to be kismet, but you're getting the same table Grace used to have. Isn't that funny?"

Syd leaned down to the woman. "Hysterical."

Dana blinked in confusion. "Yes, well. Right this way."

Syd looked at Grace. "Right this way."

Grace laughed and pulled Syd along. "Don't be cross."

"Don't start."

They were seated outside on the terrace as the night was perfect—warm and beautiful.

The waiter came up, and Sydney said, "Gin and tonic for the lady, and I'll have a very dry Bombay martini straight up, three olives."

Grace glared at her when the waiter retreated.

"What's wrong? What did I do now?" she asked, putting the napkin in her lap.

"What if I didn't want a gin and tonic?"

"I'm sorry. Didn't you want a gin and tonic?"

"Yes."

"Then what's the problem? I swear, Grace, I think you're purposely trying to pick a fight with me."

"Christ, you are so damned annoying."

She reached across the table and held Grace's hand. "Am I that bad?" She tilted her head. "Am I?"

The waiter came up with their drinks, and they sat in silence. Grace stole a glance at Syd; she looked disappointed. Grace sipped her drink. Oh, this woman!

"This is a lovely restaurant, thank you."

"Are you being sarcastic?"

"No," Grace said, hanging her head. "I had no idea we were coming here. And..." She put her hand up to Syd. "...if you ask me if I came here with Brianne, I will stab you with this butter knife."

"That's a little dark. I think Dana was right. It's kismet." She shrugged and ran her fingertip around the rim of her martini glass. "Maybe it was meant to be."

"Maybe it was." Grace took another drink. "I hope it is."

Syd smiled genuinely. "Do you? Then my night is complete." She softly drummed the table. "Let's eat. I'm starved."

"So what have you found out?" Grace asked after they ordered dinner.

"What do you mean?" Syd buttered a warm roll. "This is a mistake. It'll go right to my hips."

"Your hips are fine." Grace snagged a roll and pulled the plate of butter close.

"You've noticed my hips?"

"Yes." Grace broke the roll and slathered it with butter. "And I've also noticed you're in much better shape than you used to be."

"Well, I am older than you. I'll be forty-three—"

"Nine," Grace gently reminded her. "But who's counting?"

"So that you keep track of?" Syd mumbled as she ate her bread.

Grace laughed. "I have to admit, Syd. For a long time, I was really mad at you. I even drove to Chicago one weekend to confront you."

Syd nearly dropped her knife. "When?"

"It doesn't matter. I visited with your mother." Grace took a drink of water. "You were out with someone. So I came home."

"And talked with Brianne." Syd angrily sat back and picked up her drink.

"No. That came later when Brianne was there on business. She saw you at a club with a different woman than I saw you with."

"And she couldn't wait to come back and tell you."

"Yes. You're right there."

"Grace, after we..." She stopped, not knowing how to continue. She looked at Grace. "What did you say?"

Grace raised an eyebrow. "I didn't."

"Oh."

The server came to their table, giving Syd a momentary reprieve.

They ate in silence for a moment. Syd wasn't sure how to get back to the conversation. It didn't matter, Grace knew.

"So," Grace said, taking a forkful of rice. "You were saying?"

"What was I saying?"

"Don't do this. I believe you were about to elaborate on your life after us."

"Oh. Well, I was wrong," she said quietly.

"So you said the other day."

"Don't you believe me?"

Grace looked up and took a drink of wine. "Yes, I believe you. It was a long time ago. And you weren't ready for anything..."

"Mature," Syd said, drinking, as well. When Grace didn't save her, she had to continue. "Like I said, I was scared."

"But why? Didn't you trust me? We talked of so many things. So much we wanted to do. Why?"

Syd ate a shrimp, barely tasting it. "My father cheated on my mother every chance he had."

Grace stopped in midbite. She slowly set her fork down. "I'm sorry."

"I caught him once," Syd went on, almost in a trance. "Mother was out of town. I was eighteen, a freshman at Northwestern. I came home for the weekend. It was summer. I thought maybe he and I could go flying with Jon. Obviously, I was not expected. He was in their bedroom with some woman." Syd tossed her fork down. "For the love of God, Grace, he was in *their* bedroom. He had absolutely no shame. No consideration for my mother. Why she never left him, I don't know."

Grace ate another bite, realizing she had no appetite. Syd watched her.

"Sorry. I didn't mean to ruin your dinner."

"I don't care about the dinner, Sydney. Why didn't you ever talk about this to me?"

"Oh, who wants to hear that crap?"

"I did. You ass."

Syd laughed quietly and drank her wine.

"You're going to get angry at this. But you know I've seen Victoria from time to time."

"I know. I'm not angry. In a way, I…I'm glad. I didn't have the guts to go see you. So what did you talk about?" She absently pushed several shrimp around on the plate. "Twenty bucks a plate, and I'm playing hockey."

Grace hid her laughter in her napkin. "We talked about a lot of things. Your mother is very talkative, especially after a martini or two." She laughed along with Syd and continued, "And we talked about you and your father. She thought you were a lesbian because of him."

"Oh, good Lord," Syd said, hanging her head.

Grace laughed happily. "I know. I laughed at the time, and she thought I was nuts. "But she wasn't far from wrong."

Syd's head snapped up. "What?"

"Listen to me first before you get all crazy. He had nothing to do with your being a lesbian, but I think he had a great deal to do with your attitude on relationships."

Syd cocked her head and thought about it. Her gaze darted around the room as she realized the possibility.

Grace let out an amused laugh then. "Victoria had that same reaction. You look very much like her. She agreed with me, just as you're about to."

Syd arched an eyebrow. "You're pretty cocky, Counselor."

Grace sat back and picked up her wineglass. "Not cocky when you're right."

"Oh, you can still be cocky, trust me."

"Let's not quibble."

"Let's not. But you're probably right." She held her hand up. "Okay, okay. You are right."

Grace reached over and took Syd's hand, loving how soft and warm it felt, just as it always had. "The point is, you were scared because you didn't want to end up like your father. You didn't trust yourself. You didn't trust me, and you'd rather have bailed out at ten thousand feet than trust the future."

Syd stared at their entwined fingers. "I wouldn't blame you if you wanted nothing to do with me."

"I wouldn't blame me, either. But the truth is, Sydney Ellen Crosse, I do want you. Still after all your dumbassery. You're pretty good at it."

Syd laughed and once again hung her head. "Well, anything worth doing…"

"Let's finish dinner. And I want dessert."

"You got it."

Grace had a wonderful time. She loved the restaurant, she loved the food, she loved—well, that was enough for one night. For the first time in almost a week, she was happy and content.

The drive home was beautiful. Grace sat next to Syd, her head back and looking up at the moon.

"What are you thinking about?" Syd asked quietly.

Grace turned her head to her. "Oh, lots of things."

"Good things, I hope. And not all this mess with Jon."

"Yes, good things."

Syd pulled into her drive and cut the engine.

"Let's go for a walk on the beach," Grace said happily.

"I'd love to. And I want you to know I'll always be there for you. But now I have to go."

"What?"

"I can't explain because, well…"

"What. Are. You. Going. To. Do?"

Syd looked at her watch. "I can't tell you. You'll have to trust me."

"Trust you." Grace narrowed her eyes. "Your mother was right."

"Okay, that's something we need a long, long time to discuss."

"And you don't have time."

"Ah, no. I don't. Grace, please."

"Go, go," Grace said, holding up her hand. "I can't believe we had a wonderful night and you're just going to run off and do whatever crazy thing you do." She laughed and stepped back. "Can I at least get a good night kiss?"

"Of course," Syd whispered, pulling Grace into her arms.

The kiss was meant to be quick and gentle, but it lingered until both were practically pawing at each other. Grace moaned and ran her fingers through Syd's hair.

"Gotta go," Syd mumbled against her lips as she tried to pull away.

"Then go," Grace said, biting at her bottom lip. She successfully pulled Syd's silky, expensive blouse out of her slacks, taking a button or two with it.

Syd gasped and tried to pry herself away. "Gracie…"

"I love it when you call me that," Grace exclaimed, cupping both breasts.

"Good God," Syd cried out and roughly pushed her away. She was breathing like a bull. "Geezus, woman!"

Grace licked her lips, breathing equally ragged. "Sorry," she said with a nervous laugh. She took a step toward Syd.

"You stay right where you are!" Syd held up her hand and backed off the porch. She slipped on one step and nearly fell backward. "Stay!" she ordered Grace. "I-I'll call you tomorrow."

"Okay," Grace said, still breathing heavily. "Don't do anything stupid tonight."

Chapter 15

Syd was about to do something stupid. When she got back to Jon's, Harry was waiting in her room, pacing and watching the clock. He stopped when he saw her.

"It's eleven forty. We...what happened to you?"

Syd followed his gaze and realized her blouse was pulled halfway out of her slacks, and several buttons were missing.

"Uh..."

Harry rolled his eyes. "Never mind. We gotta get going here if we're gonna do this."

"Okay, let me change."

Harry groaned and sat down. "Make it quick, will ya?"

Syd came out in a few minutes. "How do I look?"

"How...? You look ravishing." Harry set out the rubber gloves and small flashlights.

"I'm serious."

"Syd, we're breaking into a building. You look fine," he said slowly.

"Fine. What do you have there?"

"Everything we need." Harry pulled out a case with his lock-picking utensil. "This will get us in and out."

They gathered everything and drove into town. They parked in the alley a block behind the building, turning off the headlights.

Quickly, they made their way to the back of the courthouse. Harry knelt by the lock. He put the file in, then another. He turned it gently back and forth and...

"Bingo," Harry whispered as the door opened.

"Excellent."

Harry pushed the door back and quietly crept in. The stairs were right there, and Harry led the way to the second floor. He opened the door and heard footsteps.

Sydney grabbed Harry, and they ducked into the ladies' room. They each went into a stall and stood on the toilet seat. Sydney could hear her heart pounding in her chest.

George picked a fine time to wake up, she thought angrily. The door opened, and they saw the beam of the flashlight searching the floor. Sydney held her breath while the light scanned along the floor under each stall. Christ, if I get caught in the ladies' room, my mother will kill me, she thought stupidly.

They heard his footsteps retreat down the hall as George left the restroom. Sydney stepped off the toilet and opened Harry's stall. He stood on the toilet seat, looking petrified.

"Come down from there. You look like a statue," Sydney whispered.

After making sure George was gone, they walked across the hall.

Harry whispered, "I think it's this door." He stood in front of a door and pointed.

Sydney gave him an exasperated look. "Harry, that's the men's room. This is the room," she hissed and pointed to the correct door.

Harry squinted and looked at the sign on the door. "Oh, geez. You're right."

The door was locked, and Harry knelt down and showed once again why he was in and out of jail. The door easily opened. They walked in and closed the door. Sydney went over and pulled the shades, then turned on her flashlight. They looked in every file cabinet and in every drawer. The room was small so there weren't many files.

Sydney scratched her head and looked around the room. "Where the hell is it?"

"Over here."

Sydney quickly went to his side. It was a safe.

"I bet it's in here," he whispered.

"Can you open it?" Sydney asked.

"Syd, please. Don't be insultin'." He knelt in front of the safe and rubbed his fingers against his shirt.

Sydney squatted next to him and looked around the room. Harry put his ear to the tumbler.

"This is a newer one," he said quietly.

Sydney looked at him anxiously. "Can you do it?"

"Shh," Harry said as he slowly spun the dial. "Locks are like women. You may know a lot of 'em, but when ya find the right combination," he turned it back slowly, "...of you and her, she'll open only for you. I don't mean ta be vulgar," he said triumphantly and pulled the lever. The safe opened.

Sydney was amazed once again. "You old philosopher you." Sydney patted him on the back. "But that was sexist."

They sat on the floor looking at the autopsy report. Sydney read furiously, taking in all the information. Same thing Brianne had said: sand in his lungs, mouth, and nostrils. Someone stabbed him in the back of the neck with a sharp instrument. Also, lake water in his lungs. But the cause of death was that sharp instrument to the base of his neck. There were pictures, gruesome as they were. One photo showed Jon's neck, head, and shoulders.

Syd read the description. "Listen to this. It appeared to be a thin sharp instrument that was inserted into the victim's neck and through the spinal cord. Death occurred within seconds."

Sydney flipped the page. Bruises on his back and neck. Sydney looked at another photo of Jon's face submerged in the sand. She turned the photo around and looked at it from all angles. "Christ, Jon. Who hated you this much?" Sydney said sadly.

Then Sydney picked up the evidence bag. It was marked with Jon's name and case number. Thanking God that Harry thought of the rubber gloves, Sydney opened the bag and took out the page from what appeared to be a journal. Sydney read it.

Jon was writing about Grace. He had changed his mind about the contract. He didn't know how to tell her. She was in love with him, and he didn't know how to break it to her. He wasn't in love with her, and he didn't want to go through with the contract. He'd try to tell her at dinner Tuesday. Sydney turned the page over and nothing. Then something didn't seem right about the page. But she couldn't figure it out.

"Syd, we'd better scram. You almost done?" Harry said nervously.

Sydney gently put the torn page back where she found it and closed the bag. She did the same with the report. Then Harry locked the safe.

They got out without a hitch. All doors were locked, no fingerprints, no one saw them. They walked the two blocks to the car.

"We did it." Sydney slapped him on the back.

Clouds had moved in, and it started to rain. They got the top up on the car.

"I'll put the stuff in the trunk," Harry said, and Sydney got in and started the car. Harry was taking too much time.

"Good grief," she said, exasperated. She got out and went to the back of the car to find Harry lying there groaning.

"Christ, Harry." Sydney knelt next to Harry; he continued groaning, which Syd thought was good. At least he wasn't unconscious—or worse.

Suddenly, someone grabbed Sydney and swung her around. Someone hit her square in the face, knocking her over the car and into the alley. Sydney tried desperately to stand. Through the rain, Sydney thought there were two men, but she couldn't be sure. She tried to make sure she still had all her teeth. She saw Harry still lying on the ground, trying to get up, as well. Stay down, Harry, she begged.

Syd lay perfectly still as her attacker walked over to her. He nudged her in the ribs. "She's out." Syd opened one eye and caught a glimpse of the boot. She desperately tried to remember everything she saw; there was something about the boots. But that was all she could see. She lay still until the thunder cracked overhead, and the two men walked down the alley and out of sight.

Syd quickly stood, then fell to her knees as her head throbbed. "Fuckers," she whispered and stood slowly. She made her way to Harry, who also slowly got to his feet. His forehead was bleeding.

"Harry."

"Syd." Harry groaned. "You okay?"

"Yeah, I think so."

"Holy shit, look at your face."

"The hell with that. Look at my good shirt," she said, pulling out the bloodied front of her shirt. "Damn it. C'mon, let's go to Grace's. I have a bad feeling here."

As she took a step, she faltered.

"You okay?" Harry asked, wiping the blood off his forehead.

"Yeah, yeah."

"Syd, your face."

"What about it? Am I missing a tooth?" she asked frantically.

"No, but your cheek is really bleeding. Let's get going. I'll drive."

Harry drove quickly to Grace's. All the lights were out, and only her car was there. Sydney had her head back; Harry feared the worse. He'd seen a concussion before.

He knocked on Grace's door. Finally, the porch light went on, and Grace opened it. She looked at Harry. "Irish, you gotta help, Syd is hurt."

Grace's eyes flew open. "What happened?"

"Help me get her outta the car," Harry said.

Grace ran after him to the car. She looked in and almost fainted at the sight. Syd's head was back. She looked unconscious, and her cheek was swollen and bleeding.

"God, Sydney," she exclaimed.

Between the two of them, they got her into the house and on her bed. There was blood all over her shirt.

"Geezus, she needs a doctor," Grace said, almost in tears.

Harry shook his head. "No, we can take care of her."

They got Sydney out of her shirt while she mumbled.

"I'm okay. I'm okay."

"Lie still," Grace said.

"Grace? You're all right?"

"Of course I'm all right. What the hell happened?"

"Later, Grace," Harry said. "Do ya have any first-aid stuff?"

"Sure."

Harry stopped her. "A glass of water and any pain meds? Nothing too strong."

"Okay."

Harry examined Syd's cheek. "Syd, can you hear me?"

"Yes, I can hear you. I'm not deaf. But my head is killing me."

"You got your bell rung good."

"Don't tell Grace."

Harry rolled his eyes. "You're in her bed. She knows."

"Shit."

"This is all I have," Grace said frantically.

"It's fine." Harry went to work trying to stop the bleeding under Syd's eye. It was turning a nasty blue color by the minute.

Syd winced.

"Sorry," Harry said. "Try to lie still."

"Easier said than done," Syd said through clenched teeth. She saw Grace standing behind Harry. "Hello."

"Hi. Are you okay?"

"Well..."

Harry glared at both women. "Can we do this later?"

"I'll go put on some coffee."

Harry finished cleaning the gash under her eye.

"What's the verdict, Doc?"

"You'll live. Take this." He handed Syd a pill along with a glass of water. "I don't think it needs stiches, but ya gotta stay quiet, Syd. A knock on the head is a tricky thing."

"Okay. What about you? Your forehead..."

"It's fine. I'm fine. I'll take a look at it in a minute." He sat back and took a long breath. "What do you think happened?"

"Someone knew we were in that building."

"Syd, one of them came up to me and told me to get the blankity-blank out of here and go home and take the dyke with me."

"Really?" Syd tried to sit up. Harry pushed her against the pillow. "Did you recognize the voice?"

"Nah, with all the rain and the thunder, I don't know."

Syd let out a dejected sigh. "He could have come up with something more original than dyke, I must say."

"Look, it's late. I don't feel right leaving..."

"Why not?" Grace asked from the doorway. "What's happened?" She walked into the room, wincing when she saw Syd's discolored cheek. At least Harry stopped the bleeding. In the back of her mind, she wondered how many times this had happened.

She sat on the edge of the bed, brushing the lock of hair off Syd's forehead. "You're not going to tell me, are you?"

"It's better if you don't know right now. Tomorrow, we'll get with Adam, and we'll go from there. Is that okay for now?"

"Yes," Grace said, holding her hand. "But you're to explain what's going on at some point."

"Deal." Syd tried to smile but only winced. "Harry, what did you give me?"

"Nothing. Just lie still."

"Harry's right," Grace whispered. "Try to sleep."

"Harry," Syd mumbled. "Take care of her."

"I will. I will."

They waited for a few minutes until they were sure Syd had fallen asleep.

"C'mon, you can take the couch," Grace said. "You've got a nasty bump on your forehead."

Harry chuckled and gingerly felt the bruise. "This is nothing. Last year, me and Syd…" He stopped abruptly. "Boy, I am pooped. Maybe I will take that couch. Let me check the doors."

Grace pushed him toward the couch. "I'll lock up. You go ahead. I made up the couch already."

"Thanks. Just don't go outside. And if you hear anything, wake me up."

"I will. Go."

After she locked up and shut the lights off, Harry was snoring peacefully. She went back into her room and sat on the bed. Grace put a cool cloth across Syd's forehead, and Syd moaned and opened her eyes. Grace brushed back the lock of hair off her forehead.

"Grace?" she whispered. "You're all right?"

"Shh. Yes, I'm fine. Go to sleep," she said softly.

"Harry. He's okay?"

"Yes, he's asleep on the couch."

Syd blinked and looked around the room. "Where am I?"

"Well, if you must know, you're in my bed."

"Still?" She tried to sit up and winced.

"Relax." Grace gently pushed her back against the pillows.

"What time is it?"

"It's about two thirty. Go back to sleep."

"Where are you sleeping?"

"On the chair in the—"

"Sleep with me," Syd whispered.

Grace let out a nervous laugh. "You're a flirt even with your front teeth knocked out."

"My teeth?" Her hand flew to her mouth.

Grace grabbed her hand. "I'm kidding."

"That was not funny," Syd said seriously.

"You have such a huge ego. Go back to sleep."

"No," Syd said. "Not until you get in bed. I won't let you sleep in a stupid chair."

"Fine, you colossal child. I'll be right back."

"Did you put this T-shirt on me?"

"Yes, I put the T-shirt on you. And yes…" Grace opened the dresser drawer and gathered a change of clothes. "I peeked." Grace turned out the bathroom light and made her way to the bed.

Syd was sound asleep. Grace crawled in beside her and lay on her side facing Syd. "Oh, how the mighty have fallen." She once again brushed her hair off her forehead.

She lightly kissed Syd on the lips before resting her head on Syd's shoulder.

Chapter 16

Adam stood in Grace's kitchen, watching as she made a pie. "Syd's been asleep all this time? It's nearly two o'clock."

"Start peeling." Grace handed Harry a bowl of potatoes. She dusted off her hands. "She was awake earlier, but Dr. Doogan over here slipped her another sleeping pill."

"She's no good when she doesn't get enough sleep. And I have a feeling she's gonna hafta be on the top of her form."

"What exactly happened?" Adam asked.

"Can we wait for Syd?"

"I suppose. I—"

Harry looked up from his chore and smiled. "Hey, you made it."

Grace turned around. Syd stood in the doorway, gently pulling at her T-shirt. "How did I get in these hideous clothes?"

"Well, you look rested," Grace said. "Come and sit down."

"Thanks. I feel pretty good, actually," she said and sat in a chair.

Grace handed her a glass of water.

"Thanks." She looked up at her. "What's cooking? It smells so heavenly it woke me up."

"The weather's taken a turn for the worse. It's going to rain, so I thought I'd make a beef roast, mashed potatoes, and apple pie. Comfort food."

"America on a plate. I knew I smelled apple pie. Oh, Adam. Hi." Syd gave Harry a curious look; Harry shook his head while peeling his potatoes.

"Hello. You both look like hell." He glanced at his watch then. "I want to go see the sheriff. Something's nagging me. She said she'd see me around three."

"Come back when you're finished," Syd said.

"And you'll tell me what's going on," Adam assured her.

"And stay for dinner," Grace said, walking him to the door.

When she came back, she put the pie in the oven. She sat next to Syd and Harry, who whistled softly as he peeled the potatoes.

"Okay, who's going to start?" Grace asked, looking at them.

Harry stopped whistling; Syd started to rise.

"Sit."

Syd sank back into the chair.

"Talk."

"I was born in Chicago," Syd started and flashed a smile.

"I was born in Toledo…" Harry laughed nervously but quickly concentrated on his potatoes when Grace glared at him.

"Grace, I don't want to go into anything with you. You and Adam at some point will have to talk to Brianne and the odious state trooper. The less you know, the better. You can't lie if you don't know anything."

Grace thought about that for a moment. The logic was inescapable, and Syd was right, which she hated to admit.

"You know I'm right," Syd offered. "And I'm not being smug."

"We can at least talk about what you think is happening, can't we?"

"She's got a point there, Syd," Harry said.

"It might help to get things out in the ether. I can tell you this, and it may not mean a thing. But the other morning, Harry and I went to where they found Jon's body. We looked around and found what might be important. It was one of those fancy little cigars, a cheroot."

Grace looked from Harry to Syd. "A cheroot?"

"Yes. It was wedged between the rocks."

"That's what happened to your hand? That's where you were that morning?"

"Yes. At the time, I just took it. I had no idea if it meant something." Syd leaned in then. "But the other night, you said some guy was watching you. After I left you, I went over there and skulked around, and I found an exact same cigar."

"Really? That is odd."

"I don't know what if anything it means, but I want to find out. I also want to find out about that boat. No one mentioned a boat to us. The Baker family gave that information to Brianne. And Adam didn't recall seeing any mention of it in the police report. That's why I'm going to the marina to find out what boats were out that night and who rented them. You never know, it might be a significant clue." Syd snapped her fingers. She looked at Harry. "And speaking of clues, those cheroot cigars. Harry, tomorrow, I want you to check out all the tobacco shops in town and drugstores if there are any. You know what to ask. See if anyplace sells them and if you can get them to tell you who…"

"Great idea, Syd."

"Shouldn't the police be doing all this?" Grace reached across and took Syd's hand. "I don't want a repeat of last night. Even if you're not telling me what happened. Your bruised face is enough for me. Both of you."

Syd covered her hand. "I like that you care what happens to me."

"I like that you like that. So be careful."

Syd grinned while she watched Grace take the bowls of potatoes from Harry to the sink. She rested her palm on her chin. "Ah, Harry…"

"Ain't love grand?" Harry sighed happily, putting his hand to his heart.

He got a dish towel snapped to the back of his head for the answer.

"The roast is in the oven. I have some briefs to go over. I'll be in the living room. Don't get into trouble and do not leave this house," Grace said.

As soon as she walked out of the room, Syd leaned into Harry and whispered, "Last night, the photos of Jon. There was a boot print on the back of his shirt. And whoever beat us up last night was wearing heavy worker boots, ya know like biker boots. But there was something about the boot, Harry. There was something in it or on it. Damn, I can't remember."

"It'll come to you," Harry whispered, glancing at the doorway. "I was thinking last night. The voice didn't sound like anyone I've heard, but the other guy with him carried a sidearm."

"Are you sure?" Syd asked, grabbing his arm. "Think."

"I'm sure. I saw it as they walked away."

"Oh, boy. This is not good. We have to be careful, Harry. For Grace's sake, we have to be careful. Something's rotten in Seacliff."

"And it ain't the Friday fish fry."

Grace walked into the kitchen. "Adam just called. They've released Jon's body. Tina and Keith are making funeral arrangements for tomorrow. I'd better call them back. Adam will be here in a little while."

"I'll call my mother. She'll want to be here for the funeral."

"This is happening fast," Harry said.

"It seems that way," Grace said. "And there's one other thing."

"What is it?"

"It seems I'm in Jon's will."

Harry nearly dropped his cigar. "This is like one of dem books you gave me, Syd."

Chapter 17

Syd watched Grace on the phone while she talked to Tina and Keith.

"She's in his will?" Syd said, almost absently. "I suppose that's not too unusual."

"Maybe it's about the conservation thing," Harry offered.

Syd merely nodded in agreement. Grace finished her call and sat on the couch next to Syd. "The funeral is at ten tomorrow."

"Who did you talk to?" Syd asked, reaching for her hand.

"Keith. Tina was too upset, so he said. He sounded so detached. I can't blame him." She put her head back. "This is all so sad."

"It is. But there's a matter of a murder here. Do you have any idea why Jon would have you in his will?"

"I can't imagine."

"That note, or page, said you told him you loved him and he didn't return your affections, and he was going to tell you at dinner that night that he was not going through with the contract. Right?"

Grace nodded.

"Then why would he leave you something in his will?" Syd asked. "Something is definitely not right."

They heard the car outside. "Good. That has to be Adam."

Grace met him at the door. He walked in, smiling. "Hello, all. Syd, you look much better. Must be the TLC. Something smells heavenly."

"Dinner will be ready in a bit."

Adam sat and stretched out his legs. "So I take it Grace told you about the will."

"Yes. What do you make of it?"

Adam tiredly rubbed his face. "I have no idea what's in the will…"

"But? C'mon, Adam, what are you thinking?"

"The reading of the will is tomorrow right after the funeral. I received a call from Marcy Longwood to let us know."

"Is that bad?" Harry asked.

"Depending on what's in the will, it can be done before the funeral. But given Jon's estate, it's usually done a day or two after the emotional drain of the funeral, so the family has time to get their bearings, as it were. But Tina and Keith want it done tomorrow."

"That's probably because they stand to inherit everything Jon has."

"One would think so. Grace, as your lawyer, I'd like to be with you."

"Do you think that's necessary?" she asked.

"Probably not. But in light of what happened at the police station and that note, which is still bothering me, I'd like to be there."

"Yes, you're going," Syd said.

Grace let go of her hand. "Will you stop being so bossy?"

"Was I being bossy?" Syd looked at Adam, who shrugged. "Oh, well. You're going regardless of my bossiness."

Grace looked to the ceiling and closed her eyes. "God, you're annoying. I think dinner's ready."

"This is delicious." Syd took another helping of potatoes.

"It is very good," Adam concurred. "A home-cooked meal is much better than eating in a restaurant."

"I can't wait to dig into that pie."

"Thanks. I'm glad you like it."

Syd could tell Grace was preoccupied; it didn't take a rocket scientist to figure that out. She watched as Grace picked at her food.

"I don't suppose you'll tell me what happened to both of you last night." Adam wiped the corner of his mouth on his napkin. "Keep in mind, I'm Grace's lawyer."

"Which is exactly why we're not telling you."

Harry laughed. "This is true."

"Look, someone was following us last night while we were, uh, going for a walk. And I think whoever it was knew I went to see the Baker family. I just have this itchy feeling someone is skulking around watching everyone."

"And you think whoever that is has something to do with Jon's death."

Grace and Harry cleared the dinner dishes; Harry carried the apple pie as if it were the crown jewels.

"And here's something else," Syd said, taking a piece of pie from Grace. "Thanks. I think someone is trying to frame Grace."

"But why? Why me?" Grace sat in a dejected heap.

"I don't know, but I've had that same feeling," Adam said. "But proving it is something different."

"And that's where I come in." Syd looked across the table. "And Harry."

Harry held up his fork in agreement.

"And I just know something's going to happen in that will. Whoever this is obviously wants me out of the way. I don't think they like our snooping around."

"Why do you say that?" Adam looked from Sydney to Harry. "Never mind. Go on."

"I'm going to give them what they want. So I will leave along with Harry right after the funeral."

Harry was shocked. "Syd, you can't be serious."

Grace was incredulous. "You're leaving?"

"Just for the day. We'll fly out of here. I want everyone to see us leave. And if you don't mind one more night of us, Grace, I think we should stay here tonight. Tomorrow, we'll leave, looking like two scared rabbits. Adam will take you to the reading of the will, then directly back here. My mother...Oh, hell, my mother."

Adam held up his hand. "I already made a reservation for her where I'm staying. She's coming in tonight. I'll pick her up and get her a limo in the morning to take her to the funeral. She said she'd love to stay to see what's happening, but she has some function in Evanston, and she can't miss that."

"Thank you. I truly appreciate it."

"Not to worry. So my question to you. What is the point of all this clandestine activity?" Adam looked seriously confused.

"If my hunch is right, something is going to go haywire at the reading of Jon's will." Syd looked at Adam. "If Grace was accused of Jon's murder and needed to post bail, how much are we talking?"

Adam gaped at her as did Grace and Harry.

"I have no idea," Adam said. "The evidence is slim. She has no record. If she's released on her own recognizance, the most...one hundred thousand, the least, ten grand. Why?"

"Because I think that's going to happen, if not tomorrow, then the next day," Sydney said, watching Grace, who looked like she was about to faint. Sydney took out her cell.

"Good grief, Sydney, why would you think that?" Adam asked seriously. "What are you doing?"

"I'm calling my office and making sure I have cash, boatloads if necessary."

"Do you think that will happen?" Grace asked Adam.

He watched Sydney pacing as she talked on the phone. "I won't lie to you, Grace. If they have a case, as trumped up as it might be, they may. You must be ready for that."

"Okay." Grace sighed. "I wish I knew why this was happening."

Sydney disconnected the call. "It pays to have money."

"Do tell?" Harry said, chomping his cigar.

"Oh, shush. Okay, that's settled. My office will take care of everything. They just need twenty-four hours."

"I'm sure we'll have that."

"Then let's get back to this." Sydney thought of the page from the journal, and the pieces started to fall. "Look, when you saw that page from the journal, what did it look like?" she asked Adam.

She had to be careful here, Adam couldn't know she broke into the courthouse and saw all the evidence. She noticed Harry giving her a warning stare—he thought the same thing.

"It was a piece of paper. Torn as if torn out of a book," Adam said, frowning.

Sydney nodded. "Was it legible?"

Adam got testy; lawyers hated to be questioned. "Of course it was legible. How could we know what was on it if it wasn't...?"

When his voice trailed off, Syd became hopeful that he'd figure this out without her saying anything. God, Adam, keep going, Sydney thought.

Adam stood and pondered for a moment. "Wait a minute."

"What?" Syd asked innocently.

"The sheriff said it was found on Jon's body. No, Jon almost drowned. The autopsy report said there was lake water in his lungs. That meant he was in the water for some time." He stopped; Sydney waited for his instincts to kick in.

"Sydney," Adam continued, "how could something be that legible if it were in his pocket in the water? It would have to be soaked clean through, and even if it dried, it would be illegible. It did not appear to be wet at all."

Sydney looked amazed. "Really, what does that mean?"

Grace said slowly, "It means that it was planted on him after he came ashore. The murderer must have done it after he killed him."

"You think so?" Sydney said in mock amazement.

"Of course it does," Adam said, beaming proudly. He looked at Sydney. "Why didn't you think of that?"

Sydney shook her head. "I don't know."

She looked over at Harry, and they both grinned. Grace caught them and gave them a suspicious look.

"Well, Adam, I think that gives us a reason to think someone is trying to frame Grace. My gut tells me that something is going to happen. I want cash available for her bail. So you handle it. Wire transfer any amount needed. I will not have Grace spend any time in that jail. Do you understand me?"

He nodded, smiling. "I'll take care of it. Where will you be?"

Sydney looked at Grace. "I'll be close, and I'll be watching. They need to think I'm out of the way. This will make it easier for me to do this."

"Easier for you to do what?"

Syd waved her hand. "Grace, Adam will handle your legal affairs. He will make certain that if anything goes wrong he will take care of it."

Grace gave her a worried looked. "Answer my question, Sydney. Easier for you to do what?"

"Easier for me to catch a murderer. What do you think, you silly woman? You have to keep up."

Chapter 18

After all was finalized and all the pie eaten, Adam returned to his B&B. He'd be back in the morning.

The thunder rolled while Harry made sure all the doors were locked. Syd and Grace cleaned up in the kitchen.

"This is a very domesticated scene." Syd handed the plates to Grace, who placed them in the dishwasher.

"Yep. Dull stuff."

Syd grabbed her arm, pulling her close. "Not dull at all."

"No?"

Syd smiled. "No," she said softly. She lowered her head, just about to kiss her.

"Okeydokey. All locked up. Oh, geez."

Syd and Grace jumped when Harry walked in.

"Sorry…" he said sheepishly.

"Your timing stinks."

Harry laughed. "I think I'll turn in. G'night."

"Good night, Harry. And thanks," Grace said.

"You're welcome."

"Well, it is late."

"Yes."

They both laughed then. "I feel like a teenager."

"Well, you look like you just went five rounds. Are you really all right?" Grace asked.

"I'm fine. But I like that you care."

"I've always cared."

"I have too. I've just been so stupid."

Grace grabbed her hand, leading her out of the kitchen. "I know."

"I can't wait until I get my own clothes. No offense…" Syd slipped into bed.

Grace followed, lying next to her. "None taken. You're not used to buying off the rack. And in Seacliff, we have nothing but. Go to sleep."

"I can buy off the rack."

"What store?"

"Um…"

Grace let out a snort and started laughing. "Those slacks you wore to dinner fit you like a glove."

"So you noticed?"

"I noticed." Grace yawned. "I can almost see you grinning."

Syd lay on her side to face her. "I'm not."

"Liar."

"Okay, maybe a little."

"Syd?" Grace said softly.

"Yes."

"We are not having sex tonight."

Syd laughed. "I did not—"

Grace laughed, as well. "Oh, yes, you did."

"Well, all right. Good night. Can I at least kiss you?"

"Sydney…" Grace moaned when Syd leaned over and gently kissed her. "I didn't say yes."

"You took too long."

Grace reached over and touched her bruised cheek. "I don't want you to do this."

"Don't worry. Everything will be fine."

"Why?" she asked. "Why are you doing this?"

There was a second or two of silence. "If I told you, you'd never believe me," Syd mumbled, almost asleep.

The lightning flashed, and the rain started.

"Syd?" she asked softly. "Sydney."

She was breathing heavily, sound asleep.

"Now you fall asleep." Grace looked over, barely able to see her in the darkness. She was afraid for Syd. She also had some anxiety for herself. Someone was trying to frame her, and she couldn't figure out why. She closed her eyes and tried to sleep. Who? And who would kill Jon Pickford?

Breakfast was quiet. Harry ate like he'd never seen bacon before. Syd drank her coffee, glancing at Grace, who stared out the kitchen window.

Adam arrived, looking sharp and ready for the world. "Good morning, all. Sydney, you still look like hell." He smiled and looked around the table. "Good grief, what's wrong?"

Grace smiled. "Nothing. How about some coffee? We have time."

Sydney watched her, then looked at Adam. "You understand, right?"

Adam nodded. "I've already contacted the bank. They can wire transfer whatever is needed directly to the courthouse, if need be. All bases are covered. You do what you have to. Rest easy, I'll take care of this end." He patted her on the shoulder and smiled.

"Okay, here's the game plan. Harry and I are flying out of here. Again, I want everyone to see. Make it well known that I'm scared, and I wanted my mommy. Then hopefully, whoever is behind this will feel more relaxed and in control. That's when they'll slip up. I need to check out the marina and the tobacco shops. I also want to get into Jon's house and look for that diary or journal. Now you and Grace come back here. Adam, she doesn't leave your sight." She looked at Adam, who nodded.

Grace was completely confused and frightened. This was a different Sydney Crosse. Grace wondered again what her life was like now in Chicago. Is this what she did for fun?

"Now I'll be around, as I said. However, if you need to contact me, use email, Adam. I have my laptop. Which reminds me, I'm still waiting on some information about Keith. Jack sent me some on Tina and Grace the other day."

Grace gaped at her. "You checked up on me?"

"Uh, not really checked up like checked up, more like..."

"More like you wanted to know who I was involved with."

"Uh...yes. More like that." She held up her empty coffee cup.

"Unbelievable." Grace snatched the cup from her hands.

Adam and Harry waited outside. Sydney placed her hands on Grace's shoulders. "You listen to Adam. Do whatever he says. Will you do that for me?"

Grace had tears in her eyes and threw her arms around her neck. "Yes. Please be careful. Am I going to see you at all?"

The corners of her mouth twitched mischievously. "Would you like to?"

Grace sighed heavily. "Can you ever be serious?"

"It hasn't been my strong suit as you well know." Syd pulled her back into her arms. "But I'm trying. If I can come here without being seen, I will. I'll get in touch with you through Adam's email. Hopefully, in a couple days, this will be all over." She looked down into Grace's blue eyes. "Now off you go to see what you inherited. I hope it's the plane," she said happily.

Grace stood there for a second, then kissed her thoroughly, leaving Syd breathless.

"Please be careful," Grace begged, then quickly went out the door.

Syd stood there, unable to move. She heard the car drive away, and Harry walked in.

"You okay?"

"Yes. We need to figure this out. So c'mon, you old thief. We have to get the hell out of here, so we can come back."

Sydney and Harry went back to Jon's to pack their bags and change for the funeral. As they walked downstairs, Keith and Brianne were talking in the library. They both looked over as Sydney entered the doorway.

"Geezus, what happened to you?" Keith looked horrified.

"I ran into a door," Sydney said quietly. "Look, after the funeral, I have to get back to Chicago. I appreciate the hospitality, but something's come up at the…office," she said, trying to look shamefaced. "My lawyer is with Grace. Perhaps Ms. Longwood can also help, if need be. Well, Keith, I'm sorry about Jon, I hope everything will turn out all right."

Brianne sneered at Sydney. "So, big talk. What's wrong, did Grace finally realize what you are? Big rich playgirl met her match. I knew Grace was too smart. You run along home."

Keith was shocked. "Brianne, for chrissakes." He came over to Sydney. "Look, I'll call you."

"Thanks," Syd said; she gave Keith a quick hug and walked out with Harry following.

Sydney and Harry greeted Victoria as she stepped out of her limo. She was shocked when she saw them.

"What in the world happened to you?"

"Harry and I had a disagreement. He slugged me."

"You slugged me first."

"You're both horrible liars. I have a feeling it has to do with Jon's death."

"Mother, you should have been a detective."

"Don't be insolent." She looked at Harry. "And what were you doing? You're supposed to be taking care of her. Both of you acting and looking like common hoodlums. What's going on?"

Harry said quietly, "Vic, be a good gal and get into the church." He firmly took her by the elbow.

Sydney looked over her sunglasses, shocked again to see her acquiesce to Harry. This was getting to be a disturbing habit.

Grace and Adam were at the door as Sydney walked up. Victoria looked at Grace and smiled.

"Grace, you're such a nice normal young woman. I've always liked you. What are you doing still associating with this lunatic?" She motioned to Sydney; Harry stepped out of the way.

Sydney sighed and looked to the heavens.

"Just lucky, I guess."

The service was short and simple. Grace watched Sydney and her mother. She held Victoria's hand as she softly cried. Syd was extremely gentle with her; Grace knew how much they cared for each other. Grace remembered all the nights the three of them would get together. Then it became too familiar for Syd, and her fear took over.

Grace sighed, tears springing into her eyes. She cursed herself for not putting a tissue in her purse. As if reading her mind, Sydney reached over and handed her a handkerchief.

Sydney set her attention to Tina and Keith. They looked somber as they listened to the eulogy. Then Brianne caught her attention. She was staring off into oblivion. Sydney wondered what she was thinking and what if anything Brianne had to do with all of this.

After the service, they all stood outside.

Victoria noticed Brianne, who didn't even acknowledge any of them as she passed by. "Was that Brianne Gentry? She looks dour."

"That's her natural state," Sydney said, steering her mother away. "Will you keep a civil tongue in your head? Grace was involved with her at one point," she said exasperated.

"Do you believe that?" Victoria sighed deeply. "You're hopeless."

"Yes, she is," Grace said, grinning at Sydney.

Victoria laughed along. "Oh, Sydney. Why couldn't you have kept this one?"

"I'm trying. Believe me."

"Well, don't hurt yourself in the process." Victoria winked and laughed along with Grace. "That was a good one, wasn't it?"

"Yes, Victoria. Very good."

"All right, enough of this. I would love to stay, but I need to get back to Chicago. I have another fund-raiser." Victoria pulled Sydney down for a kiss. "Behave yourself. I know you're up to something, Sydney. I can see it in your eyes."

"Go home, you meddling woman." Syd kissed her on the forehead.

"I'm serious, dear."

"Mother, I will. I'll drink my milk and go to bed early. I promise."

"Harry, take care of her. I hold you completely responsible." She looked up at him and almost smiled.

"I will do that," Harry assured her and opened the car door for her. "Good day, Mrs. Crosse." He smiled down at her.

"Good day, Mr. Doogan. Take care of yourself, you old fool." She got into the car, and it slowly pulled away. The window opened, and they heard her say, "Sydney, behave yourself!"

"Well, I think this is a good time to fly out of here." Syd looked at her watch. "We'll fly home, then we'll be back by three or so. Remember, Adam."

Adam sighed. "Sydney, I remember. Heavens, get going."

Sydney nodded, then looked at Grace. "While they're all looking, I'm going to grab your elbow. I want you to wrench away from me and walk away as if you were angry. Adam, you follow. Go now."

For an instant, their gazes met, then Grace whispered, "I love you."

Going off script stunned Sydney. "What did you say?"

Grace turned, and Syd grabbed her elbow. Grace wrenched it away as planned, but Syd would not let go.

"Wait, wait," Syd said, grinning.

"Will you let me go, you idiot?" Grace said, gritting her teeth.

She pulled away again. This time, Syd let her go. Grace then turned in a huff and marched away, with Adam following.

Syd turned to Harry, who had his hand covering his eyes. "Did you hear what she said?"

"Yeah, can we get out of here like we planned before you blow it?"

"Oh, sure, but she did say she loved me, right?"

Harry pushed her along. "Yeah, yeah. She's crazy about ya. Go…"

Chapter 19

As Grace approached Adam's car, Brianne walked up behind her.

"Grace, I'm sorry. But I told you she was no good." She watched Sydney and Harry walk away and let out a short grunt of pleasure. "What a loser. All show and no stay. You're too smart for her."

Grace wanted to slap her smug face. She took a deep breath. "You're right, Brianne. I'll talk to you later." She turned from her and got into the car.

Adam drove as Grace fumed. "Loser! Calling Sydney a loser! God, to think I was almost involved with that, that..." Words escaped her.

Adam smiled at her and said nothing. Grace was still fuming.

"Sydney has more guts..." She growled and looked at Adam. "Aren't you the least bit angry?"

Adam looked at her. "No. But then I'm not falling in love with Sydney Crosse."

Grace felt her face get hot. "Want to know the truth?"

"Of course."

"I've always been in love with that fathead."

"So it's true," Adam said as he drove.

"What?"

"Sydney told me about you. She said the same thing. Although she beat herself up over the breakup. And she didn't call you a fathead."

"Yeah, I guess that was kinda rude."

Grace, Adam, and Tina sat in Marcy's office.
"Keith's running late. He should be here any minute," Marcy offered.
They all heard a plane engine roaring overhead. Adam took a deep breath and rolled his eyes. He whispered to Grace, "That would be the red baron." Grace muffled a laugh by coughing. "What a showoff."
Keith walked in. "Sorry, I'm late."
"That's fine," Marcy said. "Well, everyone is present." She cleared her throat and put on her glasses. She took out the sealed manila envelope, opened it, and began.
"This is the last will and testament of Jonathon William Pickford. I, Jonathon..." Marcy started, and Grace only half listened, thinking of all that had happened in the past week. She was tired, confused, and felt alone now that Sydney wasn't here to annoy her.
Grace broke her own thoughts and listened to Marcy. She was not sure what was going to happen. However, she had come to trust Sydney's instincts. She was sure what was about to happen would not be pleasant. Not pleasant at all, and her life may never be the same.
Marcy finished. Keith sat there slack-jawed. Tina was furious. Even Grace was stunned.
"Well, I had thought this would be different," Keith said slowly. He looked at Grace. "I guess he really wanted to leave most of it to you." He stood and looked out the window.
Tina was not as kind. "One million? That's it? We only get one million and some stupid nature freaks get the rest?"
Keith snorted, "Well, it's something."
Tina was fuming. "He's worth twelve million. We're his family, and we split one million?"
Grace sat there not knowing what to say. She had no idea.
"And what the hell is a codicil? What was that?" Tina asked angrily.

Marcy sighed. "It's like an amendment. Jon wanted to make sure that if for any reason Ms. Morgan could not fulfill her duties, then the bulk of the estate would go back to you and Keith. However, the hundred acres would still remain in the hands of the Conservation Department. That would not be touched."

"So it's up to her?" Tina pointed at Grace. Marcy nodded. "That's the way Jon wanted it."

Adam spoke for the first time. "Ms. Longwood, when was this codicil drafted?"

She looked at him. "Two months ago, Mr. Bryson."

He nodded and stood. "Well, I think Ms. Morgan and I will get some air. Is there anything more to the will?"

Marcy shook her head. "We'll get in contact with you. Ms. Morgan will need to sign the formalities before she legally takes the inheritance."

"Understood," Adam said, collecting his briefcase.

Grace stood. "Keith, Tina, I had no idea, really."

Tina gave her a nasty look, and Keith only nodded as they walked away.

Once in the car, Adam pulled on his tie. "Well, we need to talk. Let's get back to your house."

Grace poured lemonade while Adam looked as though he was deep in thought. He looked up when Grace handed him the glass.

They sat for a minute or two. Adam watched Grace; she was still in shock. "Did you have any idea he would do this?" he asked quietly.

Grace shook her head. "All we discussed was the acreage he had."

"He left the bulk of his estate for you to manage. You had no idea he was turning his estate into a corporation? A corporation that funded environmental law?" he asked again.

Grace looked at him. "No, I didn't know he was going to do that. We discussed him leaving the acres, and that's all," Grace said, getting irritated.

"And you were not in love with him? He did not decide to change his mind about the acres he had?" Adam said, looking at her. "Because it looks like you were in love with him, and he wasn't with you. He decided to change his mind and his will, and you were the last person he saw."

Grace gaped at him. "I was not in any way in love with Jon Pickford. We were business associates. We discussed one thing, the property. I had dinner with him Tuesday. He was excited about the venture and couldn't wait to sign the contract. Then someone killed him, and it wasn't me," she said vehemently.

Adam smiled, reached over, and took her hands. "Good. Answer that question when Brianne or that detective asks you just that way. Do not elaborate or offer any other information."

Grace sighed. "I don't know any other information."

He nodded. "Sydney was right. Her instincts are very, very good. Something's rotten here. I only hope she can find out what stinks and soon."

Grace sat on her porch rocking back and forth watching the lake. Adam retreated to the kitchen, typing away furiously on his laptop. He finished, took a sip of lemonade, and looked out the huge picture window at Grace. This was going to get tense. Sydney was right, and he got a very nervous stomach. That note was planted on Jon's body. He was sure Sydney knew that, though he didn't know how Sydney knew this, and honestly, he didn't want to know. He looked at his watch—two thirty. Sydney would be checking in soon.

He thought about the will. That codicil was odd. Why would Jon Pickford leave the bulk of his estate to Grace, then say if anything happens where she can't fulfill the duties, it goes back to the family, except the hundred acres? Why? Adam was stumped. He just emailed Sydney with the whole scenario, hoping she could shed some light on it.

Although it was a hot and humid day, Adam shivered as he watched Grace. The thunder rolled off in the distance.

Things were going to happen…fast.

Chapter 20

After landing in Charlevoix, Michigan, Harry took a tour, for some reason, of the airport shops.

Sydney made a call to Judy, who seemed confused. "Just make sure you tell them I'm in town and in the office but in a meeting or whatever I usually do. Good Lord, wait, don't tell them that. Use the meeting thing."

"Okay."

"This is serious, Judy."

"Okay. You got it, Sydney. No jokes."

Then she called Jack and told him what had happened. He hoped he'd have information for later; he would send it to her email.

"Syd?"

Syd looked to see Pete walking toward her. "Hey, Pete. Thanks for coming on such short notice."

"No problem. So you want me to take your plane back to Chicago?"

"Yes. And no word of this to anyone. I mean no one. Understood?"

"Sure." Pete grinned and took off his aviator glasses. "Had a wild weekend?"

"No," Sydney said. "Just remember not a word to anyone. Not even your wife."

"Not a word." Pete shook her hand and headed to the plane.

"Okay, we need a car." She looked around. "Where the hell is Harry? I knew it was a bad idea to give him that credit card."

She whirled around when she heard a car's horn. "No…" she whispered.

Harry pulled up in a small nondescript car. Sydney looked at it with disgust as she got in.

"I thought I'd get a car while you waited. What?"

"What is this?"

"We can't be noticed. And ya said nothing flashy. If we pull up in one of those foreign jobs you drive, we'd stick out like a sore thumb," he said as he headed back to Seacliff. "Plus, I bought a few things from the gift shop in the airport. Better clothes for you, you can't dress so nice. You gotta blend. I also got us a place to stay."

Sydney put her head back and sighed. Her cheek ached; she was driving in a dirty compact car that sounded like a sewing machine. She had to wear clothes purchased by an aging, colorblind petty thief. Sydney decided she did not like undercover work at all.

Harry pulled the car off the highway alongside a motel.

"We're staying...here?" she asked pathetically.

Harry checked them into the motel outside of South Haven. Sydney looked around the small room. Two twin beds, a phone, and a TV.

"We're staying in the same room?"

Harry nodded. "Trust me, it's for the best. No one would expect you to be staying in a place like this. But the best part, it has that Wi-Fi thing you needed."

Sydney plopped her bag on the bed, which bounced precariously, and sighed. She looked at her watch—two o'clock. At least she could plug in her laptop with the Wi-Fi thing. The room was like a furnace. She looked around in horror.

"Harry, where is the air conditioning?"

Harry looked around. "I guess we don't have any."

"Yes. Who needs air conditioning in the middle of summer?"

"Look, Syd, take a nice shower. You'll feel better. I'll go get us some ice and a couple of sandwiches," he said and was gone.

Sydney sat there looking around. "Oh, my God. It's a rat hole."

She tentatively walked into the bathroom and flipped on the light. "Well, it's clean." She took a shower. The water had a slight tint of brown to it for just a moment. Usually, she could stand in a shower forever. Now, she quickly washed and got out. She slipped into a lightweight T-shirt and a pair of shorts. When she was finished dressing, she needed another shower.

"This will never do." She sat on the bed, put on her glasses, and plugged in her laptop. She was itching to get to her email.

First, she read the email from Adam and frowned deeply. She read it twice to make sure. The first thing she noticed was the codicil. Why would Jon do that? If for some reason Grace was unable to do as he wished, then why not find someone else? According to Grace, this was his life's dream, finally to do something worthwhile. There had to be some other avenue he could take instead of giving it all back to Keith and Tina. Something wasn't right. However, she agreed with Adam. This did look like Grace was a scorned lover and killed Jon before he could change his will. That detective might be waiting just for this.

Keith and Tina must be livid. Sydney took off her glasses and rubbed her eyes. Then she responded to Adam. Told him all she was thinking and reiterated her need for Grace to stay out of jail, no matter how much it cost. She was going to check out the marina and try to find out something about this journal. She didn't hold much hope about the cigars she found but would give it a shot anyway. Sydney typed quickly, not wanting to forget anything. Finally, she asked Adam to take care of Grace. She'd be in touch later and not to worry. She sent the email and closed the laptop.

She looked at the bag Harry purchased at the airport. Opening it cautiously, she was not too offended by what she saw. A pair of jeans and T-shirts mostly. Mercifully, the colors were not glaring. She opened the windows in the room. No breeze, it was hot and humid—and no air conditioning.

Harry came back about a half hour later. Sydney chuckled as he came in with three bags and a huge fan.

"There's a little store down the road. I got bourbon for me and the fixings for martinis for you." He smiled triumphantly and picked up the bucket. "I'll get us some ice."

Sydney watched him leave. "Old thief," she said, smiling, plugging in the fan.

"It works!" Harry announced. "Got the ice."

"Then let's get to work."

Harry agreed and made two drinks. They sat in front of the fan, sipping their drinks and eating ham sandwiches.

"So the old man left the bulk of his money for Grace to manage, huh? That must've sent those two brats into a tizzy."

"One would think so. However, according to Adam's email, they took it quite well. Although Tina was angry and whined. Adam thought it strange they didn't show more emotion. I have to agree," she said, sipping her martini.

Harry shrugged. "Maybe they're in shock. It'll sink in, and they'll show their true colors."

Sydney shook her head and checked the time. "Okay, I'm going to check out the marina. You check out the tobacco shops. There should be plenty of people in town. Hopefully, we'll blend in."

Chapter 21

Grace sat on the porch rocking. She looked over to see Brianne come on the porch.

"Grace, how are you?" she asked quietly.

"I feel better than you look." She looked at the lake and kept rocking. Brianne looked guilty and ashamed.

"Grace, in light of what's happened this morning, I need to ask you a few questions. I need you to come with me."

Grace noticed how uncomfortable she looked, but she couldn't muster any pity for her.

"You think I did it, don't you?" she asked sadly.

Adam came out and stood there.

"Good afternoon, Sheriff."

Brianne's face clouded over, and she stared at Adam. "Counselor," she said, then looked at Grace. "Would you come with me?"

"What do you need from Ms. Morgan?"

Brianne gave him a disgusted look. "As I explained to Ms. Morgan," she said sarcastically, "in light of recent occurrences, I need to ask her a few questions."

Adam sat down. "Fine, go right ahead."

Brianne stood there gaping at him. "I'd prefer you'd come down to the station."

"Are you going to charge my client with anything? If not, you can ask any questions you like right here."

"Under the law, I can have Grace come with me. But I don't want to make this a circus." Brianne glared at him and turned to

Grace. "Okay, Grace. Did you have any idea that Jon would be leaving you his estate?" she asked her and glanced at Adam.

Grace said honestly, "He didn't leave me his estate, Brianne. He wants it made into a corporation to fund lobbying for environmental law. I am to manage this corporation. I don't own anything."

Adam smiled and looked out at the lake. Good girl, he thought.

"However, I did not know he was going to do this," she finished and continued rocking.

"Were you at any time involved with Jon sexually? The page from his journal suggests that you were, and he not only refused you, but had changed his mind about this whole contract business." She ran her fingers through her hair. "Christ, Grace, he shows up dead two days later. Don't you know what that looks like?"

Adam said nothing but watched Grace.

"Yes, Brianne. I did not kill Jon. I have nothing more to say," she said. "I don't know what else I can tell you but the truth."

"This would be so much easier if you cooperated," Brianne said, frowning.

Now Adam bristled. "Cooperate or capitulate? Ms. Morgan has told you the truth. I find it hard to believe how a friend who has known Ms. Morgan all her life is so willing to believe her guilt. Why is that?" he asked quietly, looking at Brianne.

Brianne took a menacing step in Adam's direction. "Being the sheriff, I don't have that luxury. I have to go by the facts."

"Well then, when you have the facts and not speculation, please come back. Until then, my client has nothing further to say," Adam said, ending the conversation.

Brianne stormed off the porch and peeled out of Grace's driveway. The engine roared as she drove off.

"She's pissed."

"You did just fine," Adam said and put a hand on her shoulder. "She'll be back, though. Hopefully, they won't get any lab results for a couple days. That'll give Sydney some breathing room. Speaking of which, she told me to take care of you. So how about dinner?"

"All right. Where is she?" She looked out at the lake.

"Some 'rat hole,' as she put it, but she didn't say where. Just to say she was close, and she'd be watching you." He chuckled, pulling at his earlobe. "I don't know what you've done to that poor woman, but she never stayed in a rat hole for a woman before."

"It'll be good for her character. I wonder what she's doing now."

Sydney stood by the marina. There were people everywhere, thank goodness. She fit in well enough. Harry made her wear a baseball cap. She felt ridiculous; she adjusted it and walked into the small trailer.

A woman sitting behind a desk looked up. "Hi, need a boat?"

Sydney smiled and sat down. "Yep. I need it for the day. I was here last week. The one I wanted was already taken. Someone rented it for the night. It had the downriggers on it and ship's bell. My husband liked it," she said apologetically.

"Really? We usually don't rent at night. Let me look." She leafed through a couple of pages. "Well, I'll be darned, we did. Hmm." She looked closer at the date. "No wonder, I was off that day. Wait till I see Jerry. He's not supposed to do that. I'm sorry, I can give it to you for the day, but we have to have it back by seven. The one you want is here. I know exactly which one."

They walked down the pier, and in the slip was the boat, just as Mike Baker had described it. "Mind if I take a look at it?"

"Climb aboard. Only I have to apologize, it's been here since it was brought back. I haven't had a chance to clean it. If you wait…"

Sydney put her hand up. "No, that's fine. I'll just take a look." The woman looked back at her office when they heard the phone ring.

"If you have to go back, I'll just look around and let you know," Syd offered, giving her most charming smile.

"Sure. That's fine." She turned and walked away.

Sydney jumped on the deck and started looking around. Nothing out of the ordinary. She checked the live well and under the seat cushions. Then she saw it, in the corner. A crumpled package of cigars. She gently picked it up and took out a handkerchief, wrapped it up, and put it in her pocket. "What is it with these cigars?" She frantically looked for anything else. Then she saw the woman walking back. She jumped off the boat and smiled at the young woman.

"So no one has used this boat since last week?" Syd asked as they walked back to the office.

"Nope, and I feel terrible that it hasn't been cleaned," she said as they sat down.

"That's all right."

"Well, when would you like it?" She was interrupted by one of the workers who needed her outside. "Excuse me, just a moment."

Sydney waited for her to close the door, then quickly picked up the ledger. She found the date and looked for a signature, Jon Pickford. She recognized the signature. She heard the woman come back in and put the ledger back.

Sydney stood. "Well, I'll talk it over with the husband, er, my husband and see when he wants to go out. I'll let you know, would that be all right?"

"Just fine," she said.

As she was leaving, she noticed one of the workers. It was Jerry. Sydney wanted to take credit for great detective work, but his name was on his shirt. "Excuse me? See that boat over there?"

The boy looked and turned red. "Yes, don't remind me."

"Why?" Sydney asked.

"I made a huge no-no. I let it go out at night and just caught hell from Sandy."

Sydney patted him on the shoulder. "The old guy probably wanted to impress the girl he was with." Sydney waited for his reaction.

The boy stared at her. "What old guy, what girl? Some young guy rented it. He was alone. Signed for it himself. At least I got that right. He paid cash, more than the price. I thought I was doing somethin' good. Man, was I wrong. She almost fired me."

"Don't worry. Hey, what did this guy look like?" Sydney asked casually. The boy shrugged.

"Normal looking, not too tall. About five-eight, I guess. Smoking a nasty cigar, he blew it right in my face twice."

"Anything else?"

"He wore these funky boots. Ya know the black biker boots with the chain across the heel? Handed me a wad of money and told me to scram. Come to think of it, he was a jerk."

Sydney chuckled. "Was the jerk alone?"

The boy nodded. "Yeah. Well, I gotta get back," he said and walked away.

Sydney walked back to the car and waited for Harry. What was going on? Cigars again. But the boots—that was interesting. She leaned against the hood of the car. The sun had come out, and someone turned up the humidity. She gingerly touched her cheek; it ached again. She took off the baseball cap, tossed it on the seat, and immediately scratched her head.

She heard a whistle and saw Harry walk down the street. They got in the car and drove out of town.

"Syd, you look pooped."

"I am pooped. And I want a decent shower."

"You need to eat."

Harry drove to a small nondescript diner.

"Well, it's food."

"It is?" Syd looked down at her burger and doused it with ketchup.

"So what did ya find out?" Harry ate his chili dog as if he'd never had one.

145

Syd winced as she watched him. "Found out someone signed Jon's name to the register, but it looked to me like it was his signature. I found another damn cigar, well, the package, and the kid that works there said the guy was a jerk, about five-eight, smoking the cigar and wearing biker boots."

"Wow. He was a wealth of information."

"He was a kid. They don't care."

"Lemme see the pack."

Syd pulled the crumpled pack out of her pocket.

Harry laughed. "Ha! Take a look." He pulled out a package of cigars. The boxes were identical.

"Harry, where did you find these?" Sydney asked, amazed.

"I went through every store in town, see? Only one sold these. That's gotta be them. The lady behind the counter said they never sell them. Not until a week or so ago. Then all the sudden, they're selling. A guy and woman come in regular, like, to buy 'em," he said proudly. "But they haven't been in for two days. Last time, the blonde bought four packages, so she figures not to see 'em for a while."

Sydney beamed at him. "You're amazing. Harry, tell me you got a description of these people."

Harry nodded. "Indeed I did. A blond woman, older, she says, but looks like she comes from money. And some guy who was always rude, she said. Average height, dark hair. Then she says, he always had on these work boots. Even when he wore shorts."

"Boots again. Well, this was a great day's work."

"What are we gonna do?"

"I'm going to email Jack. Give him this info and see if he can cross-reference and maybe come up with someone. I wish we had more."

Syd sat back and looked out the dirty window.

"Syd?"

"Yeah?"

"You gonna eat that?" Harry motioned to the half-eaten burnt burger.

"No, you go right ahead."
"Really?"
Syd gave him an incredulous look. "Really. I insist."
"Thanks. They got good eats here. Ya gotta try the chili dog tomorrow."
"I'll make a note of it." She picked up her iced tea in a red plastic glass and set it down. "I hope Adam is taking Grace someplace nice for dinner."
"Good steaks at Ernie's," Harry said, eating the last of the burger.
Syd grinned and tilted her head. "I adore you."
Harry turned bright red. "Tell your mother. I need a good word."
"Ahh. I can imagine a steak at Ernie's."

Grace watched the lake from their table. Adam brought her to Ernie's.
"We should be as normal as possible," he said.
Grace agreed. As she gazed around the restaurant, the scene reminded her of a night long ago with Syd.
"What are you thinking?" Adam asked. "You have a lovely smile right now."
"Oh, I was thinking of a time with Syd. She invited me to Chicago for a charity dinner her mother was chairing. We actually danced almost all night. She's a marvelous dancer."
"Yes, she'd have to be. Sydney is nothing if not socially apt. Victoria saw to that."
"I know, but she's more than that."
Adam smiled as he watched her. "Yes, she is."
"She's smug, arrogant…"
"Don't forget pompous and petulant."
"But she's putting herself in harm's way for me."
"Who do you think might be doing this?" he asked, drinking his wine.
Grace shrugged. "I have no idea. I know Keith and Tina spend a lot, and half a million to them doesn't seem like a lot."

She laughed genuinely. "Half a million doesn't seem like a lot. What is this world coming to?" she asked, looking to Adam for an answer.

He smiled. "Sydney and I had this same discussion two weeks ago over dinner. I know it sounds ludicrous coming from a woman whose net worth is well over twenty million," he started, and Grace gaped at him.

"You've got to be kidding me."

He laughed quietly. "Shocking, isn't it? I'll bet you think Sydney sits around all day at the pool or at the club swilling martinis and chasing women."

"I used to."

"I'll tell you something. When her father left her TeleCrosse Communications, its net worth was nine million. In six years, Sydney has almost tripled the net worth. Believe me, she knows absolutely nothing about big business," he said positively and drank his wine.

Grace was completely intrigued. She leaned forward. "Then how did she do it?"

Adam leaned forward. "Instincts. You can't teach them, you can't learn them. She just has them. Plain and simple. Do you know she spent a small fortune hiring the men and women she has now? She knows people. Maybe because she was left on her own when she was younger. I don't know. However, I would trust her instincts above anyone else's." He chuckled and added, "That's not to say she's not a colossal pain. She can be most unmanageable at times."

They finished dinner, and Grace found herself thinking about Sydney even more than she had in the past week.

"You're in love with her, aren't you?" Adam asked, signing for the bill.

"Yes. You know, she's four years older than I am. And when we met, I thought she was younger. She acted so…"

"Childish?"

Grace laughed. "Not in a bad way. She definitely knows how to keep things lively. But in doing that, she avoids the hard decisions of life. The gritty, 'choose a side' part. You know what I mean?"

"Yes, I do. It's sometimes better to help others, especially if it deflects the attention from yourself and your loneliness." Adam laughed then. "You spooked her."

Grace threw her head back and laughed along. "She reacted like a horse in a burning stable. She couldn't get away fast enough. Thank God we were in Chicago at the time. She would've had to swim across Lake Michigan."

"She's a good swimmer but not that good. No, don't give up on her. Syd loves you. I know it."

"It will be her decision. When this is all over."

They both grew serious then. When will this be over?

Chapter 22

"When will this be over?" Syd whined as she sat in front of the fan, pulling on her T-shirt.

"It'll get cooler tonight." Harry had a wet white handkerchief wrapped around his head as he sat next to Syd on his bed.

"You need to get some sun." Syd stared at his white legs beneath the red plaid shorts. "You look anemic."

Harry chuckled and took a drink of bourbon. "This is the life. A cool drink, some TV, a good meal. And a friend to share it with."

Syd knew her mouth dropped to the floor. She said nothing, just sipped her martini. She didn't even have olives. She felt like crying...

"Well, you got the friend part right. But I can't watch another episode of *I Love Lucy* or *The Rockford Files*. I'd better email Adam."

She typed away, telling Adam about her day. Reminding him to take care of Grace. She would try to stop by Grace's later that night, if possible. Then she signed off. She closed the laptop and set it on the table between the beds. "I still can't believe we're sharing a room."

"I'm telling ya, it's all they had. And this is the best we should do. We gotta keep a low profile."

Syd took her glasses off. "Harry…Does a woman of my age staying in the same room with a man of your age in twin beds seem like keeping a low profile?"

"Hey!" Harry sat on the side of his bed and took the laptop. "I told 'em you were my daughter."

"Wha—? Never mind." She sat back against the headboard. She noticed Harry looking at the laptop.

"How does this thing work?"

"You turn it on and poof...the world at your fingertips."

"Interesting," he said.

Sydney smiled. "Want to send an email?"

Harry gaped at her. "To who? I don't know nobody."

"That's a double negative, and of course, you do. You can send one to my mother," she said quietly with her eyes closed. She opened one eye and peered at Harry, who was looking at the laptop.

"Nah, your mother wouldn't want to hear from me."

"Well, I promised I'd email her, but I'm really not feeling up to it. I wanted to let her know how I was. I know she's worried. I'll do it tomorrow," Sydney said tiredly.

Harry looked at her. "You promised your mother? Syd, that ain't right."

Sydney yawned. "Well, I'll walk you through it. It's like writing a letter, that's all."

Harry picked up the laptop and plugged it in. "Okay, go slow," he warned.

Sydney smiled. "It's like flying the plane."

Harry laughed. "And we saw how well that went."

Syd talked him through how to get to the email. "Now just type like you'd write a letter. Mother will get it and probably read it tomorrow. Maybe even tonight." Sydney smiled, watching Harry.

He rubbed his hands on his shorts and started. He typed a few letters, then looked up and thought for a minute, then smiled and looked back at the keys and slowly typed. Sydney smiled, watching him with that ridiculous white handkerchief on his head and the white basketball undershirt.

Harry smiled, typing away, then finally, he stopped. "Okay, wanna hear what I got?"

"If you want. Sure."

"Okay." Harry cleared his throat. "Dear Vic. Ha ha. I mean Victoria." He looked at Syd. "'Cause she hates it when I call her Vic."

"I get it."

"Anyway. How are you? Sydney is resting, so I thought I would write to you instead. She is fine. We went to a nice diner to eat. I had a chili dog. But no onions as they give me gas."

Syd hid her grin and listened.

"Syd will email you tomorrow. I hope you have a peaceful night full of stars." He looked up. "Was that too much?"

Syd felt tears sting her eyes. "No," she said softly. "That was perfect. Use the mouse pad on the keyboard like I showed you and click send."

He fiercely concentrated, then let out a relieved sigh. "Okay. I did it."

"You did. I'm proud of you. Now go to sleep."

Harry handed her the laptop and stretched out on the bed. Syd turned off the lights and lay back. Unbelievably, she fell sound asleep.

Sydney woke up with a start. She looked at her watch—eleven o'clock. She was wide awake as she sat on the edge of the bed. It was still hot and humid. Harry was sleeping peacefully. She quietly stood and slipped into her deck shoes. She didn't want to turn on any lights and wake him up.

After writing Harry a note, she turned the fan on him and slipped out quietly.

She drove to Grace as quickly as she could in the sewing machine. As she approached the house, she slowed and turned off the lights. She parked a block away and walked. It was cooler near the lake, and she was grateful when she felt a little breeze, although she was still sweating. She looked around and saw no one as she crept onto the porch. She knocked softly, and the door opened immediately.

"Sydney," Grace said quickly.

Sydney frowned and whispered, "What the hell are you doing answering the door like that? Good grief, woman, there's a murderer about, and you're opening your door to anyone."

"I knew it was you," she hissed quietly. "Who else could it be, for chrissakes? What are you doing?"

Sydney chuckled. "Ignoring an irresistible urge to kiss you."

"Well, go jump in the lake. That should quell it," she whispered.

"Don't be like that. Let me in."

She followed Grace into her house. "Do you have any apple pie left? I'm starved," she said emphatically and walked in the dark to the kitchen.

Grace groaned and closed the door. She followed Syd to the kitchen and turned on the small light by the stove. And nearly laughed out loud.

"What in the world are you wearing?"

Syd looked down at her shorts and tie-dyed T-shirt. "What? I'm a fashion statement. I'm trying to blend in with the vacationers."

"Don't tell me, Harry picked it out."

"Yes. He also rented the sardine can, which is parked a block away."

Grace looked at her and didn't like what she saw. There were dark circles under her eyes, and she looked tired and drawn. However, her eyes still sparkled as she looked at her.

"Well, where's the pie?" she asked sincerely.

Grace sighed. "Between you and Harry, you ate it all. Sit down. I'll make some eggs."

"Bacon?"

"Ham. I know that may make you self-conscious," she said sweetly.

Syd returned her sweet smile. "Good enough. We're staying at some..."

"Rat hole."

"Oh, right. I put that in the email."

"So tell me what happened after you left." Grace hauled out the carton of eggs, butter, and leftover ham and got to work.

"Did I know you could cook?"

Grace glared at her. "Yes. I cooked for you many times."

"Hmm."

She told Grace of the day's exploits, including the diner and the motel. The story had Grace laughing while she cracked the eggs in the sizzling pan.

"Harry had the right idea, God bless him," Grace said over her shoulder. "So what do you think is going on?"

"So I'm thinking whoever killed Jon must have an accomplice." She leaned forward. "Here's my theory. Somebody hired the boat, I think Tuesday night. Whoever it was signed Jon's name. They somehow got him on the boat and cracked his skull. The coroner's report said there was an injury to the back of his neck. Then they tossed him overboard. Jon, being a good swimmer, came to and got to shore. Unfortunately, someone was waiting for him. He stepped on Jon's neck and forced his head into the sand. Jon breathed in all the sand, and knowing he wasn't dead, the murderer took some object and jammed it into the base of his neck, making sure he was dead.

"This guy smokes little squared off cigars, they're called cheroots. I mentioned that to you. Harry and I found them at the crime scene. I found them where the man was watching you, and I found a crumpled pack on the boat."

Grace put a glass of milk in front of her. "No coffee."

"Thanks. So it's a theory, but I need proof. I need a big break here. Damn it." She looked at Grace then. "There's something else. The other night, when we came to your house after we got beat up, Harry said one of them wore a sidearm. Like a cop."

Grace turned around to her, spatula in hand. "You mean Brianne?"

"Yeah, I think so. The ham is burning."

"Oh." Grace prepared two plates and set them on the table. "But you're not sure."

"No, I'm not. That's why we need a break. We need something concrete. I sent an email to Jack Riley in Chicago. I gave him everything I had. He's going to cross-reference and see if anything comes up. I'm also waiting on some info on Tina and Keith."

"Eat."

They ate their breakfast in silence. When Syd was finished, she was exhausted. "Thank you, Grace. That was again delicious."

"You need sleep," she said quietly.

"I do. I'll leave. Thanks for the breakfast."

"Why don't you stay?" Grace asked.

Syd reached over and gently stroked her cheek. "Because I wouldn't want to leave."

"Is that bad?"

"No. But right now, I need to focus on this. And honestly, since the first time I saw you last week, I-I can't get you out of my mind. Your face crowds my vision. If I let myself go, I could stay right here in your arms and never leave." Syd sniffed back the tears and coughed softly. "So I have to go for now. What?"

"You've never talked like that before. Sydney Crosse, I could grow to love you all over again. Cross my heart." She grabbed Syd, pulling her in for a scorching kiss.

Syd stumbled forward, nearly knocking the chair over. She frantically tried to hold on to Grace and the kiss.

Grace pulled back and laughed at the stunned expression. "You may go."

"Huh? Oh. Right. Go. Okay. Which way?"

There was a promise of a beautiful day as Sydney drove back to the rat hole. She felt rejuvenated after seeing Grace and completely aroused after the kiss.

Harry was snoring away peacefully as Sydney quietly plugged in her laptop. It was still humid, but at least when she stepped into the shower this time, the water was not brown.

"How does one get brown water?"

Afterward, she dressed in the bathroom—so humid. Harry was still sleeping. "How can he sleep in this heat?" she whispered and logged on to her computer.

There were several emails. One was from her mother to Harry. "How adorable." She read the email from Adam. This codicil was still worrying Adam. And Syd had to agree. Why have that put in? Why not have another alternative? Something wasn't right. Why would Jon do that?

Sydney agreed with everything Adam was saying. She answered his email, typing quickly, and asked Adam to find a way to get Tina and Keith out of the house for a while that day. Maybe lunch, whatever. She needed to get back into the house and look for that journal. The police didn't have it yet. If they did, they surely would have contacted Grace. Sydney mentioned her fears concerning Brianne. She then told him her theory about the accomplices and to keep his eyes and ears open. Someone knew something. She could not believe Tina and Keith would go gentle into that good financial-meager night without screaming and yelling.

She opened the email from Jack Riley. He started by telling Sydney she owed him big-time for this. It took him three days to compile this info and promises for everything from Bears tickets to playoff tickets, if there were any. It was too much for an email. Jack needed to get it faxed to her. There were pages of information on this little punk, as Jack put it.

In a nutshell, Keith had a scam going on in the ivy-covered halls of Harvard way back when. A small extortion business. Get a fax number quick.

Sydney sat there thinking, a fax. She had no printer. She emailed Adam for Grace's fax number at her office. Immediately. Then she opened Jack's last email, he was still begging for a fax number.

Sydney sighed, then laughed. She thought of Mike and Tommy playing football on the beach. She responded to Jack. *Hold your water...will have a fax number this morning. Don't be a wiener, Jack.*

She opened the last email from Adam. The subject line read, *From Grace.*

Syd's heart illogically jumped in her chest. "Good Lord, Sydney. Calm down." She wiped the palms of her hands on her shorts and opened the email.

Syd, Just wanted to tell you how lucky I am to have you on my side. Whatever happens here, I will always know you are a wonderful person to help me. Thank you for coming over last night and letting me know you were all right. There are so many things I want to say but not in an email. Sufficient for now, just to say thanks again for all you've done. Please give Harry a kiss for me, and be careful, please. Grace.

Syd grinned and read the email again. She let out a contented sigh and closed the laptop. "I think she might love me." She put her hands behind her head and laughed out loud, waking up Harry.

"Oh, sorry. Good morning, Harry. You snore like a steam engine. Get out of bed, you lazy man. We have things to do."

Harry just lay there. "Morning, Syd. Did ya sleep? You look better," he said, yawning and stretching but still not getting up.

"You have an email."

Harry's eyes flew open, and he sat up. "You're kiddin' me."

"Nope. Read it."

Harry sat there staring at the laptop. He reached for it, then stopped. "Wait, I gotta take a shower." He rushed into the bathroom.

Sydney gave him a bewildered look. "She can't see you," she called after him.

Syd had to admit, breakfast was much more edible than the previous night's cement on a bun, which, Syd remembered, Harry devoured.

"So how is my mother?" she asked while buttering her toast.

"She's fine. She thanked me for letting her know how you was, er, were. She worries about you." Harry then leaned over to Sydney and quickly kissed her head. "That's from your mother."

Sydney laughed and returned the gesture, kissing him on the top of his bald head.

"That's from Grace. Ah, Harry. Isn't it wonderful to be alive?"

"Yep. And I'd like to keep it that way. So let's just do what your mother and Grace said and be careful."

Chapter 23

Grace paced back and forth in front of her desk while Adam typed his email to Sydney.

"I wonder what information she's got." Grace walked up to her office window and gazed out at the quiet street below.

"We'll find out soon enough. Want to say anything to her?"

Grace chuckled quietly. "No, we don't have that much time. Just tell her…" She stopped and laughed again. "No."

"She'll read this immediately, I'm sure. I don't know if she'll come here, but we can get the fax and find her. Jack must have called in a good many favors to get this information, if it took him three days to compile it. Sydney has very loyal friends." He chuckled and closed his laptop. "Jack would do anything for her."

Grace smiled. "I'm sure Syd has a way of making a lot of people do anything for her, charming as she thinks she is."

Adam laughed. "She does have a healthy ego." Adam's computer signaled he had incoming mail. "That was quick." He opened his email and read Sydney's response. "Okay. She sent Jack the fax number. He's sending it within the hour. He must be busy."

"Well, I'm sure the poor man is busy. He's a police lieutenant. The world doesn't stop for Sydney Crosse."

"Oh, I don't know. She took credit for the solar eclipse last year."

Grace tried not to find that amusing, but it did sound like Syd.

Adam laughed and looked at Grace. "She said to tell you to make sure there's paper in the machine. She knows how forgetful you are."

"What a colossal…"

Adam waited. "Is there—?"

"Yes, Adam. There's paper in the fax."

"Sorry." Adam laughed. "She is funny, I have to admit. So we read it when it comes. She wants to meet at that restaurant where you two had dinner. High noon, as she put it." Adam laughed and closed his laptop.

"You really like her, don't you?" she asked curiously.

Adam smiled. "Yes, I do. With all her faults. And believe me, she has many. I truly think she's turned out to be a good woman. Better than her father could ever imagine or be himself. I know I've said this to you before, but Sydney is not what she appears to be, and that's the way she likes it." He let out a genuine laugh.

They sat staring at the fax machine for nearly an hour when it started. It was almost noon. Finally, it produced three pages of information. Grace and Adam stood there watching the pages print. The cover page from Jack read, *This kid was a punk. Sorry, Sydney. The info is correct, so don't even think it's not. Let me know if you need anything else. Call me to let me know you're alive!*

Grace read it, then put the pages together. Then they both ran out the door.

Sydney and Harry sat at an outdoor table and waited. Sydney drank her iced tea and looked at her watch. "Where are they? It's ten after twelve."

Harry sighed. "Syd, they'll be here."

Sydney got up and paced. The waitress came outside and set the beer in front of Harry.

"Thank you." He grinned and took a long drink. "Ah. That's good. It's a beautiful day. Less humid but still sunny."

"You should have been a weatherman."

"Sit down, Syd. They'll be here. Grace would never leave ya hanging."

"What's that supposed to mean? Like I left her hanging?"

"Oh, geesh," Harry said, taking another drink. "You'd best get over this. You two are on the verge of being happy again. Don't blow it."

Syd frowned deeply and sat down. "I don't want to blow it. I can't believe she's even talking to me after..."

"Can I give ya a little fatherly advice?"

"I'd love some. Better late than never."

"Don't think about all the yesterdays. Think about the tomorrows. Tomorrow don't have any guilt or regrets," he said softly. "I think I read that in one of the books ya gave me. But it's true."

Syd felt the lump in her throat. "Where were you six years ago?"

Harry laughed and drank his beer. "Probably getting out on bail."

Syd looked at her watch again. "If anything happens to either one of them, I'll—"

"You'll what?"

Sydney jumped up when she saw Grace's wonderful smiling face; Adam was right behind her.

"Where have you been?" she asked anxiously.

Adam smiled. "Good grief, woman, we're only ten minutes late."

Grace smirked. "Now, Adam, Sydney isn't used to such behavior. Why, the world would stop spinning if no one listened to Sydney Crosse."

Sydney laughed out loud and held the chair for her. "My adorable Ms. Morgan, how you put me in my place."

Grace sat and looked across at her. "It's just that I don't find you as irresistible as the rest of our gender."

Sydney put the napkin in her lap and said simply, "Of course you do. You're just more stubborn than the rest of our gender." She looked up then at the glare she received.

Adam cleared his throat. "Sydney, read this before you need Grace's salad fork surgically removed from your forehead."

Harry chuckled and reached across and gently took the fork from Grace. "One murder's enough, Irish."

Grace smiled at him and nodded. "For now."

Sydney read the pages with disbelief. "Well, Keith was busy at college. Blackmail, extortion, forgery. Good heavens, he *was* a punk. According to this, Keith Pickford had a small business at Harvard. He extorted money from fellow students by blackmail, pictures and the like. He also forged the signatures of these students on their credit cards. Identity theft. Good grief, what a little monster."

Sydney read further and was shocked. "My Lord, over two hundred thousand dollars in one year. Tax-free. You and I are in the wrong business, Adam." Her face grew dark. "Jon Pickford paid back every penny and then some to keep it out of the papers and keep Keith out of prison."

"Keith hung around with a dangerous crowd, according to this." Sydney finished and put the paper on the table. "Jack's working on more. I already emailed him earlier." She looked out at the lake trying to see if this fit at all.

"An extortion ring in college. Boy, I missed out. All I did was study," Grace said sarcastically and drank her tea.

"This codicil is bothering me." Sydney looked at the papers again. "Adam, this amendment to the will. Why would Jon do that?"

Adam shook his head. "I've been trying to think of a reason, and to be honest, I can't figure it out." He looked to Grace.

"I have no idea what's what anymore. All I know is that last Tuesday Jon Pickford was elated at the prospect of this contract. He gave me no clue that I was in his will. He never said a word to me."

"Grace, I don't think he had any intention of dying soon. His will was the last thing on his mind," Sydney said, then leaned back in her chair.

Grace watched her. "What? You've got that ah-ha look."

Sydney held up her hand. "He wasn't thinking about dying. He had no intention of telling you about his will. Isn't it a coincidence that he put that codicil in just before he died?" she asked almost absently. "I've got to find his journal."

"Well, I've called Marcy Longwood. She agreed to meet Grace and me at two o'clock in her office. Keith and Tina will be there. I gave her some reason, just to get them out of the house, so you have some time. Be careful, I don't have to remind you there's a murderer walking around Seacliff. If he spots you again..."

Grace suddenly was very worried. "Can't you go to the police?"

"I'd love to, darling, but I'm not at all sure Brianne isn't part of this somehow."

"Then the state police. That Detective Webster."

"We have no proof, just speculation and an old report on Keith," Adam said.

"Adam is right. Harry and I will see if we can find anything at the house. You go with Adam and meet with Marcy."

After lunch, they agreed to meet at Grace's later that night. On the way out, Sydney took Adam aside.

"I'm very worried about Brianne."

"I know. She bothers me, as well."

"Please watch Grace. I don't want her alone with that nitwit sheriff for an instant."

"Sydney, whoever is doing this wants Grace out of the picture legally. They have made no attempt on her life. They're very smart."

"I know. I have to get to the bottom of this before they set whatever they have planned in motion. I have a very bad feeling Brianne is in some way involved. I just know she is. Stay close to Grace. Let nothing happen to her." Sydney turned to see Grace standing there.

"Why do you think Brianne is involved in this?"

Sydney sighed. "Didn't your mother ever tell you it's not polite to eavesdrop?"

"Why, Sydney?"

"Because I know her," Sydney blurted out angrily. "My gut tells me that Brianne is involved in this. Either that or there was something wrong with that Caesar salad I just ate. Now please do as I ask and stay away from her."

"I can handle Brianne," she said confidently.

For the first time, Sydney was truly angry and scared. "No, you cannot handle Brianne. You will do as I ask and stay away from her. I am dead serious about this." She started to say something, then leaned down and kissed her lightly on the lips. "I will see you later this evening."

Syd turned and walked away. Harry kissed her on the cheek. "She's just a little tense."

"And very much arrogant."

"Well, there's that, too."

"How does Sydney know Brianne, Adam?" Grace watched as Sydney drove out of the parking lot.

"I was wondering when you'd ask that. We'll talk about Brianne after this meeting."

He wasn't looking forward to telling her this, and he knew she wasn't going to like hearing it.

Chapter 24

Harry stood at the back door and took out his lock pick case.

"Harry..." Sydney reached under the potted plant and took out the key. "Been here forever."

"Geesh, that's so unsafe."

Sydney opened the back door and walked in.

"Do you know how many homes are broken into because people are dumb enough to hide the keys? And this is no bungalow."

"I know, but Jon was a trusting sort. Okay, quickly now. You take the library. Be careful, leave everything as you found it. Look for a journal, you know. Like a diary, something you'd write in, or anything of Jon's. I'll go check the bedrooms," Sydney said, and they split up.

Sydney went to Jon's room. She looked around and went over to his desk. She rummaged through the drawers and slots, pulling out everything and finding nothing.

"Well, if I was a journal, where would I be?" She looked around, then went over to the nightstand. Jon's reading glasses were there, as well as his watch. Sydney frowned and wondered if anyone had even come into this room since his death. She felt creepy, but she sat on the bed and opened the drawer. There, at the bottom was a small leather-bound book. Sydney's heart beat quickly as she opened it.

It looked like the same paper as the note. Leafing through it, she saw a page was torn out at the end of the journal.

The first few pages had writing on them. She recognized Jon's script. The dates on the journal, however, were almost six months old, and only a dozen or so pages were filled out. She wasn't sure what if anything it meant, but she tucked the journal in her shirt and put the room back in order. She smoothed the quilt on the bed and was about to leave when she saw an ashtray on Jon's dresser.

"What the hell?" She was shocked to see a small end of the same cigar and two cigarette butts in the ashtray. She picked up the cigarette butt. *Newport* read the brand name on the filter. "Does anyone even smoke these things anymore?" She placed it back in the ashtray, then went to Harry, who sat at the desk in the library.

"Harry, let's go. I've got it."

Then they heard someone at the front door.

"Damn it."

She and Harry bumped into each other as they rushed through the kitchen and out the back door. They ran across to the hangar and ducked behind the door. Sydney leaned against the hangar wall and wheezed. "That was close."

"No one saw us. I'm sure." Harry peeked around the corner of the hangar.

"Okay, let's get the hell out of here."

Once back at the car, Harry got behind the wheel and drove off.

"So ya found it. Is there anything in it?" Harry asked anxiously.

Sydney smiled. "Well, not much. I didn't get to read it. Let's drive by Grace's. If she's not back yet, we'll go to our mansion."

Sydney was extremely happy Grace was home; she hated to go back to the rat hole.

"You don't know how happy I am that you're here," Sydney said, walking onto the front porch. "This porch is getting a workout."

"We were worried we didn't give you enough time," Adam said. "I was at a loss for the reason we were there." Adam laughed quietly. "So I winged it. I'm not as good as Sydney in the charm department. I had to come up with something quick. At least it had something to do with the will."

Grace had to agree. "You should have seen the looks from Tina and Keith. They were very confused."

"You, Adam? You winged it? I'm impressed."

"So impress me now. Did you find anything?" he asked.

"Did she!" Harry announced, sitting in the rocking chair.

Sydney grinned and produced the book.

Adam's eyes widened. "You took it?"

Sydney nodded. "Yep. And what's more, I hope they realize it. That should get them moving, although I don't think there's anything in there worth much."

Adam opened the journal. He read a few pages. "Nothing about the will, nothing about the contract, and nothing about Grace. It's all about himself, how his life had turned out. How he wanted it to change."

He handed it to Grace, and she read it, as well.

"So now what?" She looked at Sydney.

"There was a page torn out of the back. So I believe this is the journal, but there's nothing of any use in it." She leaned against the porch railing. "Grace, do you remember what brand of cigarettes Brianne smokes?"

She thought for a moment, then shook her head. "I have no idea. I only know she's been trying to quit for years."

"I do," Adam said proudly. "I saw the pack when she lit up after the funeral. Newport."

"Are you sure?" Syd asked. "You must be sure."

"I am. I remember thinking my father used to smoke the nasty things. Why?"

"I found the end of two in the ashtray in Jon's bedroom. Jon did not smoke."

"Cigars and cigarettes are our only clues? Who is this guy?" Grace said impatiently, if not angrily. "I'm sorry. This is just getting to me. If they want to charge me with murder, why don't they?"

Sydney was quickly at her side. "Grace, how about something to drink? Would you mind?"

"Sure. It'll take my mind off this." She got up and went into the house.

"Fellas, she's at the end of her rope. I think I'm going to pay a visit to Brianne. You two stay with Grace."

Harry said anxiously, "Let me go with ya."

Sydney shook her head. "No, I need to do this alone. Stay with Grace."

"I thought you weren't supposed to be around. You're putting yourself right in the line of fire. This is unwise," Adam said emphatically.

"I won't be seen. Give me the journal. I'll be back in an hour or so." She took the journal and left.

Grace came out with iced tea and looked for Sydney.

"Where did she go?" Both men were silent. "Okay, what's going on?" She looked around, and the journal was missing. "What is she doing?"

"I don't know. She'll be back in an hour. So let's just sit tight," Adam said.

They sat on the porch, and Grace looked at her watch. "Adam, tell me about Brianne and Sydney," she said seriously. Harry got up. "Sit down, Harry."

Harry sat back down.

Adam sighed. "I knew you'd ask sooner or later." He drank his iced tea and looked out at the lake.

"Long ago, when Sydney was in college, Brianne was on the police force in Gary, Indiana. I'm not sure if you knew that."

"I'm four years younger than Syd and Brianne. I was in high school, more than likely. But I didn't know Brianne well until after I graduated and came back here. What happened?"

"The short of it…A friend of Sydney's had driven through Gary one night and was pulled over. A verbal altercation ensued, one thing led to another, and the young man was pulled from his car by one officer and beaten severely while the other one watched. They took him to the station, charged him with speeding, resisting arrest, and a minor drug charge. The young man said he was framed and that the police planted the packet of cocaine. Sydney paid a great deal of money to help him. The city of Gary didn't want any publicity. After a cursory investigation, they dropped the charges, dismissed the offending officer, and reprimanded the rookie officer. It was then forgotten. Sydney wanted her friend to press charges. He declined. The rookie officer involved was Brianne Gentry. Sydney's friend was Jack Riley."

Grace sat there blankly staring at the lake. "I can't believe it."

"You may, Grace. It's true. Brianne left the Gary department some months later with only a slight reprimand on her record and came home. Jack Riley finished college at Northwestern with Sydney and is now a lieutenant with the Chicago Police Department. Other than Harry and me, Sydney never told a soul about it. Not even her mother."

"So can ya see, Grace, why Sydney was so hard about you seeing Brianne?" Harry asked her.

"Yes. I do now. She could have told me this. I would have listened."

"You two ain't actually been on speaking terms in recent years," Harry gently reminded her.

Grace sighed, knowing he was right. "Where did she go?"

"She took the journal. I think she's gonna force their hand. Bring 'em out if she can. That's what I think, anyway," he said and chomped on his cigar.

Grace got a nervous feeling in the pit of her stomach. "If anything happens to her, I'll kill her," she said, anxiously looking out at the lake.

Chapter 25

Sydney drove to the edge of town and parked across the street and out of sight. She sat there for a moment and watched the police station. Brianne's cruiser was parked in back. It was a busy day in Seacliff; tourists were everywhere. She put on her baseball cap and sunglasses, then nonchalantly walked to Brianne's patrol car. Sydney couldn't believe her luck when she saw the window was left open. Either Brianne was careless or would not be gone long. So without stopping, Sydney tossed the journal onto the driver's seat. She kept right on walking back to her car.

She didn't have to wait long at all. Actually, she was lucky she made it back to her car. Brianne come out of the station, flicked her cigarette, and opened the door. She stood frozen, then looked around in every direction.

"I knew it, you slimy..." Sydney whispered.

Brianne looked horrified. She picked up the journal, jumped into her car, and peeled out. When she drove toward Sydney, Sydney ducked low in the seat. Syd then followed at a safe distance.

She wanted to be surprised to see Brianne pull into Jon's circular driveway. With all her suspicions confirmed, she drove back to Grace's.

"What a scumbag."

Grace met her at the porch. "Are you all right?" She threw her arms around Syd's neck. "I was so worried."

"I'm fine. Boy, I should do this more often."

Grace pulled back and slugged her shoulder. "What's the big idea?"

Syd winced and backed up. "Are you bipolar?"

"Where did you go?" Adam asked.

"I went to the police station and threw the journal on the front seat of Brianne's cruiser."

"And?" Grace asked slowly.

"She looked terrified when she saw it and drove directly to Jon's."

"You sure you weren't seen?" Adam asked.

"Yes, Mother. I'm sure."

"Then you're all right?" Grace said, frowning.

"Yes. I assure you, I'm fine."

"Good. Now you listen to me. I appreciate your help, but I do not want you going off by yourself anymore. Do you understand me? You didn't tell anyone where you were going. What if something happened to you?" she said angrily. "Are you listening to me?"

"How can I not?" Syd asked. "The decibel level is quite annoying."

Grace looked like she might explode. "All right then, go get yourself killed," she said heatedly as her voice cracked.

Syd's head shot up as she heard the emotion in her voice. Grace stormed off the porch and walked down by the beach.

Syd watched her, then glanced at Harry, who gave her a disapproving look.

"Sydney, you scared the hell out of her. She was worried about ya."

Sydney felt like a heel. She looked over at Adam, who was frowning.

"You were rather insensitive. Go to her right now and apologize," he said fatherly.

Sydney sighed and stood. "I didn't mean to be insensitive. I..."

Harry gently pushed her off the porch.

Grace kept walking as Syd followed her. "Grace, wait."

"What?" she asked with her arms folded across her chest, looking at the lake.

Syd finally reached her. They stood side by side staring at the lake. "Say something."

"Why? Won't my voice be too irritating?"

She hid her grin. "I'm sorry, truly I am."

"Adam told me what happened between Brianne and Jack Riley."

"He did? Why?"

"The question is, why didn't you tell me?"

"Well I…Brianne was your friend, and you and I, well..." Sydney ran her fingers through her hair. "I should have. I wanted to, many times. You said you weren't involved with her, so I thought it would just come off as gossip, and I didn't want that. There were so many conflicting emotions when I first saw you. But you're right. I should have told you."

"We're not the same as we were back then. We have a lot of catching up to do. If you want to."

"Of course I do. I'm just not used to a woman caring about my well-being. I know that sounds pathetic." She laughed nervously.

Grace kicked at the sand. "Well, that's the type you associate with."

"This is true, but it's no excuse. I'm sorry."

Grace looked at her. "I was worried, that's all. You go off half-cocked."

Syd put her hands on her shoulders, forcing Grace to face her. "Ah, Grace. I don't deserve your kindness."

"Yes, you do."

Syd felt like her heart would explode. She bent down and kissed Grace tenderly. Grace sighed, returning her kiss. Her arms went around Syd's neck, her fingers gently ran through her hair. That old feeling came flooding back for Syd. The memories of them lying in each other's arms.

"I love you, Grace," she whispered against her lips. "Always have. Never stopped."

The kisses grew more passionate. Grace parted her lips, and Syd took the invitation and pulled Grace incredibly close.

It was Sydney who pulled away, mainly because she could no longer breathe. "I'm lost in you," she whispered and kissed her forehead.

"I'm a little lost myself right now."

"C'mon, let's walk," Syd said, putting her arm around Grace's shoulders. They walked along the beach in silence.

"You're too quiet. What's wrong?" Grace asked softly.

"I was just thinking of something Harry said earlier."

"Harry? Oh, boy."

Syd laughed. She grabbed Grace's hand as they continued walking. "He told me to forget about yesterday and concentrate on tomorrow. Because, in his words, tomorrow don't have any guilt or regrets."

"That's very profound." Grace lightly swung Syd's hand. "And he's right."

"I know. It's what I've been doing for a long time. Regretting and feeling guilty over how I left you."

Grace stopped. "No more. All right?"

Syd smiled and lifted Grace's hand, lightly kissing her palm. "All right."

"And…?"

Syd laughed then. "Cross my heart."

"Good. Let's get back before they send out a search party."

They found Harry and Adam in the kitchen; Harry's head was in the refrigerator.

"Hungry?" Grace asked.

"There you are. We were gonna send up a flare. Yes, I'm starving. All the pie is gone."

"You ate most of it," Sydney said.

"What do we do next?" Adam sat at the kitchen table across from Syd.

"By now, Brianne has told Keith about the journal. I wasn't sure if Keith was involved, but now, I'd have to say he is. I have no idea about Tina," she said and drank the iced tea Grace set in front of her. Then she looked at her glass. "Good heavens, it's after five." She gave Harry a scowl.

Harry sighed. "Martini?"

"Naturally."

"I never would have believed Keith would be involved in this," Grace said. "Liquor cabinet above the stove, Harry."

"Gotcha."

"Where money is concerned, you can believe almost anything," Adam said. "I might as well have a martini also, Harry."

"Coming up."

Sydney nodded. "We're missing a player, though. Someone is still out there. Brianne's not that smart, and I don't think Keith has the stomach to kill someone. Extortion? Yes. Murder? Not so much."

Harry set the cocktails in front of everyone and sat down with a beer for himself.

Sydney grinned. "Harry, you must never leave me."

"No bleu cheese olives," Harry said.

Sydney gave Grace a scathing look.

"Sorry."

"Okay, let's put together all we have," Adam said.

"We got a guy who smokes little cigars. He wears boots all the time. He's average everything, dark hair. And he's with a blonde," Harry said.

"Someone hired a boat and signed Jon's name to it. The guy who smoked those cigars had to have been on board at some point," Sydney said positively.

"Jon leaves almost his entire estate for Grace to manage. However, he makes a strange amendment to it. That's my big question," Adam said, sipping his drink.

"The page from the journal was obviously planted on Jon after he was on the beach. My guess is Brianne, just from past experience. But why?" Sydney looked out at the lake. "Why would Brianne be involved in this? That's a puzzlement."

Adam said logically, "I say money, pure and simple."

Grace smiled sadly. "I guess she must hate me. I never really thought she did, but to do this, she must."

Sydney gazed out at the lake. Why would Brianne do this? She knew what she was capable of, but this was different. Well, Sydney played the card by exposing the journal. Now she had to see what they were made of.

She shivered, thinking of that old saying about being careful what you ask for...

Chapter 26

Adam left after dinner. "I hope I don't hear from you until tomorrow. Everyone, have a peaceful night."

Harry grinned as he rolled his unlit cigar. "Well, we should be getting back, Syd. I need a shower and bed."

Grace coughed gently and avoided Sydney. "Well, if you want, you can stay here. I know it's hot, and that motel room has to be an oven."

"We don't want to inconvenience ya, Grace." He looked at Sydney. "Do we?"

Sydney was watching Grace, who fidgeted with her wristwatch. "No, we do not want to be an inconvenience."

Grace looked up at Sydney then.

Harry coughed softly. "Why don't I go back to the motel? You two have things to discuss. I'll get all our stuff in order in the room. Then I'll come back in the morning." He looked at Grace. "You wouldn't mind, Grace?"

Grace looked at him. "What? Oh. N-no, I don't mind."

"Great. Then I guess I'll be goin'." He gave a fatherly look to Sydney and kissed Grace on the cheek. "Sleep tight, Irish."

They stood there on the porch, looking out at nothing in particular. Sydney cleared her throat.

"Sydney, I don't want to talk about all this anymore tonight."

"You don't?"

She shook her head, walked by Syd, and opened the screen door. "No, I don't." She took her hand and led her into the house.

Grace closed the front door; they stood for a moment in the darkness. Without saying a word, Grace reached up and caressed her bruised cheek. "I can't believe what you've done for me. And we haven't seen each other in so long. It's like you barely know me."

Syd took her hand and, turning it over, kissed her palm. "Oh, I know you. I've never forgotten you," she whispered in the darkness. She then bent down and kissed her deeply.

Grace reached in and started unbuttoning her shirt.

"Grace," Syd whispered passionately, kissing her neck. Her hand lightly passed over Grace's breast. "I miss the feel of you."

"I miss your touch," Grace said in a ragged voice. She grabbed Syd by the hand and practically ran down the hall to her bedroom.

Suddenly, they were both on her bed, each struggling for control.

"I need to feel you." Syd nearly stripped Grace's blouse off, then her bra. She peppered feverish kisses over her breasts.

"Yes, Syd." Grace reached over and pulled at Syd's shirt, lifting it over her head.

All of the sudden, Syd heard a noise coming from the back of the house. She tried to ignore it, but Grace jumped when it happened again.

"Damn it." Syd pulled her T-shirt back on while Grace searched for her blouse.

They both stood still; Sydney put her finger up to her lips. They heard it again. Grace gave Sydney a worried look and grabbed her robe. Sydney went toward the door and listened.

Someone was in the kitchen. She motioned for Grace to stay, then walked out into the hallway. As she heard a chair being moved, she looked around for something to hit the intruder with and found nothing. Grace was right behind her.

As Syd walked up to the kitchen door, it swung open. Grace let out a screech as Sydney fell backward into her, knocking both of them to the floor. Someone rushed out of the kitchen and through the open back door.

Both scrambled to their feet. Syd was the first to the back door. She saw no one. She quickly closed and locked the door.

"Are you all right?" Grace asked anxiously.

"Yes. Are you?" Syd ran her hands over Grace's body.

"Yes, yes. God, Syd. That scared me to death. Did you see him at all?"

"No. It happened too fast." Syd looked around. "What the hell was he doing in your kitchen?"

Grace sighed and looked around. "Leftover pie?"

Syd blinked for a moment, then laughed. "Talk about a mood killer."

"We will continue this," Grace said confidently. "However, I think it best we call Harry and Adam."

"I think we should call Brianne. She's the sheriff. I'm sure Adam will tell us we need a police report on this."

Harry and Adam arrived almost at the same time as the police. It was not Brianne, however, but a young deputy.

"Where's the sheriff?" Adam asked.

"Off duty." The young man took notes and looked around the house. Then he took Grace's statement and Sydney's. He asked a few questions and took names.

"Come by tomorrow, and we'll finish up with the police report. You'd better get that lock fixed, as well."

"Thank you. We'll be in tomorrow."

The deputy looked at all of them, then left.

"Well," Adam said, looking around the kitchen. "Suffice it to say, they know you're back."

Sydney shrugged. "I don't care at this point. If I wasn't here, who knows what would have happened." Grace shivered.

Harry patted her hand. "Well, I guess we're staying."

"Wrong," Sydney said. "Grace stays at the inn with Adam." She looked at Adam, who already had his phone out.

"I will not be intimidated, Sydney. This is my house."

"I know it's your house. However, someone broke into it for God knows what reason. You are not staying here tonight," Sydney said, unwavering.

Grace put her hands on her hips. "Look. Between your bossy arrogance and this murder, I've just about had it. Quit telling me what to do," she raised her voice.

Adam closed his phone. "All set." He shrank back when Grace shot him a dangerous glare.

Sydney stood there and sighed. "Grace."

"I mean it, Sydney. I will not be chased out of my own home. I'm staying," she said, standing her ground.

For the first time, Sydney lost her cool. She slammed her hand on the table, knocking over the coffee cups, and all of them jumped.

Harry said anxiously, "Syd."

Sydney put her hand up to him as she stared at Grace. They stared and glared at each other while Adam and Harry just watched in silence. Sydney took a deep breath, realizing her hands were shaking with fear and anger. She rubbed her hands together and closed her eyes tightly as if concentrating. Finally, she let out a breath and regarded Grace.

"Will you please go with Adam? I care far too much to have anything happen to you. Do this for me, please," she said calmly.

Grace took a deep breath and looked into those eyes she remembered, that now pleaded with her.

"All right. I'll pack a bag."

"Thank you."

"You're welcome. This does not mean, however, that you are right," Grace said and turned away.

"Damn it! Must you always have the last word?"

"No, not always." Grace marched out of the kitchen.

Syd let out an irritated growl and picked up the coffee cup, shaking it furiously.

Harry gently took the cup out of her hand. "Now, Syd. At least she's leaving."

Sydney lay awake the rest of the night. They had gotten Grace settled in the last room available, and she was satisfied she was safe and Adam was there. Grace, on the other hand, was cool and distant when Syd kissed her cheek and said good night.

Syd desperately tried to piece things together. It all revolved around the damned will and the codicil, she was sure of it. Keith, Brianne, and possibly Tina were all involved. Syd figured Brianne planted the note on Jon's body. There was no way that the note could have been in his pocket while he was in the water. She knew that. She also knew Jon did not write the note. Just as it was not Jon's signature on that boat receipt.

She was also sure it was Brianne who was the missing accomplice who beat up her and Harry. All to frame Grace. Why?

Maybe she was looking at this from the wrong angle.

Sydney wondered how much Keith knew. Thinking about his college exploits, she figured he must be involved somehow, but murder? She thought Keith too weak to be able to kill someone. Extortion was more his racket.

For some reason, her mind kept going back to the boot that she and Harry saw. And she remembered the boot print on the back of Jon's shirt. It had to be the same guy at the marina. And perhaps he was the same guy who broke into Grace's house that night.

"Damn it. I need to figure this out," she said, drifting off to sleep.

An hour later, her watch alarm went off. "Are you kidding?" She turned off the alarm and rubbed her face, trying to wake up. Feeling drugged, she pulled herself out of bed and woke up Harry.

"C'mon, you old thief," she said hoarsely.

Harry sat up. "Oh, what a beautiful morning. I think I'll sleep in."

"Don't you dare," Syd said as she stumbled to the bathroom.

She let the water run for a second or two to get the brown tint out of it, then stepped in. For a moment, she let the warm spray wake her. She quickly showered, remembering Jack probably sent her another email.

After sidestepping Harry at the bathroom door, she quickly dressed in the abysmal shorts and T-shirt. She grabbed her laptop and opened Jack's email.

"I made coffee," Harry called out from the bathroom.

"We have coffee?" Syd sniffed the air and found the pot.

Sitting with her laptop and a cup of coffee, she opened Jack's email.

Apparently, Keith had a college mate who did his bidding for him. Jack could find no name, no description. Keith would not divulge that information, which Jon paid for, as well.

However, Jack did find one young man who was a victim of Keith's game.

Sydney smiled. "Jack, you're getting an enormous bonus when I get back."

As she read, she saw that Keith had photos of this young man with another gentleman in a compromising situation, to put it nicely. Blackmail soon followed, and a great deal of money was exchanged. However, not before this young man was threatened, beaten, and scared to death as was his partner.

Sydney frowned as she read. "What a little monster."

Jack figured that was his M.O. Sydney chuckled. "M.O.? Cop talk." She joked, but Jack was probably right. Keith found the right people to extort and got down to his dirty business.

Although this all happened quite a while ago when he was in college, Sydney was sure he was using his Harvard education someway. She needed to find out how.

For some reason, Tina came to mind. She hadn't seen Tina in a few days. Syd wondered where she was. Too much going on, she thought.

She typed a response to Jack, thanking him for all his help and telling him if he got anything else to let her know.

Syd was about to close her laptop when she got a notification of another email.

It was Adam.

Get over to Grace's right away. Brianne is coming with a search warrant.

Sydney grabbed a half-shaven Harry and ran out the door.

Chapter 27

"Harry, you stay out of sight. When they get here and go inside, see if you can watch them. But do not let them see you."

"Gotcha, Syd."

Harry had barely stopped the car when Syd jumped out and ran to Grace's door.

She didn't even get a chance to knock. Grace opened the door and flew into her arms.

"They have a warrant, Syd."

"I know, honey. It'll be okay." Syd looked over Grace's head to Adam.

"Brianne came by with Webster. They wanted to search the house. Of course, I asked for a warrant."

"And of course, they didn't have one," Syd said, kissing Grace's forehead.

"They're coming back with one."

"Here they come," Harry called from the side of the house.

"Okay. You know what to do, Harry. Don't let them see you."

Brianne's cruiser pulled next to the house.

Syd gave Grace a quick kiss. "Don't worry. Do whatever Adam advises." She then sat on the rocking chair and lazily rocked.

"Sydney, you're going to piss her off," Grace whispered.

"I know," Sydney whispered back as she rocked. "That's the plan."

Brianne appeared on the deck with Webster; Brianne was shocked. "What the shit are you doing crawling back here? Haven't you done enough?"

Sydney smiled and batted her eyelashes. "I'm just a masochist for love."

When Adam walked out, Grace sidestepped to make room on the porch.

Webster raised an eyebrow. "Geezus, did you sell tickets?"

Adam spoke first. "May I see the warrant, Sheriff?"

Brianne fumed as she took the warrant out of her pocket. Adam looked at it and handed it to Grace, who examined it and disgustedly threw it at Brianne.

Sydney hid her grin while Brianne bristled as she tried to catch the flying paperwork.

Webster seemed thoroughly amused watching Brianne pick up the warrant.

Grace opened her door. "Go right ahead. Please remember, I know the law, too, officers," she warned as they walked in.

They sat on the porch waiting, and Grace's hands shook. Sydney's heart ached for her, and she stood next to her and took her hands and held them gently. "Be over soon, Gracie," she whispered affectionately.

"Don't let them see you lose it." Adam stood on the other side of her and smiled.

"Thanks, both of you," Grace said.

After they searched the entire house, Brianne came out with something in a plastic bag. The inspector followed her out and gave all of them a smug grin. Sydney looked at the bag, and it looked like a kitchen utensil. She shot a disgusted look at Brianne. That was what the intruder was doing in Grace's kitchen.

Brianne looked at Grace. "This yours, Grace?"

"What is it?" she asked logically.

"It looks like an icepick, doesn't it? It also has blood on it. How do you explain that?"

"I don't own an icepick," Grace said, glaring at them.

Adam stepped forward. "Where did you find that?"

Brianne was looking at Grace. "In the kitchen, between the refrigerator and the counter."

Syd looked at the item in the plastic bag. It did look like an icepick. Then she looked at the wooden handle. That was when it hit her. The boot—that was what she couldn't remember. It was the handle of the icepick she saw in the top of the boot. Harry was right; it would come to her, and it did.

And as sure she was of the boot and the icepick, she knew Jon's blood would be all over it. Now Sydney got very, very nervous.

"How utterly convenient," Sydney said lightly.

"Watch it, Crosse. I'd like nothin' better than to take off this badge and kick your ass," Brianne said.

Sydney smiled. "Now, now, Wyatt. It's not nice to threaten the public. Makes for bad press. Besides, you usually stand by and watch."

Brianne took a step toward her, but Webster stepped in. "All right, that's enough. I think we found what we needed." He looked at Grace. "I'm afraid you'll have to come with us, Ms. Morgan."

Sydney's heart broke when Grace looked terrified. "She doesn't have to go with you now…"

"Keep out of this," Brianne said to Sydney.

Adam stepped in, putting a hand up to stop Sydney. "I'll go with her."

"I'm going too," Sydney said, glaring at the smug look on Brianne's face.

"No, you stay here. You have things to do. I'll be in touch."

Sydney walked over to Grace and took her by the shoulders. "Adam will go with you, honey. I'll be right outside that jailhouse. You will not stay in there long."

Grace tried to smile as she nodded.

"Detective, can you give us a moment?" Adam asked. "Don't worry, we're not going to hide her in a suitcase."

Webster looked at all of them and nodded. "You got two minutes." He and Brianne walked off the porch.

Adam turned back to them. "Quickly now. The arraignment will be swift, I'm sure. Sydney will have the bond money, and you unfortunately may have to spend one night in jail, Grace."

Sydney made a move to walk off the porch; Adam stepped in front of her. "Sydney, Grace needs you here more right now. This can't be helped. We cannot give them any fuel for this fire," he said gently but firmly. "I'll go and get my briefcase. You two say goodbye quickly."

Grace grabbed onto Sydney and sobbed. "I can't believe this is happening."

"Shh. Now listen to me. Nothing will happen to you. You're their scapegoat for whatever reason. They won't let anything happen." She lifted her chin and whispered, "I love you, Grace. Please trust me." She kissed her tenderly and brushed away her tears.

"Figures, you say you love me on my way to jail."

"Gotta go, Grace," Brianne said quietly.

Grace tried to back up, but Sydney pulled her into her arms. "I will figure this out. This will have to hold you for a while," she whispered against her lips. She pulled back after the kiss; she was elated to see Brianne fuming.

Adam walked out with briefcase in hand. "Grace…"

Grace caressed Sydney's bruised cheek. "See that doesn't happen again. Promise."

"Cross my heart," she whispered. She then stepped back, giving Brianne a contemptuous sneer. "This won't be like Gary, Indiana," Sydney said to her. "You swine."

Adam stepped in between them. "This will serve no purpose now, ladies. Good grief, there's an overflow of testosterone between you. Enough."

Grace walked off the porch with Brianne. Adam turned to Sydney. "Honestly, Sydney. You swine? Did you see the hatred on her face?"

"I saw it, and I hope she stays that way. She'll be so anxious to get at me again, she's bound to slip up," Sydney said confidently. "Although I have to admit, I did see a little spittle fly. Go, Adam. Please take care of her. Don't leave her alone in that place."

"I won't. You just make sure you have bail."

"It's all set, whatever you need."

Sydney stood on the porch and watched them drive away.

Harry came from behind the house. "Coast clear?"

Sydney nodded. "What did you see?"

"I did just like you said. I looked through the kitchen window, and you were right. Brianne, the lowlife, scum-suckin' sonofa...."

Sydney interjected. "Yes, we're all aware of Brianne's forefathers. Cut to the chase."

"Well, there she was. She tells Webster to check the other rooms. She'll take the kitchen and living room, she says. She comes into the kitchen and goes directly to the spot. Sees it, then she waits for Webster to come in. They look around, and she finds it. Like she ain't never seen it," Harry said.

"Harry, you'll never get to first base with my mother if you don't stop with the double negatives." She patted Harry on the back. "Good job."

"Okay, so let's go nab her," Harry said.

"Unfortunately, there's no proof. All we have is speculation. And it would be your word against hers. They have evidence, as false as it is. Right now, they have a motive. Grace is a scorned lover who finds out Jon's refused her and reneged on the contract. She kills him and now they have a note in Jon's handwriting and the possible murder weapon." Sydney sighed heavily. "It is the murder weapon, I'm sure of it. The other night in the alley. I remember seeing a boot, and when I just saw the icepick, I remembered seeing the top of it in that guy's boot." She explained about the boot from the other night. "So I'm sure it has Jon's blood all over it."

"So now what?" Harry asked. "I can't believe this is happening to Grace."

"It is, and we'll just have to figure it out." Sydney looked out at the calm lake. "We just have to."

Chapter 28

The arraignment was swift; it was later that day. Grace pleaded not guilty. She stood tall and confident as Sydney waited in the back of the small courtroom.

"Your Honor, since my client is a well-respected member of this community and has no prior record, I'd like to see her bond set or have her released on her own recognizance. If you would agree," Adam said.

Adam always amazed Sydney. She watched the judge look sadly at Grace; Sydney figured they knew each other, and he nodded.

"I agree…" he started.

The State's Attorney interrupted him. "Your Honor, a man has been murdered."

The judge now interrupted him. "Counselor, just because we are a small community, do not presume that we don't know what this case is about. Normally, I am not opposed to moving things along. We do have a backlog. But for some reason, I feel this is moving fast. And do not interrupt me again," the old judge said and continued. "As I was saying, I agree. Bond is set at one hundred thousand dollars. And the defendant is released on her own recognizance. The trial begins on Wednesday, July 15, at nine a.m." He banged his gavel and got up and left the courtroom.

Grace sat and put her hands over her face. Adam put a reassuring hand on her shoulder. "You go with them, Grace.

You'll be released once Sydney settles your bail. I'll be there when they release you."

Sydney quickly paid her bond. Harry waited outside on the steps of the courthouse. When Brianne walked out, he casually spit on the ground in front of her.

She stopped for a moment. "Be careful."

Harry grinned. "Yes, Sheriff."

Sydney walked out of the courthouse, folding the paperwork. "Best money I ever spent. They're not out yet?"

"Give it time, Syd. They gotta process her, and Adam's gotta do his thing. She'll be all right. We're lucky this didn't happen on a weekend. Grace might've been sitting in a jail cell. As it was, she was just in a holding cell for a while. Don't worry, she'll be no worse for wear. She's a game gal."

"I know. But it breaks my heart that she had to go through that."

Harry put a hand on her shoulder. "Don't get all mushy now. She needs ya."

They waited for at least a half hour while Sydney glanced at her watch every few minutes.

At last, Adam and Grace walked out of the courthouse.

Sydney ran up the steps, meeting them halfway. She pulled Grace into a fierce hug. "Are you all right?"

"I'm fine, really," Grace said. "It could have been much worse, I suppose."

"It coulda been, trust me," Harry said. "Sorry I wasn't in there, Grace. Courthouses give me the willies."

"I don't blame you at all," Grace said as they walked down the steps. "Well, I'm a jailbird. Are you sure you should be seen with me?"

Syd laughed. "I don't know. Adam, what do you think?"

"Well, she has a mugshot."

"I guess it pays to know a rich playgirl." Grace stopped and faced Sydney. "Thank you. I don't know how I'll be able to repay you."

"Repay me? Don't be insulting. We'll call it your dowry, or I'll take it out of Adam's salary," she said lightly. "C'mon. Let's get the hell out of here. We need to celebrate."

"Oh, hell. Syd, I checked your email. Jack said he was gonna fax something about Keith."

Sydney stopped. "Okay, Grace and I will go to her office. We'll meet you at Ernie's."

They headed for Grace's office.

"Dowry?" Grace asked.

"Yes. It's a common word. It means a gift, a bridal..."

"I know what it means. I don't know why you said it." She stopped and turned to her. She looked down at her and smirked.

"I don't know."

They stopped in front of Grace's building; she unlocked the door. "Liar."

Syd laughed as she followed Grace to her office. Grace took the pages off the fax, handing them to Sydney before she walked over to the window.

"Thanks." Sydney sat at her desk and put her feet up.

Grace turned around. "Make yourself at home."

"Okay," she said absently. She put on her glasses and read the pages. "Well, Keith had help, as Jack said before. However, this guy seems whacko. Damn." She looked at the pages again. "A great deal of scattered information that I'm not sure means anything." She took off her glasses and looked at Grace. "What are you doing all the way over there? Come here."

Grace walked over to her and allowed Syd to pull her onto her lap.

"Hello." Syd grinned, then kissed her.

"Hello," Grace said sarcastically.

"I know that tone. What have I done?"

"Nothing. I'm just wondering what you're really like. A benefactor, an amateur detective, a rich playgirl...a lonely woman."

"Grace..." Sydney shifted uncomfortably and stopped.

"Yes?"

Syd said nothing for a moment. "What? Did I say something?" she asked innocently.

"You said my name, as if you were going to say something else. Perhaps something serious and not laced with sarcasm or pomposity. If that's possible."

"It's possible. More than possible. It's probable."

"Hmm. You're a changed woman? How'd that happen?"

Syd reached up, caressing her cheek. "I don't know. Maybe the love of a good woman."

Grace closed her eyes, leaning into her hand. "Anyone I know?"

"A wonderful, caring woman, who I think is a little cray-cray to still love me."

Grace chuckled, resting her head on Syd's shoulder. "She must be crazy."

"I thank God for that. Though I'll probably have to have a psychiatrist test her. Not sure I want to fall in love with a psycho—Ouch."

Grace let go of her hair and laughed. Syd laughed along and tried to pull her closer. Grace gently pushed her hands away and stood, offering her hand. "That's enough. I need a drink. Let's go before your brain implodes."

Sydney took her hand as Grace pulled her out of the chair.

The restaurant was packed, and they were lucky to get a quiet table overlooking Lake Michigan. Well, Sydney slipping the hostess fifty dollars didn't hurt. Sydney ordered champagne.

"Don't you think you're overdoing it?" Grace asked.

"Nope. I want everyone to know we're not giving up. Especially Brianne and Keith and whoever else is lurking around." She poured four glasses. "We're going to need another bottle."

"I know we're celebrating of sorts. But I've been thinking about Marcy Longwood," Adam said. "Can we throw something around for a minute and see if it sticks?"

Syd smiled. "Why, Adam, you sound positively human. Go on."

They all leaned in and listened.

"What's the biggest question so far?"

He looked at Sydney, who said immediately, "The codicil."

The waitress came over and took their order. "Hi, Grace."

"Hi, Jenny," Grace said, trying to smile.

"Grace, I don't believe a thing about you and Jon Pickford."

"Thanks, Jenny."

"If they should question anybody, it should be Marcy."

Sydney nearly spit up her champagne; she started coughing. Adam slammed her on the back. "Why is that?"

"I shouldn't say anything, but they were, ya know." Jenny looked around the table. "Ya know."

"Foolin' around?" Harry offered when no one did.

Jenny nodded. "I heard the girls talking about it. She and Mr. Pickford were quite the item a long time ago. Almost three years. She's so much younger than him." She looked at Grace. "You knew that, didn't you, Grace?"

Grace was stunned, yet again. "No, I didn't."

"Well, he stopped seeing her. The girls said she took it hard, but then she took up with his son all of the sudden."

"That I knew," Grace said evenly.

"Keith was strutting all over when they started. You know how guys are."

"The little dears." Syd sipped her champagne.

Jenny leaned in and whispered, "He even had a picture."

Now all four of them leaned forward. Adam was the first to speak. "A picture of what?"

"Whattaya think?" Harry said to him.

"Exactly." Jenny looked around. "I heard from Bill that it was a picture of him and her, ya know."

"Who's Bill?" Grace asked, rubbing her temple.

"The bartender." Jenny looked around again. "Hell, I better take your order before I get fired."

"We'll take another bottle of champagne and order later."

They waited until Jenny walked away before they all leaned in, nearly knocking heads.

"It seems Keith has a penchant for taking dubious photos," Adam whispered.

"What's Debbie doing here?" Grace noticed her up at the hostess desk.

"This place is hopping," Syd said.

When Grace waved, Debbie looked relieved and quickly made her way to their table.

"What's wrong? You're as white as a ghost," Grace said.

Harry stood and offered his chair. Debbie sat. "I tried your cell. When I couldn't get you, I figured you might be here. Have you heard?"

"Heard what? Debbie, if you don't spit it out..." Grace warned her.

"Marcy Longwood committed suicide. An overdose, they say."

"What?" Grace nearly screeched. She leaned in and said more quietly, "What?"

"You heard me. It's horrible."

Grace was shocked. "She's dead?"

"When and where? Do you know?" Syd had a horrible feeling in the pit of her stomach.

"They found her this morning in her bed. Alone," Debbie added. "I talked with one deputy. They figure she'd been dead for about six or seven hours. Her office called the cops after she was a no-show for her eight o'clock appointment and couldn't get in touch with her at home. She was lying in her bed...dead," she said morbidly. "Grace, I heard she was seeing Keith Pickford."

"I know," Grace said slowly. "How did you know?"

"Well, it was kinda common knowledge, though nobody ever really saw them. But I'm dating a deputy. He told me Brianne let it slip they were lovers."

"Brianne..." Grace looked at Sydney.

"He also told me about the search warrant, Grace. And you're the main suspect in Jon Pickford's murder. You should have told me."

Grace reached over and covered her hand. "I'm sorry. The arraignment was this morning."

"What? Are you serious?"

"As a heart attack. You're going to hear a lot of crazy shit, I think."

"I date a cop. I always hear a lot of crazy shit. What do you want me to do?"

"Check my calendar. Cancel any appointments. Then take a vacation, I guess, until this is cleared up."

"I can't believe this. What asshole thinks you killed Jon Pickford?"

Grace chuckled sadly. "Sheriff Gentry for one."

"What? That's crazy."

"I know. Just do as I ask, okay? Lock up the office. I'll call you in a few days."

"You call any time if you need anything."

"I will. Thanks."

Debbie took Harry's glass of champagne and slugged back its contents. "Sorry. Okay, I'll talk to you later." She walked over to Grace; they hugged for a moment. "Call me," Debbie whispered, then she left.

"Marcy Longwood killed herself." Suddenly, Sydney felt like vomiting. "Well, I wanted them to play a card. I had no idea," she said sadly.

Grace reached for her hand. "You're right. You had no idea Marcy might be mixed up in this. Don't go blaming yourself."

"Why in the world would Marcy Longwood kill herself?" Adam asked. "Good God, what next?"

"I wonder," Syd said absently and drank her champagne. "As tragic as this is, it certainly adds a wrinkle to this mess. I think things are unraveling, girls and boys."

"What do you mean?" Harry asked.

"This could be very interesting." Sydney took a drink and thought for a moment. "If what Jenny says is true, and I'm sure it is, then Marcy was having a fling with Jon. Abruptly, he stops it. Then just as quick, she starts seeing Keith." He looked at Grace. "At any time in the years you and Jon were working, did he ever mention Marcy or Keith?"

Grace shook her head. "The only time he talked about Keith was when he was spending a good deal of money. He mentioned how spoiled they both were, but he never mentioned Marcy in any other way except professionally."

"Why would a successful lawyer, an attractive woman, kill herself?" Sydney asked curiously. "I have a wild guess."

"I'll bet it's not too wild," Grace said. "What is it?"

"My gut tells me that she was in this, as well. She wanted out and couldn't get out. So maybe she took the only way that she felt was left to her," she said sadly.

"The codicil," Adam said. "That's what I was getting at earlier. She's a lawyer. Jon's lawyer. She knew what his will was like. Somehow, and I feel I'm right here, that codicil is the key. We sit here trying to figure out why Jon would put such a strange amendment to his will."

"Perhaps he didn't," Sydney interjected. "That would make sense."

"But very difficult to prove."

Harry grunted while he ate a piece of bread. "Not if things keep unraveling like they are. One of 'em is goin' to break. My money's on the sheriff. I think I can get her to a point where she'd gladly spill her guts just to make Syd look bad."

"I don't like that look in your eye, Sydney," Adam said.

Grace agreed. "Neither do I. Brianne is at a point of no return, I think. Please don't do anything to push her past that point." She gave Sydney a worried look.

"Careful, Grace. You sound like you might care for me."

"But I do. If anything happened to you, I'd have no bail."

Harry laughed. "She got ya there, Syd."

Chapter 29

Grace wanted to go back to her home, but the rest of them agreed it would be better if she continued to stay at the inn for another night. She reluctantly agreed.

After Sydney made sure Grace was safe and she got Harry a room, as well, Sydney needed time to think on her own. Grace was a constant distraction; she kept fighting the urge to hold her hand. She needed alone time to figure out what to do next.

She borrowed Adam's rental and drove back to Grace's, just to make sure the house was locked up. Then she walked along the beach. The night was warm and full of stars. This put her in a good state of mind.

And now she got down to it. Her first thought was of Marcy. Her instincts told her one thing: Marcy Longwood was in over her head, so there was no other way out. Whoever was behind this wanted to portray Grace as being the scorned lover, when in truth, it was probably Marcy.

She was in over her head in what, though? There were too many scenarios running around in Syd's head. Her mind drifted back to what her criminology professor at Northwestern had said to her and Jack. When searching for a motive and inundated with many possibilities, cut through the muck, and you'll find that the simplest explanation is usually the correct one.

Sydney thought the simplest explanation in this mess was money. That was usually a great motivator. However, Marcy didn't need money. Being Jon's attorney and having other clients, as well, Syd was sure she was financially set. Her offices and her home showed that. There had to be another reason Marcy would even consider being involved in this.

Sydney, however, found money to be a perfect reason for Keith and Tina. She almost forgot about Jon's murderer. She was sure neither Keith nor Brianne had the stomach for murder. Or Tina for that matter. She then made a mental note to talk to Keith the next day and find out where Tina had been all this time. She was at Marcy's but other than that, Syd hadn't seen her around town or at the restaurant. It wasn't like Tina to keep a low profile. Syd hadn't seen her all week. Then she'd try to get into Marcy's office. She might need Harry for that. She chuckled openly then—another night caper.

Somehow, she had to tie all this together. Money was the reason; she suspected all of them. She just needed to prove it—quickly.

She decided to stay at Grace's. If anything else was going to happen there, she might catch someone in the act.

She started to walk back to the car, confident that somehow she'd come up with something concrete. She hoped anyway.

Sydney drove to Millie's the next morning. It was a quaint bed-and-breakfast nestled in a grove of oak trees. Small but elegant, Sydney thought as she drove up the tree-lined drive. She found Adam's room and knocked.

Adam opened it quickly. "Good morning. I saw you pull up. How's Grace?"

"I haven't seen her yet. I-I spent the night at her place."

"Why?" Adam asked. "Why not stay here?"

"Because I needed time to think about this mess, and Grace distracts me."

Adam laughed out loud. "You sound like a teenager."

"Shut up."

"She said, proving my point." He went on when Syd glared. "Okay, what is on the agenda for today?"

"I want to find out what's happened to Tina."

Adam frowned. "Tina? What's the matter with her?"

Sydney frowned and shook her head. "I haven't seen her in days. One minute, she's there, and now she's gone. Where is she?" She sighed deeply. "I have a bad feeling about this, as well. I'm going over to the house. I purposely left my jacket and a few things there, good excuse."

"You must be careful. If what you suspect is true, these people either killed or had Jon killed. Their own flesh and blood. They will not think twice about you."

"I will be careful, and I will show extreme caution."

"I don't believe you. What do you want me to do?"

"Stay with Grace today. Let her sleep in. I'm sure she's exhausted. I have a few things to do. I'll meet you at Ernie's for lunch at one." Sydney turned.

"We're going to own that restaurant. Oh, and no arguing, I'm getting you a room here."

"Thanks." Syd laughed along. "Now I have to wake up the snoring beast. What room is he in?"

"Right down the hall. Room seven."

"Lucky number seven." Syd walked past Grace's room, quelling the urge to go to her and stay in bed with her all day. Once this is over…

She knocked at Harry's door. She smiled when she heard him whistling.

He opened the door, looking rested. "Good morning, Syd. You look pooped." He grinned slightly. "Where did you sleep last night?"

"Shut up. I was at Grace's."

"Why?"

"Why does everyone keep asking me that? C'mon, we got things to do."

"Okay, okay." Harry grabbed his key and followed her out.

"I want you to follow Keith today."

"All day?"

"I can't do both. Now be a good thief and do as I ask." Harry sighed and agreed. "Be careful. I don't want anything to happen to you. Understand?"

Harry smiled. "He won't even know I'm there. Can I take Adam's car?"

"You cannot. You get the sewing machine."

"And keep those lock picks close. We're going to take a look at Marcy Longwood's office tonight."

Harry's eyes lit up, and he rubbed his hands together. "Now you're talkin'."

Syd drove back toward town and headed for Jon's; she pulled into the circular driveway. No cars. She wasn't sure if that was a good sign or not. She looked around, went to the front door, and turned the knob. That it was unlocked surprised her, so she cautiously walked in the foyer.

"Keith, Tina?" she called as she walked down the hallway. There was no one in the kitchen or the library.

However, out on the patio, she saw Tina lying in the chaise lounge. She was appalled at the way Tina looked. Syd stood frozen, staring at her.

Tina's eye was blackened and her upper lip cut. She wore shorts showing a bad bruise on her thigh. What in the hell happened to her? She was staring out at the yard, drinking iced tea. When she painfully stood, she saw Sydney. She looked stunned, then terrified.

"Tina, what happened?" Syd met her at the French doors.

"What are you doing here? I thought you were in Chicago."

"What happened?"

Tina quickly walked past her. "Get out of this, Sydney. Go back to Chicago and forget this."

Sydney grabbed for her, but she scooted out of her way. "I mean it!" she yelled and ran upstairs.

"What the fuck is going on?"

Syd didn't know what to do. She knew Tina wasn't going to talk. There was nothing to do.

She drove away, staring at the road ahead. God in heaven, what happened to her, she thought. Someone beat the hell out of her, that's what happened. Tina may be many things, but no one deserves that kind of physical abuse.

Grace and Adam sat at Ernie's, waiting for Sydney and Harry. Adam watched Grace curiously.

"Sydney stayed at your house last night," Adam said.

"Is that where she was? She could have stayed…"

"That's what I said. But she said she needed to think, and you were a distraction."

Grace smiled. "She did?"

"Yes. Sydney never talks to me about the women in her life. But with you, she can't shut up. She also told me about your relationship and how it ended. She blames herself."

"I know. We were both shocked when we met again after so long. I've kept in touch with Victoria, but Syd never…oh, I don't blame her. At first I did. But I understand her. She certainly has changed."

"All grown up. It's about time. I think it began when she started working with Jack Riley."

"Working with him?"

Adam suddenly realized what he said.

"Is she a…"

"No, no. She is not on the police department. Good Lord." Adam laughed at the idea. "She knows many people who have many problems. She helps them when she can. Jack offers his assistance when he can. Those two really love each other, brother to sister. It's nice to see."

"I thought something like that. Victoria and I have had many conversations about her. She noticed things about Sydney. Staying out late, being secretive. I think she knows more than she's letting on."

"That sounds like Victoria. Sydney thinks she's being so clever with her."

"And that sounds like Sydney."

They both laughed at the comparison.

"This is not good, you're both laughing."

Grace looked up to find Sydney walking to the table.

"Well, you look rested." She smiled at Grace and sat next to her.

"Thanks, I am. But I have to say, you looked tired. But the bruising is less." She reached over and gently touched Syd's cheek. "Sorry. I just need contact with you."

"Don't ever apologize for that."

Adam gently cleared his throat.

"Did you hear something?" Syd asked Grace. She looked at Adam. "Oh, hello, Adam."

"Hello. Where have you been?"

"I stopped by Jon's to see if anyone was there. I found Tina out on the patio." Sydney stopped for a moment to collect her thoughts. The images of Tina still disturbed her. "She's into something bad. More than likely related to this. Someone used her as a punching bag."

"What?" Grace asked.

"She had bruises on her face and her thigh, her lip was cut, and she looked terrified to see me. She told me to leave and forget this. I tried to talk to her, but she ran upstairs."

"Good Lord," Adam said. "This has to stop. We have to figure this out."

"I don't know, but I just have a feeling..." Grace shook her head.

"What feeling?"

"Don't you feel it? It's in the air. Like electricity. I feel jumpy and anxious."

"Like something is about to happen. I wish it would," Adam said.

"I think it will. Whoever it is and whatever is going on, they're on to us. I know it. And I think Marcy knew it, and that's why she killed herself. Tina is into something with this, and maybe she wanted out and got the hell beat out of her. Probably by the guy who did the same to me and Harry." Syd sat back. "All this information about Keith and this guy back in college.

All the extortion. It has to be connected. There's no other explanation."

"So the motive is money?" Grace asked.

"What else?" Sydney nodded. "Money."

"However, I don't think Marcy was in it for the money. I knew Marcy, not well, but I knew her," Grace said. "Something else motivated her, or something forced her. I think Marcy wanted out, and they wouldn't let her. In her mind, this was the only way. If I can find out why she killed herself…"

With that, Sydney's cellphone went off. "It's Harry… Harry? Where are you?"

"Syd, I'm at a clinic on Broad Street. Someone tried to run me over."

"What?"

"I'm okay. Just come and get me. The sewing machine won't start."

"I'll be right there."

"What happened?" Grace asked.

"Someone tried to run Harry over. Do you know where the clinic is on Broad Street?"

Grace jumped up. "Yes."

There was Harry, lying on a table with a young nurse holding his hand. He grinned as they ran up to him.

"Harry, what happened?" Syd looked to the nurse. "Is he all right?"

"He's fine," she said.

The side of his head was bruised and scraped; his right ankle was wrapped and iced. Other than that, he appeared to be okay.

"A bump on the head and a severe sprain." She smiled at Harry. "He can still flirt. He'll need to stay off the ankle for a couple days." She patted his shoulder and left.

Sydney watched him anxiously. "Harry, are you sure you're all right?"

"It was nothin', really. I was trailing Keith, like you said, keeping outta sight. When all the sudden outta nowhere, this red sports job comes screaming around the corner. I turn and just had enough time to jump outta the way." He shook his head. "It was close, though. I tried, but the car wouldn't start. This place was close by."

"C'mon, let's get you back to the inn."

They got Harry situated on his bed with his foot propped up.

"Are you okay?" Grace asked.

"I'm fine. Geesh, this stinks."

Grace laughed and kissed the top of his head. "I need to check in with Debbie. Then I'm taking a long hot bath. Can I leave you two alone?" She didn't wait for an answer as she walked out.

"Syd, how are we going to get into Marcy's office tonight? I don't think I can walk on this foot."

"True." Sydney frowned and thought for a moment.

"You could ask Grace to go with you."

"The woman is out on bail. I'm not sure it would go over well if she gets caught breaking and entering."

"Oh, right."

"Well, I'll have to do it myself. Show me."

For the next hour, Harry showed Sydney his lock-picking expertise. Sydney tried it on Harry's door, and it worked like a charm. He handed Sydney the small case. "There's every size you need. If it's like the rest of the buildings around here, you should have no problem."

"I'll wait till everyone's in bed, then sneak out." He looked at Harry. "Do not tell Grace. Or Adam."

Harry looked horrified. "I would never. But how are you going to keep this from Grace? She's right down the hall. And your room is right next to hers. Geesh, this will never work!"

"Oh, don't be so pessimistic."

"All we have to do is make it through dinner. We'll have dinner here in your room, then you say how tired you are, and we'll go make it an early night."

"How are you gonna stay away from Grace? You know she's gonna want to be all over you."

"You think so?" Sydney grinned at the possibility.

"Oh, will you quit grinning and think?"

"Don't worry. I'll think of something. And I'll be back before anyone knows I'm gone."

"I don't think this is going to turn out well."

"Don't put the kibosh on this. Relax. Now it's five thirty. I'm going to take this stuff to my room and take a shower. Call me around seven. I'll tell Grace and Adam you still can't walk, so we'll have dinner brought to your room. We'll all eat, then off to bed."

Sydney gathered everything she needed and took it to her room. She then reveled in the longest, hottest shower she'd had in days. All she needed were her own clothes. These jeans and T-shirts were getting a workout.

She had just finished dressing when someone knocked at the door.

Grace stood there, grinning. "Hello. I hear you're staying at our inn. I'm just making sure you don't have a woman in there."

Sydney laughed and pulled her into her arms. "I do now." She kissed her, pulling her close in her embrace. "You taste like toothpaste."

"Thank you." Grace kissed her again, then walked into her room. "Nice. It's bigger than mine."

"Well, Adam made the reservation this morning. He knows what I like."

"I'm sure he does." She sat on the bed and patted the mattress.

Syd swallowed with difficulty and glanced at her watch. When her phone went off, she grinned.

"Who could that be?" Grace asked, sounding completely deflated.

"Why, it's Harry." Sydney shrugged. "What's up?"

"Whattaya mean? You told me to call ya at seven," Harry said.

"Oh, really? I'm sorry, Harry. What?"

"What, what?" he said.

"Sure. Why don't we have dinner in your room?"

"Who are you talking to?" Harry asked. "I'm so confused."

"It's no problem at all. Grace is here, I'm sure she won't mind. I'll take care of it." She disconnected the call before Harry started crying in confusion.

"We're having dinner in Harry's room?" Grace asked.

"Well, the poor guy can't walk, and he's feeling lonely. You know."

Grace narrowed her eyes. "Yeah, I know. What's going on?"

"Nothing. Good grief, you're paranoid. Must be your time spent in the slammer. Let's go." She walked over and pulled Grace to her feet.

Sydney ordered dinner from Millie's restaurant and had them bring it to Harry's room. Millie did not offer room service, but Sydney offered a nice tip to change their minds.

"This is unusual," Adam said. "But this has been an unusual week so far."

Sydney made sure she yawned through the entire meal. Harry did the same.

By nine thirty, Harry was practically snoring. Syd called to have the dishes removed. And like clockwork, Adam retired to his room, which left Grace and Sydney standing in the hallway with Sydney yawning.

"Well, you'd better get to bed. I don't want you falling asleep in the hallway."

"I'm sorry, Grace. It must have been that hot shower and a good meal."

"Mm-hmm. I still don't trust you." Grace reached up and kissed her. "Good night, I suppose."

"Good night. I'll see you for breakfast. Have a good sleep. And try not to worry about anything."

She waited a second after Grace closed her door, then ran to her room and gathered what she needed. She ran to Harry's room and knocked.

"Who is it?"

Sydney looked to the heavens. "Open the door," she whispered.

Harry laughed as he opened it. "Ya can't be too careful nowadays."

They spent the next hour going over the instructions again and again. Syd looked at her watch. "Okay, I'm going."

"Don't dawdle there. In and out."

Sydney nodded, fighting the anxious feeling she had. "Right."

"And don't forget to put the rubber gloves on and the baseball cap. It's an old building, so I don't think there's a camera. I'm sure there's a security light, though. If there's a camera, you might want to skip this. Check it out when you get there."

"Got it."

"If there's a camera and you go through with this, don't look up and keep the hat on."

"Right."

"Now if you can't get in, forget it. Don't force the lock. Just do it gentle like I showed ya," he warned.

"Okay, okay. You're making me nervous."

Harry looked at his watch. "Okay, I figure it shouldn't take more than ten minutes to get there. Park a block away. You shouldn't take longer than five minutes to get in. Give yourself about twenty minutes to find something. Then you leave it exactly as you found it. Lock the door and scram. Turn off your cell."

"Good idea." Syd turned it off and put it in her pocket.

"Leave it in the car. If it falls out and you don't know it, you're screwed."

"Then why am I turning it off?"

"Because if it rings, someone'll hear it. And what if Grace calls ya? Just turn the damn thing off and leave it in your car. Call me from the car when you're finished. If I don't hear from you by, say, one thirty, I have to tell Adam."

"Okay. That gives me plenty of time. That's a plan."

"Be careful."

Sydney smiled. "Email Mother, will you? I told her you'd be checking in." She plugged in the laptop and put it on the dresser next to the bed. "Keep the foot up, I'll be back. Remember, do not tell Grace. Hopefully, she's sound asleep."

"Okay, be careful."

Sydney waved him off. "Will you quit saying that?"

Chapter 30

Sydney parked a block away as planned, then walked to Marcy's office. She went around back. There was no visible camera, but there was a security light. She had to be quick in case someone drove by. She knelt by the door. Putting on the rubber gloves, she took out the case and selected the correct lock-picking files. Slowly, she inserted one, then the other and gently turned.

"Locks are like women," she whispered, repeating Harry's words of wisdom. She turned the knob—it was still locked. She wiped her brow and looked around before she tried again. She took a deep breath to calm her shaking hands and tried again.

Then she turned the knob, and it opened. "Thank you, Jesus." Though she was not sure she should be invoking his name while doing something illegal, she quickly went in and closed the door. She turned on the flashlight and walked to Marcy's office. Gratefully, the blinds were closed.

"Let's do this quickly, Syd."

She checked Marcy's desk, and surprisingly, it was opened. She looked in every drawer. She looked through everything, but nothing stood out. Then she found a small flat tin like the ones used in a bank vault only smaller. She took it out, and of course, it was locked. Gently but quickly, she took out the lock pick files and picked the small lock. It opened so fast, she was amazed and chuckled. "Well, if anything happens to the company, I can become a petty thief."

In the tin, she saw an envelope. It was closed but not sealed. She opened it and was shocked at what she saw. There were pictures, six or eight of them, all showing Marcy and Jon in various sexual positions. She was appalled and surprised that Marcy would keep them in a place so easily found. Why hadn't she destroyed these? If she could find these, surely...then she thought for a moment and looked in the box.

There was a key, and Sydney knew right off it was to a safety deposit box. She'd seen enough of them in her time. Christ, what bank? There was one bank in town, but it was small. She worried that it was too small to have a safety deposit area.

There was also a note, *You do your part, you get the negatives.* It was typed, not handwritten. Someone was very, very clever. So she was being blackmailed, Sydney knew it.

Suddenly, she heard a noise. Damn it, she thought, and put everything back in the envelope, including the key, and tucked it in her shirt. Someone was in the hall. She quickly and quietly closed the desk drawer, then stood behind the door.

The doorknob gently turned, and the door opened. Sydney was plastered against the wall, waiting. Do it now, Sydney thought. She quickly pushed the door, and a man groaned and stumbled into the room. Then all of the sudden, the man swung something at Sydney and caught her right in the face. She muffled a cry of pain as it caught her under her right eye—again. She fell against the wall, then grabbed at the intruder.

"You ain't getting me!"

Sydney heard the familiar voice and grabbed the man. "Harry?"

"Syd?" Harry asked quietly.

Sydney turned him around. "What in the hell are you doing here?"

Harry sighed. "Geezus, you scared the hell outta me."

Sydney closed the door and turned on the flashlight and shined it in Harry's face.

"Are you insane?" she whispered.

Harry had to chuckle. "I thought I'd come over and see if you were all right."

"Good God, man. You hit me." She felt her cheek; it was bleeding all over. "In the same damned spot. You're fired," she said emphatically.

Harry took the flashlight and turned it on Sydney. "Aw, geez, sorry, Syd. Reflexes."

"Let's get out of here before anyone else shows up. What the devil did you hit me with?"

Harry smiled sheepishly. "My cane. The nice nurse gave it to me."

"I'll give it to you. Let's go."

They checked the room and made sure all was put back together. Then Syd ushered Harry out the door.

"How did you get here?"

"I called a cab."

"How did you get in?"

"A good thief always has spares."

Once back at Millie's, they crept up the stairs to their rooms. In the hallway, Sydney whispered, "Now say nothing of this to anyone."

"Okay," Harry whispered in return.

With that, Adam and Grace came out of Adam's room, and both of them jumped. Harry let out a small scream and held on to Sydney's arm.

Sydney looked down at him. "Unhand me, you fool."

The red-faced thief let her go. Grace was shocked at Sydney. "What in the hell happened to you?" She put her hand on her cheek. "Again?"

Adam was frowning. "What have you two been up to?"

"Can we get out of the hall?" Sydney said. "Let's go to my room."

Grace put Harry in a chair and put his foot up. Then she went into the bathroom and came out with a cold compress and unceremoniously pushed Sydney back onto her bed. She gently put the cloth over her cheek and put Syd's hand on it. "Hold it and shut up."

Adam was scowling at both of them. "All right, let's hear it."

"Legally…" Sydney started.

Adam groaned as he put up his hand. "I don't want to hear anymore. Tell Grace. I'll be in my room. Come get me." He walked out and closed the door.

Grace sat on the bed and looked down at Syd. "What did you do? And don't lie to me."

"I...let myself into Marcy's offices. Grace, I found the reason she was involved. Adam can't know about this. He's too straitlaced. And more importantly, he's a lawyer."

Grace put her hand to her forehead. "Sydney, darling, if you broke into Marcy's office and took something, you're right— Adam can't know about it. It's called breaking and entering. In case you didn't know, it's illegal. However, I can see it. Adam just cannot know where it came from."

Syd looked up at her and smiled. "You called me darling." She ignored the groan from Harry.

"A momentary lapse. Tell me what happened."

Syd retold their evening. Grace looked at Harry, who gave her a weak smile and shrugged. Grace continued to listen without interrupting until she had finished.

"So we have the evidence that could possibly clear you."

"And almost get killed in the process. You're bruised on top of your bruise."

"Well, I would have been in and out…" Syd gave Harry a scathing look.

Grace took the cloth off Syd's face and took it into the bathroom.

"Syd, I felt bad you goin' alone."

Grace called from the bathroom. "Both of you, keep quiet."

They stopped, but Sydney scowled at Harry, who shrugged helplessly.

Grace returned with a clean cloth and gently put it back across Syd's cheek.

"Thank you." Syd gave her a weak smile.

"Show me the pictures," she said.

Sydney frowned. "They're very graphic."

She rolled her eyes. "Good grief, I'm not a schoolgirl."

Syd took them out of her shirt and handed them to Grace.

Grace opened the envelope and leafed through the pictures. "Really, you treat me like a child, for heaven's sake. Oh, my God." She quickly put them down.

"Told you," Syd said childishly.

"Well, I haven't seen 'em," Harry said, frowning, and Grace walked them over to him. He looked at all of them with eyebrows raised. He then turned them around and looked again from a different angle. "How do ya suppose they got in that—?"

"Okay, okay," Grace said, snatching them out of his hands.

"So it's obvious she was being blackmailed. There is also a note and a safety deposit box key. My guess is they blackmailed her into doing something with the will. When she had fulfilled her part, she was to get the negatives and perhaps money, but I'm guessing about that. I would say the negatives would be put in the safety deposit box," Sydney finished and tried to sit up. Grace simply pushed her back.

"Well, who's doing the blackmailing?"

"My guess again would be Keith. He is the likely suspect, having done it in college." Sydney thought for a moment. "It seems a little strange that she'd be sleeping with him, though," she said absently, staring at the ceiling. "I mean, going from Jon to his son." He looked at Grace. "How well did you know Marcy?"

Grace shrugged. "Only professionally. She seemed nice enough, although I had no idea she was in love with Jon. As I said, he never said a word to me about her. However, Jon was an honorable man. You must have known that."

Sydney nodded. "Indeed he was. He was a good, solid man," she said sadly and continued, "I remember when I was younger,

Jon was the one who helped me. He was more of a father than my own father."

Grace watched her. "You loved him, didn't you?"

Sydney looked up at her. "Yes, I loved him. So did my mother. When I was younger, I wanted him to be my father. Silly, I know. I wished my father would go away with one of his many women and leave my mother in peace. Do you know that after Emily died I secretly prayed that my mother and Jon would fall in love? I was a grown woman, I know. It was silly."

Grace gently kissed her forehead. "It's not silly at all."

There was a knock on the door, and Adam came in. "I couldn't stand it much longer. You must have done something awful to take this long to explain." He was actually frightened.

Sydney chuckled. "No, Adam, really. Let's all go to bed. We'll figure it out in the morning."

Harry got up and took Adam by the arm. "Help an old thief to bed."

Grace sat on the bed looking down at Sydney. She took the cloth off her face and frowned. "It looks like it hurts."

"It's fine, really. I can still see you with one eye. You only look half as adorable."

"You scared me tonight," she said, looking at their hands. "I woke and went to your room, and you weren't there, and neither was Harry. So I went to Adam, and we sat there for an hour waiting. It was the longest hour I've ever spent." She put her hand over her eyes and cried softly.

Sydney was shocked. She sat up and leaned on her elbow. "Gracie, I'm so sorry. I thought I'd be back without anyone the wiser."

Grace leaned away. "I don't hear from you for years. You come back into my life and now look at us. I'm a felon, and you're all beat up."

Syd started to get up when Grace quickly walked to the door. "Grace, please. It's almost over. I can feel it."

"How much longer, Syd? What has to happen—me going to prison or you getting killed?"

"You're not going to prison."

Grace sighed and walked back to her bed. She gently cupped Syd's face. "I hope you're right. I look horrible in orange. Go to sleep."

"Stay with me?"

Grace smiled and kissed her uninjured cheek. "Not now. We'll talk about us when this is through."

"Okay," Syd said and lay back. "I'm sorry I worried you."

"I'm sorry Harry hit you."

They both laughed; Grace kissed her softly on the lips. "Good night."

"Good night." She watched Grace close the door behind her.

Chapter 31

The next morning, Sydney was the last to come down to breakfast. Grace caught her breath when she looked at her face. Her right eye wasn't as swollen, but the gash underneath it was turning black and blue again.

"Good morning," she said tiredly and sat. "Ah, coffee."

"Good morning." Adam watched her. "So I've come across some interesting photos."

Syd's head shot up. "What, um, what?"

"They were left at the desk for me this morning. I can't imagine who would leave them. However, they are unbelievably helpful. I was so curious, I opened them right there, in front of the desk manager." He looked for their waitress and beckoned her.

She came over. "What can I get you?"

"May I see the manager, please?" Adam said.

"Is something wrong?"

"Oh, no, no. Nothing like that."

"What's going on?" Harry asked.

Sydney shrugged and drank her coffee. "Ooh, are those scones?"

"Yes, they're heavenly. Have one." Harry offered the plate.

The desk manager came over to their table and looked at Adam. "Can I help you?"

"Sir, you didn't see who left that package last night, did you?" Adam asked.

"No, sir, I'm sorry. I walked away to get some coffee, and when I returned, it was on the desk with your name on it," he said honestly. "My night manager and I made sure it was kept for you."

"And I opened it in front of you."

"Yes, sir."

"Thank you. I was just telling my friends here that I haven't a clue who sent it. It appears to be some pictures and a key of some sort," he said.

"I wouldn't know, sir. I didn't look inside."

Adam nodded. "It's good to know that." He held up the key and looked at Sydney. "Well, perhaps you can shed some light on it. Actually, if anyone knows what it is." He looked around the table.

The desk manager shrugged. "I don't know, sir."

Adam shrugged, as well. "Well, thank you. You do a magnificent job. Very professional." The desk manager smiled and walked away.

Sydney chuckled. "Very good, Adam. Now give me the key." Adam laughed and handed it over. Harry was confused.

It was Grace who explained to Harry. "We now have a witness that none of us had any idea what the key was and how the package got to Adam. If any questions arise, Adam knows nothing." She smiled at Harry.

He watched Adam and Sydney talking. He leaned into Grace and whispered, "Who sent him the package?"

Grace said with childlike innocence, "Harry, I have no idea."

Harry stared at her and winked. "Grace, you have the makings of a first-class thief."

After breakfast, they gathered in Syd's room.

"So we can assume Keith blackmailed Marcy to help with Jon's will?" Adam asked.

"I think so. But we have to figure out Brianne's part in all this." Syd was about to go on when her phone rang. "Oh, good. It's Jack. Jack? What's the word?"

"I've got some good news."

"Hold on, let me put you on speaker." Syd placed the phone on the table; they all huddled around it. "Okay, Jack. Go ahead."

"I got a name. One Charles Harris. He's the scumbag friend of Pickford. This guy is good, Syd. He only has two priors, but both dismissed, which is why it was so hard to get a name. Both were for extortion and illegal wiretapping. Here's what I came up with. This guy was a genius. He had graduated from Harvard in the top two percent when he was nineteen. Electronics expert, and he has the ability to scare the hell out of people. He's also a wiz with surveillance. That's how he blackmailed a few of his college friends. He had no pictures, no documents. He used surveillance, heard every word, every telephone conversation. Then blackmailed the poor slob. Syd…?"

"Yeah?"

"I'd be careful with the phone in Grace's office. This guy used to tap phones, he might try that with you."

"Okay. Anything else?"

"Yeah. According to the victims, he and Pickford would blackmail with compromising pictures. However, one victim couldn't figure out how they knew the one particular thing they used to blackmail. Like I said, they had no pictures, no documents, but they knew what he did. The victim had no idea how Keith and this fellow found out. Syd, I got a picture of this guy. I don't want to use the fax machine at Grace's office anymore, just in case. I'll send it to your phone. I think with all this, you might be able to go to the locals. It's still all speculation, but they might look into it."

"I don't know, Jack. I told you who the local sheriff is."

"Yeah, I know."

"And I think she might be part of it."

"Be careful then. You know how she is. I'm sure I'm not the only one it's happened to."

Syd glanced at Grace, who had such a deflated look on her face. "I will. Thanks."

"Okay, Syd. Bye."

Syd looked around the room. "Well, I think we need to get to the bank and see if the safety deposit box is there. What do you think?"

"Great, let's go," Grace said.

"Um, when I said we, I meant me," Syd said evenly.

Grace put her hands on her hips. "Look, quit being so bossy. It's my life, you know."

Sydney sighed. "Yes, I know, and I'm trying to keep it alive for our future."

Grace would not give in.

"Grace," Adam said. "Syd is right. Why don't we go to Ernie's? We've never been there."

Grace tried not to laugh, especially when Harry snorted. "I don't want to leave you alone again," she said to Syd. "There's just so many times you can get punched in the face."

Syd grinned in spite of the situation. "I love a woman who can keep her sense of humor."

"Well, being involved with you, what choice do I have? All right, I'll go. But you'd better come back in a hurry."

"I will. Now come over here, so I can kiss you."

Grace rolled her eyes, but she walked up to her. "This is going to be what it's like in the future?"

"I don't know. We'll have to find out, won't we?"

"When this is over, no more bossing me around."

"Deal. That'll be your job and my mother's."

Grace laughed, then kissed her. "Please, please be careful."

"I'm going to the bank in broad daylight. What could happen?"

"Ooh, don't say that," Harry chimed in.

"All right, that's enough sentiment. Syd, go. We'll meet you at Ernie's." Grace let her go and stepped back. "Go before I change my mind and go with you."

Syd walked across the street to the bank. It was a small building in the middle of Seacliff. She approached the nearest desk.

"Excuse me. I have a question regarding safety deposit boxes."

"Certainly, would you like to purchase one?"

"Well, no. I have key, and I'd like to see if it belongs to this bank."

The woman raised an eyebrow. "May I?"

Syd handed her the key. After examining it, the woman nodded. "It's one of ours. I take it it's not yours."

"Well, that's the problem. I know who owns the box. She gave it to me for safe keeping, and now…Can I be honest with you?"

"I wish you would."

"It belonged to Marcy Longwood."

The woman's eyes grew comically wide. "I see. Well, I'm very sorry, but she'd have to sign to open the box, and considering she can't, you'll have to get legal authorization for yourself. Wait, let me check on this." She walked over to a gentleman who looked at Syd, then approached her.

"You knew Marcy? I'm Dean Tanner. How do you know her?"

"Only through Jon Pickford, he's an old friend of the family. My name is Sydney Crosse, I own TeleCrosse Communications."

Dean held out his hand. "The one who just transferred all that money here?"

"Yes. That's me."

"And that's the company Jon Pickford owned, correct?"

"Yes, it is."

"Can I see some ID, please? I don't mean to be rude."

"Of course not. Certainly." Syd fished her wallet out of her jeans pocket and produced her license.

Dean examined it. He absently chewed at his bottom lip.

Syd gave him a hopeful look and waited.

"Jon was a good man. Marcy was a friend of mine," he said quietly.

"Mr. Tanner, I'm just trying to find out what's happened to both of them. You can accompany me and watch as I examine the box. I'll take nothing from it."

"This is highly irregular. I could lose my job."

"Trust me, you will not lose your job. I'll see to that."

Dean chuckled reluctantly. "I believe that. All right. Follow me."

Syd breathed a sigh of relief as she followed him to the back of the bank. "In here."

Syd followed as he walked into the room. He found the box and pulled it out. As he stepped back, she cautiously put the key in and opened it. The negatives were there and a white envelope.

True to his word, he stood by and watched as Syd examined the contents. There was a letter, signed and notarized from Marcy Longwood. Sydney read it, amazed. It explained everything—her culpability in Jon's murder, the blackmail, the pictures, the money she received. Syd looked further and saw almost five grand in the box. But she made no reference at all about Keith and this Charlie Harris or Brianne.

Sydney took a deep sad breath and closed the box. "Thank you, Mr. Tanner."

"Does it help?"

"It helps enormously. I'm sure the police will be around at some point."

"I hope I did the right thing."

"You did, trust me. Thanks again. I'm going to keep this key if that's all right."

"Yes. See that the authorities get it, won't you?"

Syd shook his hand. "I will."

Syd ran to Ernie's. Finding them at the table by the window, she quickly joined them.

"Good grief, are you all right?" Grace asked frantically.

She nodded. "Fine, fine."

"Well, what did you find?" Adam asked urgently. Sydney drank an entire glass of water.

"She had a letter, signed and notarized, explaining her part in all this, but she did not implicate anyone else."

"Damn," Adam said. "We need that information. I can take what we have to the prosecutor, but…"

"We need to know who," Syd said.

As she was about to continue, Brianne and Keith walked in and sat the bar. Both watched their table.

"It's like they're daring us," Grace whispered.

"They are." Syd had an idea then. She thought quickly. "Listen to me. They know I came from the bank. They must know I have the key. We're going to split up again. Grace, listen."

"What?"

"We're all going to stand, and I'm going to grab you. You slap me. But on the other side of my face, please."

"What? Why?"

"Shush," Syd said severely. "Just do it. I'll storm out of here, and they'll follow, I'm sure."

"But, Syd…" Harry said.

"Harry?" Syd looked him in the eye. "GPS."

"What?"

No one had time to argue further. Syd stood and pulled Grace to her feet and into her arms. Syd ran her hand over Grace's breast. Grace let out a screech.

"Now," Syd whispered.

Grace reared back and whacked her across the face.

Syd's head snapped back, completely surprised. "Good grief."

Harry jumped up to Syd, who whispered to him again, "Evanston."

She then stormed out of the restaurant past Brianne, who laughed out loud.

Adam quickly drove them back to the inn, making sure no one followed.

Harry limped along with his cane. "My room," he said over his shoulder.

"What in the world is going on?" Adam asked.

Grace was still shaking. "I have no idea."

Once in Harry's room, he started to chuckle.

"Harry, please don't lose it at this stage," Adam said.

"Where is she? Why is she doing this?"

"And what the hell does GPS and Evanston mean?" Adam asked.

Harry held up his hand. "Evanston is a city outside of Chicago."

"We know that!" Adam said.

"Syd and me were doing something, and we, well, we had to hide something, see. And well…" He stopped and rubbed his nose. "Grace, look in your, well, Syd put the key…" He turned bright red; he pointed to her chest.

Grace looked at him like he was nuts.

"What the hell are you saying?" Adam asked from behind him.

Grace looked into her blouse and reached in. There it was. She pulled out the key. "How in the hell did she get it in my bra?"

"Ya don't wanna know. That's what we had to do in Evanston. We obtained evidence that was less than the appropriate way. It was a good idea. They never searched the woman's bosom."

"I can't believe I slapped her."

"Well, she told ya to. But you really clocked her good." Harry took out his phone. "And for GPS. Before we left to come here, Syd got me this new phone."

"With GPS tracking." Grace ran up to him.

"Only I don't know how it works."

"Give it to me," Grace said.

After a minute of Harry and Adam standing over her, she had it. "There…"

"All right, I've had enough of this. It's time to call that state detective before Sydney gets herself killed."

Grace fell back into the nearest chair.

"Oh," Adam said. "Sorry, Grace."

Chapter 32

Sydney knew what was going to happen. She knew Harry would get her clues and call the state police. But she needed to bring Keith and the rest of them out or it wouldn't mean a thing.

She walked to the edge of town before she was stopped. Brianne's cruiser pulled in front of her, nearly running her over.

Brianne got out, smirking. "Just couldn't butt out, could you?" she said. "You just couldn't fucking butt out. Turn around."

"Why?"

Brianne pulled her weapon. "No one would convict me if I shot you right now. Turn around."

Syd obeyed. "You know you're really giving the police a bad name. Haven't you been reading the papers lately?"

Brianne roughly handcuffed her and nearly threw her in the back of the cruiser. She then headed down the street.

"Why, Brianne?"

"Shut up."

"Just tell me why you would do this to Grace. Because she doesn't want you?" Syd could see her eyes in the rearview mirror. She narrowed them.

"Just shut up and sit tight. This isn't funny anymore, Crosse. You've really put your foot in it this time. There's no turning back."

Brianne pulled up to what looked like an abandoned house. Brianne hauled her out of the cruiser, pushing her up the walkway. The inside looked as if it were indeed abandoned.

"Downstairs," Brianne said.

"Naturally."

As she slowly descended the rickety stairs, two sets of legs came into view. One set wore the boots she remembered.

"Hello," a man said. "Welcome."

Sydney walked into the musty basement. The only light was hanging precariously from the ceiling. Then she noticed Keith, who looked shamefaced but angry at the same time.

"You must be Charles," Syd said. "Can I call you Charlie or Chuck?"

He threw his head back and laughed. "Oh, I'm going to hate to kill you. Why can't the two of you be as amusing as her? Yes, I'm Charlie, and I prefer Charlie. How did you find out about me? I'm very impressed, and I don't impress easily."

"I have a friend on the Chicago police force. Brianne knows him."

Charlie shot a glare at Brianne, then shook his head. "Really?"

"Yes, tell him, Brianne. Tell him how you watched your partner beat up a poor college student, then plant coke on him. And thought you'd get away with it."

"Well, that's our Brianne." Charlie jumped up and sat on the workbench, swinging his legs. "That's how I got her. She can't help herself. You don't see that kind of hostility in women much. But Sheriff Gentry has it. And I got her."

"Blackmail?" Syd asked.

"Well, yeah," Charlie said, snorting sarcastically. "And by your visit to the bank, I figure you know about Marcy." Charlie shook his head sadly. "No one gave her permission to kill herself. She went rogue. How'd you get the key?"

"I broke into her office and found it, along with some pretty disgusting pictures."

Charlie glared again at Brianne. "Do you do any policework in this town? Breaking and entering and you know nothing?"

"What about you, Keith?" Syd asked.

"Give them the key, Sydney," Keith nearly begged her.

"How did they get you?" Syd asked.

Brianne pulled up an old chair and threw Syd in it.

"Temper, temper," Charlie said to Brianne. "You seem to have your finger on the pulse of the situation. How do you think I got to Keith?"

"My guess is that Keith found out about the will from Marcy, and like the cowardly scum that he is, he blackmailed her into helping you."

"The blackmail was my idea," Charlie said happily. "The poor woman loved Jon, so she allowed herself to be blackmailed to avoid any scandal for the old geezer. She even broke it off and hooked up with Keith, to save Jon. So we had her add that change to his will. I forged his name. I'm good at that."

"Well, anything worth doing…" Syd said, staring at Keith.

"I know, right?" Charlie said. "What else did you find out? I'm fascinated."

"Oh, come on," Brianne said.

"Oh, shut up," Charlie said, waving her off.

"You planned Jon's murder."

"I did."

"How did you get him on the boat?" Syd asked.

"That was Keith. He told his old man he had a business venture. Charter fishing on Lake Michigan. Keith was going to start his own business, finally make something of himself, and he wanted to show Daddy the boat. Laid it on thick so papa would be proud. Keith got him to the marina and on the boat. Afterward, I got Brianne here to plant the note on Jon's body."

"Which she bungled by putting it on after he was fished out of the lake. The note was dry and not smudged at all."

For the first time, Charlie looked really agitated. He glared once again at Brianne. "You really are worthless. What did I tell you?" He looked at Syd then. "So I guess you know she planted the icepick in your girlfriend's house too. Right?"

Syd nodded.

"God, I hate you right now," Charlie said to Brianne.

"What about Tina?" Syd asked. In the back of her mind, she wondered where in the hell Harry was.

"Well, surprisingly enough, I couldn't find anything on her. But she does scare easily and reacts to pain in a positive way, for me anyway. So she went along with everything without a whimper. Well, maybe a whimper or two. Now we come to poor Grace Morgan. Truly the most innocent of dupes."

"She's your scapegoat," Syd said softly.

"Yes. We knew right away blackmail would never work on her." Charlie laughed and pulled at his earlobe. "And actually, we couldn't find anything. So we had to use her. Very clever, though, I thought."

"It is. You change the will to make sure that if for some reason Grace couldn't fulfill her duties, like being convicted of murder, it all reverts back to Keith and Tina. You almost had it accomplished. Almost."

"Almost? Oh, it's gonna work. You're gonna hand over the key. And by the time anyone finds you and anything else, I'll be in some South Pacific island drinking rum."

"You can't be that stupid to think I'd keep it on me, do you?" Sydney asked seriously.

"Actually, yes, I do." He motioned to Brianne.

Brianne hauled Syd to her feet and frisked her. She pulled out her wallet and looked through it, tossing it on the floor. She took out her cell. "You won't need this anymore." Brianne threw it on the floor and stomped on it.

Syd's heart skipped a beat. She only hoped Harry had her location on the GPS. If not, she was screwed. She started to think of a way to get out of this.

"She's clean."

"Are you sure? She's been leading you around by your hormones since she got here."

"She's frisked enough people in her time," Syd said. "I don't have the key."

"Now from what Brianne and Keith said, they watched you the entire time."

Brianne laughed. "Grace even slugged her when she tried…"

Charlie laughed again. "Hating you, hating you," he said to Brianne. "So you handed the safety deposit key to the Morgan chick."

"I'll find her," Brianne said.

"No, ya won't," Charlie said, looking at Syd. "So your cop friend found out about me?"

"Yes. He also did a check on Keith. That's where he put things together. Jon got Keith out of quite a bit of trouble, very expensive trouble during his college days. My friend found out all about your extortion and blackmail." Syd looked at Keith, who looked as though he wanted to vomit. "Your father helped you when he should have written you off. He loved you and Tina, and this is what you did to him." Syd looked back at Charlie, who watched her intently. "As for finding out about you? My friend did some good old-fashioned policework—"

"Brianne, dear? You might want to listen to this," Charlie said. "Go on."

"He dug up all the information on you. He put it all together." She looked at Brianne. "Funny how things have a way of turning around."

"Yeah, karma is a loveless bitch, Brianne," Charlie said with a sigh. "How'd you find out about the note on Jon's body?"

"I saw the police report. That's where you found me the other night."

"That's what you were doing? We couldn't figure that out," Charlie said with a wry chuckle. "So you put it together and came up with Brianne's boneheaded move of planting a dry note on a wet body." He gave Brianne a disgusted look. "Brianne was certain the Morgan woman was sleeping with Jon."

"She was," Brianne said nastily.

Syd laughed. "She was not. What? Just because she didn't want you, poof! She's straight?"

Charlie laughed and swung his legs. "She got you there, Brianne."

Brianne pushed Syd so hard, she flew back into the chair, nearly falling backward.

"Brianne, that's how he got you? You did all this because he told you they were lovers? Oh, man. You are stupid."

Brianne looked at Charlie, who shrugged. "She's right. The Morgan chick wasn't sleeping with Jon, dumb-dumb. But you wanted to believe it, so I couldn't break your heart." He smiled. "Now don't get all weepy. This will work out, and you'll get a handsome paycheck. That should assuage your conscience."

Sydney laughed rudely, looking at Brianne. "Geezus, Brianne, you honestly think this guy is going to give you any money? Why should he when he can blackmail you for the rest of your life? Christ, use your head."

Brianne looked from her to Charlie. "She has a point."

Charlie sighed. "Don't be stupid. If I wanted to, I'd kill you right now. You'll get your money."

Brianne didn't look so sure anymore, and Sydney continued.

"Sure you'll get your money, then he'll either kill you or use the information. I read his file, Brianne. He and Keith are in this together. It's a fifty-fifty split. You make it uneven."

"She's lying, Brianne." Keith stepped up.

"By the way," Syd said. "Which one of you smokes those little cigars?"

"Good grief, you found out about that too. What do you do—sit around reading murder mysteries all day? Man, I am impressed. Brianne, take the cuffs off her."

"What?"

"You heard me. Take 'em off. She's not going anywhere, and she's a formidable adversary. I think she deserves to defend herself when you try to kick her ass."

Brianne walked up behind Syd and hauled her to her feet. She stood behind her and breathed in her ear, "I'm going to enjoy this." She roughly took the cuffs off.

Syd rubbed her wrists. "Now what?"

Charlie had a gun pointed at her. "It won't be that easy. Sorry."

With that, the light above them went out, and Charlie groaned. "Geezus, what now? Keith, go see."

In the half-light of the basement, Charlie watched Syd. "Sit down, please."

Syd continued to rub her wrists and sat.

"What's taking him so long? Shit, you people are worthless. Brianne, go see where that fathead is," he said disgustedly.

Sydney strained in the darkness and saw Brianne's figure climb the stairs. Sydney figured it was now or never. Though Charlie did have a gun pointing at her.

"Well, I hate to see this end…"

The volley of gunfire heard outside scared the crap out of Syd. It also stunned Charlie. In that moment, Syd took the chance and dove at him. But…she missed and went flying into the corner, buried in a barrage of falling boxes. She heard screaming and yelling and someone on a bullhorn. For an impossible moment, it sounded like Grace. She then heard a couple of shots fired in the room, figuring it was Charlie.

Then she heard a wonderful screech.

"Sydney! Sydney! Where are you?" Grace cried out.

"I'm over here in the UPS section."

Chapter 33

It looked like a war zone when Syd and Grace came up from the basement. Police cars, a helicopter. There must have been three dozen policemen from all over the tristate area.

"Wow. Who did you call?" Syd had her arm firmly around Grace's shoulder.

"Well, I guess I went overboard."

Harry came running, well limping, up to them with Adam right behind him. Adam's shirt was ripped, and he sported a nice bruise on his jaw.

"What happened?" Syd asked. "Are you all right?"

Adam showed his torn pants at the knee. "I got a grass stain. I pulled that thug down myself."

Syd tried not to laugh at his serious posture. Grace chuckled and held on to Syd.

"He did, Syd. Grabbed Keith right around the back of the collar and held on for dear life until I clubbed him with my cane."

"Where were the police?" Syd looked at Grace. "You said you overdid it?"

"Well, we got here first and waited, but we saw Brianne and Keith come out, so we figured we'd get the drop on 'em."

"That was very dangerous," Syd said seriously. "You could've been killed."

"Dangerous?" Grace asked, stepping out of her embrace. "Look who's talking. You've been throwing your body all over the place for a week now. You've got some nerve after we saved your life."

Syd's mouth dropped. "I-I…"

"I, I, I…" Grace finished for her. "Adam even ripped his pants for you."

"Thank you," Syd said to Adam.

"I broke my cane," Harry said.

"I'm sorry," Syd said solemnly. "Truly."

"Ms. Crosse?"

Syd looked up to see Detective Webster standing there with several other policemen. "You'll all need to come down to the office whenever you're ready." He looked at Grace. "I want to personally apologize to you, Ms. Morgan. If your lawyer will come down to the station, we'll make sure it's all taken care of."

"Thank you, Detective," Grace said.

As he walked away, he stopped. "Oh, by the way, the FBI agent wants his bullhorn back."

"So someone fill me in," Syd said slowly.

"Let's get back to the inn."

"Our home away from home," Adam said. He put his arm around Harry and walked away.

After they all cleaned up, they sat in Syd's room; it was the largest. Harry manned the bar, making cocktails for all.

Grace sat on Syd's lap, not wanting to let her go, which was all right with Syd.

Syd took the martini from Harry. "Thanks," she said with a wink. "Now who wants to go first? Okay, I will."

Grace rolled her eyes and sipped her drink.

Syd explained her ordeal from start to finish. "I was getting a little nervous when you guys didn't show up. Everything we thought about all of them was true. Expect Brianne. She honestly thought you were sleeping with Jon. She was jealous and wanted revenge."

"Oh, my God," Grace said.

"Well, that Charlie fella knew how to play people. And Brianne was an easy mark. In all the excitement, I didn't see her. You say you got Keith."

"Yeah, he and Brianne were arguing over the money. That's how we got Keith. Brianne surrendered. She threw up her hands, and that was it," Harry said.

"Webster said they were picking up Tina. He wasn't sure what they'd charge her with."

"So sad." Syd shook her head. "Well, anyway, when the lights went out and we heard the shots, I took the chance and dove for Charlie."

"Really? That was pretty brave, Syd."

"Well, I missed him and ended up underneath a pile of boxes, which probably saved my life. Other than you guys, of course." She looked at Grace, who leaned down and kissed her. "So, Harry, you got my clues?"

"Naturally. I knew right off. Grace found the key in her um…"

Syd laughed and felt her jaw. "You hit me really hard there."

Grace let out a nervous laugh. "Sorry. It must have been all that adrenaline."

"Well, I got the GPS but not right away. It took a few minutes. Then we saw where you stopped, but it went blank."

"Brianne stomped on my phone while they were frisking me for the key."

"When that happened, well, Grace," he said with a laugh. "Grace went a little…"

Syd looked at Grace. "Cray-cray?"

"Just a little," she conceded.

Adam laughed. "An understatement. She called the state police, the FBI, and if we were any closer to the water, the Coast Guard would have been there. I'm not too sure she didn't have the Marines on speed dial."

"My hero," Syd whispered. "Thank you."

"Well, someone has to look after you. My God, you're reckless."

"Want the job?"

"I'm not sure. What's the pay like?"

"Well, since you've had experience in that department, I think a big fat promotion is in order."

"I'm not cheap, Sydney Crosse."

"That you ain't. Thank God."

"Well, it's all over. Good job," Adam said, raising his glass to them.

They finished their drinks; Syd was very grateful when Harry and Adam excused themselves.

"And then there were two," she said to Grace.

Grace walked into her open arms. "So you need me?"

"Desperately," she said. "Not to sound desperate, mind you."

"You broke it off once." She looked up at Syd, shocked to see tears in her eyes.

"It was one of the more stupid things I've done," she said, caressing her neck. "I have a feeling I'm going to spend the rest of my life making up for it."

"If you're lucky."

"I feel lucky." She lowered her head and kissed her tenderly.

Grace sighed and put her arms around her waist. "Well, we've got the room for the weekend, and I think we have some unfinished business to attend to." Grace kissed her jawline down to her neck.

Syd caught her breath and whispered, "I believe you're absolutely right."

Her hand traveled down Grace's back and slowly slipped under her blouse.

"God, Syd. That feels good." She sighed and reached up, pushing Syd's shirt off her shoulders, caressing the top of her breasts. "Sydney, I do want you," she whispered as she stripped the shirt off.

"Grace Morgan, you're a wicked woman." She slipped her blouse off, then reached inside the waistband of her shorts.

Grace easily stepped out of them. Syd stepped back. "My God, I've never forgotten how beautiful you are." She lowered her head and kissed her, tenderly at first, then with more passion as her tongue parted her lips.

Passion was quickly taking over, as it did before. Both women struggled for dominance as they stumbled to the bed, never breaking their kiss.

"God, Grace," Syd mumbled, cupping Grace's breast. She easily laid Grace against the pillows.

Standing over her, she slipped off her bra and the rest of her clothes.

"Wait, let me look at you for just a moment," Grace said softly. "Just as I remember."

"A little older."

"But no worse for wear." Grace opened her arms. "Come here."

Lying next to Grace, Syd's caresses became more eager. She rained kisses down one side of her neck and up the other.

Gasping, Grace arched her back, eagerly offering herself to Syd.

Syd cupped her breasts and whispered, "Perfection." She kissed and caressed every inch of her, leaving her body quivering from her touch.

Grace parted her legs. "Please, Syd."

Syd kissed her way down her torso. She kissed the inside of each thigh, reveling in the memory of Grace and her love.

Grace gasped when she felt Syd's tongue touch her. She reached down and ran her fingers through her hair, holding her there. "Like it was yesterday," she whispered, gasping every time Syd touched her. She could feel her orgasm rising, and when Syd slipped two fingers deep inside, that was all she needed. She cried out, nearly whimpering as Syd controlled her.

Finally, she pulled Syd up to her, kissing her passionately. She rolled Syd onto her back, pinning her arms over her head. "God, I love you. You're the only one who makes me feel alive."

"I—"

That was all she got out. Grace smothered her next words with a scorching kiss. "I need to feel you. All of you." Her hand roamed freely over Syd's body. From her breast to her hips, and when Syd parted her legs, she felt like she was home. "No one but me."

"No one. Only you," Syd said in a strangled voice.

Grace slipped two fingers in, feeling the inner walls contract around her fingers. She kissed Syd's dry lips, murmuring over and over how she loved her.

"Grace," Syd cried out her warning. Her back arched into Grace's touch.

"Yes, Syd. Yes." Grace remembered the signs: Syd's body as tight as a bow, her breathing nonexistent, her beautiful body glistening. "Now, please," she whispered against her lips.

Syd did not wait, that was all she needed to hear. Her orgasm rippled through her, once, twice then she had to push Grace's hand away. "God, no more…" she said coarsely.

Grace relented and slipped her fingers away. She cuddled close to Syd, who wrapped her arm around her. Grace pulled the quilt over them.

"Give me five, no ten minutes," Syd whispered.

"Yeah, right. I remember you, Crosse." Grace kissed the top of her breast; both of them fell sound asleep.

They made love throughout the day and long into the night, leaving the bed only to get room service. They had no idea what happened to Adam and Harry.

Sydney was exhausted. "Grace, we need to get out of this bed. Don't we?"

Grace smiled. "Yes, but where are we going?"

She looked down into her blue sparkling eyes. "Anywhere you like. As long as you're with me."

"Well, we can start by visiting Chicago. We have to tell your mother and get her blessing."

"Oh, she adores you."

"It's not me I'm worried about," Grace said.

"You have a point. But she's my mother, she has to adore me. But where will we live?"

"Live?"

"Well, yes, like live together."

"Don't you think that's a little soon to be talking about living together? I mean, you've been on your own for so long."

"Well, at some point, we'll have to live together. When we get married…"

Grace sat up then. "What did you say?"

"I've never been married. Who takes whose name? Do we have to do that? I guess I can be Sydney Morgan. Although I don't know if I like the sound of that. What?"

"Married?"

"Look, toots, you're marrying me, and that's final," she said, placing her hands behind her head.

"You know what this means, don't you?" Grace asked sweetly. She reached down and cupped her breast.

"Y-yes, we get a license, and you get to legally nag me," she said with her eyes closed.

Grace slapped her shoulder.

"Ouch. See, you're beating me up already."

"No more running around?" Grace asked firmly.

"Well, that depends on where I'm running, don't you think?"

"No more womanizing," Grace said. It was not a question.

Syd opened her eyes and looked up. There was a trace of doubt in Grace's sparkling blue eyes. Sydney pushed her onto her back. "I can see it will take a bit of time and a great deal of affection to prove to you that you're the only woman for me, that you've always been the only woman for me." Syd smiled down at her as she slipped between her soft thighs. She moved her body against Grace, slowly and sensually. "Cross my heart."

Grace reached up and caressed her smiling face. "Well, you'd best get started."

Chapter 34

Harry poured Victoria a martini. He then refilled Syd's glass and Grace's.

"I'm glad to see you two have come to your senses," Victoria said, eating an olive. "Grace, will you stay here in Chicago?"

Grace looked at Syd's questioning grin. "I think I might for a little while. I'll have to go back to Michigan every now and then. I've hired Debbie to oversee Jon's property. The Conservation Department took over the contract. All the forests and woods will be taken care of. So there isn't much for me to do. I'll see what future clients I get. But I want to keep my hands in environmental law."

"We can certainly use you here in Illinois," Victoria said. "With the idiot governor we have. Republicans…"

"Well, to be fair, Mother, Illinois hasn't exactly been the poster child for good governors."

"Vic's right, Grace," Harry said, sitting on the couch next to Victoria.

Victoria looked at him. "What have I told you about that nickname?"

"Only in private."

"That's right."

Syd nearly spit up her martini. "I don't even want to know what's going on between you two. But I see, Harry, you're spending more time at my mother's house than here."

"We have sort of an agreement," Harry said. "I don't bug her, and I can hang around once in a while. Ya know, take her to bingo…"

"I do not go to bingo." Victoria huffed indignantly.

"Your mother goes to bingo." She looked at Grace. "That was a good one, wasn't it?"

Grace laughed and nodded.

"Anyway," Victoria continued, "Harry has agreed to be my driver when I need him."

Harry stuck his nose in the air. "Driving Miss Victoria."

"But…" Syd stopped when her phone pinged, announcing she had a text. She looked at it, then looked at Harry.

"Aren't you going to answer it?" Grace asked, sipping her drink.

"Oh, I'll get it later. I'd rather spend time with my girl." Syd looked at Harry over her glass.

"I'll be right back. Nature calls," he said and walked out of the living room.

"I'm hungry," Grace said. "Victoria, how about we put something together?"

Victoria stood. "Good idea. I can't drink on an empty stomach. Well, I can, but I shouldn't."

Grace walked up to Syd and ran her fingers through her hair. "Want anything special?"

"Only you on a plate." Syd wrapped her arms around her waist.

"That'll come later." Grace kissed her soundly and followed Victoria to the kitchen.

Syd waited a second before she ran out of the living room, nearly knocking Harry over.

"Was it Jack? What's he got for us?"

"Something on Clark Street." Syd looked down the hall. "They're in the kitchen. Let's go."

They ran upstairs to Syd's bedroom, then into the drawing room where Syd pressed the bookshelf and opened up her private computer room.

Syd stopped short; Harry grunted as he ran into her.

Grace sat at the desk, peering at a computer, with Victoria standing right behind her.

"Uh, how, when…" Syd stammered.

Grace turned to her and raised an eyebrow. "You forget why and how. Some detective."

"But…" Syd couldn't formulate a complete sentence.

"So where are we going?" Grace asked sweetly, rocking in the desk chair.

"We? Going?"

Victoria rolled her eyes. "You are an imbecile. What do you take Grace and me for? We're more than pretty faces. You know I'm aware of what you and Jack do. But did you really think you could build this room without my knowing it?"

"Uh…yes."

"Good heavens, Sydney, I know every contractor in this city. You do need someone to take care of you. Thank God for Grace. Harry, go get the car."

Harry dropped his cigar. "Syd…?"

Syd looked at Grace. Their gazes locked; Syd had never been so in love or so out of control. She shook her head and laughed.

"Harry, go get the car."

About the author

Kate Sweeney, a 2010 Alice B. Medal winner, was the 2007 recipient of the Golden Crown Literary Society award for Debut Author for *She Waits*, the first in the *Kate Ryan Mystery* series. The series also includes *A Nice Clean Murder, The Trouble with Murder*, a 2008 Golden Crown Award winner for Mystery, *Who'll Be Dead for Christmas?* a 2009 Golden Crown Award winner for Mystery, *Of Course It's Murder, What Happened in Malinmore, A Near Myth Murder, It's Not Always Murder, Recalculated Murder,* and *Dead in the Water.*

Other novels include *Away from the Dawn, Survive the Dawn, Before the Dawn, Residual Moon*, a 2008 Golden Crown Award winner for Speculative Fiction, *Liar's Moon, The O'Malley Legacy, Winds of Heaven, Moonbeams and Skye, Sea of Grass, Paradise, Love at Last, Someday I'll Find You, Moon Through the Magnolia, Stone Walls, Second Time Around, Love in E Flat, One Night in Paris, I Love You Again, Buoyed out on the Foam of the Sea, Build Me a Dream, Mistress of Peacock Walk, Who Wouldn't Love Me?* and *Hypotenuse of Love.*

Born in Chicago, Kate moved to South Carolina, and this Yankee doubts she'll ever get used to saying y'all. Humor is deeply embedded in Kate's DNA. She sincerely hopes you will see this when you read her novels, short stories, and other works. Email Kate at ksweeney22@aol.com.

Printed in Great Britain
by Amazon